RESOUNDING ACCLAIM FOR *NEW YORK TIMES*
BESTSELLING AUTHOR

LISA SCOTTOLINE

"SCOTTOLINE IS A STAR."

Time Magazine

"Lisa Scottoline has been added to my shortlist of
must-read authors. Her stories are FILLED WITH
TEETH-GNASHING SUSPENSE, her characters are com-
pelling, and her humor cuts to the heart of the issue
with laserlike accuracy."

Janet Evanovich

"Scottoline's writing style is SHARP, INTELLIGENT,
FUNNY, AND HIP."

USA Today

"Scottoline rocks!"

Nora Roberts

"Scottoline SETS OFF PLOT LINES LIKE FIRECRACKERS.
She gets a half dozen of them arcing at a time, bedaz-
zling the reader."

Philadelphia Inquirer

"Lisa Scottoline writes RIVETING THRILLERS THAT
KEEP ME UP ALL NIGHT, with plots that twist and
turn—and an array of characters I get a crush on."

Harlan Coben

By Lisa Scottoline

LISA SCOTTOLINE

FINAL APPEAL

HarperTorch
An Imprint of HarperCollinsPublishers

This is a work of fiction. Names, characters, places, and incidents are products of the author's imagination or are used fictitiously and are not to be construed as real. Any resemblance to actual events, locales, organizations, or persons, living or dead, is entirely coincidental.

HARPERTORCH
An Imprint of HarperCollins*Publishers*
195 Broadway
New York, NY 10007

Copyright © 1994 by Lisa Scottoline
ISBN: 0-06-104294-3

First HarperTorch paperback printing: January 2001
First HarperPaperbacks printing: November 1994

HarperCollins®, HarperTorch™, and ❦™ are trademarks of HarperCollins Publishers Inc.
Avon Trademark Reg. U.S. Pat. Off. and in Other Countries,
Marca Registrada, Hecho en U.S.A.

Printed in the United States of America

Visit HarperTorch on the World Wide Web at
www.harpercollins.com

40 39 38

To all my parents, and to Kiki

FINAL APPEAL

1

At times like this I realize I'm too old to be starting over, working with law clerks. I own pantyhose with more mileage than these kids, and better judgment. For example, two of the clerks, Ben Safer and Artie Weiss, are bickering as we speak; never mind that they're making a scene in an otherwise quiet appellate courtroom, in front of the most expensive members of the Philadelphia bar.

"No arguing in the courtroom," I tell them, in the same tone I use on my six-year-old. Not that it works with her either.

"He started it, Grace," Ben says in a firm stage

whisper, standing before the bank of leather chairs against the wall. "He told me he'd save me a seat and he didn't. Now there's no seats left."

"Will you move, geek? You're blocking my sun," Artie says, not bothering to look up from the sports page. He rarely overexerts himself; he's sauntered through life to date, relying on his golden-boy good looks, native intelligence, and uncanny jump shot. He throws one strong leg over the other and turns the page, confident he'll win this argument even if it runs into overtime. Artie, in short, is a winner.

But so is Ben in his own way; he was number two at Chicago Law School, meat grinder of the Midwest. "You told me you'd save me a seat, Weiss," he says, "so you owe me one. Yours. Get up."

"Eat me," Artie says, loud enough to distract the lawyers conferring at the counsel table like a bouquet of bald spots. They'd give him a dirty look if he were anyone else, but because he works for the chief judge they flash capped smiles; you never know which clerk's got your case on his desk.

"Get up. Now, Weiss."

"Separate, you two," I say. "Ben, go sit in the back. Argument's going to start any minute."

"Out of the question. I won't sit in public seating. He said he'd save me a seat, he owes me a seat."

"It's not a contract, Ben," I advise him. For free.

"I understand that. But he should be the one who moves, not me." He straightens the knot on his tie, already at tourniquet tension; between the squeeze on his neck and the one on his sphincter, the kid's twisted shut at both ends like a skinny piece of saltwater taffy. "I have a case being argued."

"So do I, jizzbag," Artie says, flipping the page.

I like Artie, but the problem with the Artie Weisses of the world is they have no limits. "Artie, did you tell him you'd save him a seat?"

"Why would I do that? Then I'd have to sit next to him." He gives Ben the finger behind the tent of newspaper.

I draw the line. "Artie, put your finger away."

"Ooooh, spank me, Grace. Spank me hard. Pull my wittle pants down and throw me over your gorgeous knees."

"You couldn't handle it, big guy."

"Try me." He leans over with a broad grin.

"I mean it, Artie. You're on notice." He doesn't know I haven't had sex since my marriage ended three years ago. Nobody's in the market for a single mother, even a decent-looking one with improved brown hair, authentic blue eyes, and a body that's staying the course, at least as we speak.

"Come on, sugar," Artie says, nuzzling my shoulder. "Live the dream."

"Cut it out."

"You read the book, now see the movie."

I turn toward Ben to avoid laughing; it's not good to laugh when you're setting limits. "Ben, you know he's not going to move. The judges will be out any minute. Go find a seat in the back."

Ben scans the back row where the courthouse groupies sit; it's a lineup that includes retired men, the truly lunatic, even the homeless. Ben, looking them over, makes no effort to hide his disdain; you'd think he'd been asked to skinny-dip in the Ganges. He turns to me, vaguely desperate. "Let me have your seat, Grace. I'll take notes for you."

"No."

"But my notes are like transcripts. I used to sell them at school."

"I can take my own notes, thank you." Ten years as a trial lawyer, I can handle taking notes; taking notes is mostly what I do now as the assistant to the chief judge. I take notes while real lawyers argue, then I go to the library and draft an opinion that real lawyers cite in their next argument. But I'm not complaining. I took this job because it was part-time and I'm not as good a juggler as Joan Lunden, Paula Zahn, and other circus performers.

"How about you, Sarah?" Ben asks the third law clerk, Sarah Whittemore, sitting on my other side. "You don't have a case this morning. You can sit in the back."

Fat chance. Sarah smooths a strand of cool blond hair away from her face, revealing a nose so diminutive it's a wonder she gets any oxygen at all. "Sorry, I need this seat," she says.

I could have told him that. Sarah wants to represent the downtrodden, not mingle with them.

A paneled door opens near the dais and the

court crier, a compact man with a competent air, begins a last-minute check on the microphones at the dais and podium. Ben glances at the back row with dismay. "I can't sit back there with those people. One of them has a plastic hat on, for God's sake."

Artie looks over the top of his paper. "A plastic hat? Where?"

"There." Ben jerks his thumb toward a bearded man sporting a crinkled cellophane rain bonnet and a black raincoat buttoned to the neck. The man's collar is flipped up, ready for monsoon season, but it's not raining in the courtroom today.

"It's Shake and Bake! He came!" Artie says. His face lights up and he waves at the man with his newspaper. "Go sit with him, Safer, he's all right."

"You know that guy, Artie?" I ask, sitting straighter to get a better look. The bearded man grins in a loopy way at the massive gold seal of the United States courts mounted behind the dais, his grubby face tilted to the disk like a black-eyed Susan to the sun.

"Sure. He hangs out at the Y, plays ball with me and Armen. You oughta see his spin move, it's awesome when he's not zoned out. I told him to stop by and see the judge on the bench."

Ben's dark eyes widen. "You *invited* that kook to oral argument? How could you do that?"

I don't say it, but for the first time I agree with Ben. I am becoming a geek, a superannuated geek.

"Why shouldn't he come to court?" Artie says. "It's a free country. He's got rights." He stands up and signals wildly, as ill-mannered as a golden retriever puppy; Artie's the pick of the litter out of Harvard, where they evidently do not teach common sense.

The lawyers in the first three rows of the courtroom crane their necks at him, and I tug at the rough khaki of his sport coat. "Artie, don't embarrass me," I say.

Sarah leans over. "Artie, you're crazier than he is. Sit down."

"He's not crazy," Artie says, still signaling.

"He's wearing Saran Wrap," I point out.

"He always does. It's Shake and Bake, man. You gotta love it."

"Fine," Ben says. "You like him so much, *you* go sit with him."

"Don't mind if I do. Party on, Safer." Artie claps Ben on the back and walks toward the back row.

"Please rise!" shouts the crier, standing behind a desk at the side of the dais. "The Honorable Judges of the United States Court of Appeals for the Third Circuit."

A concealed door to the left of the dais swings open, and the judges parade out, resplendent in their swishing black robes. The federal courts decide appeals in three-judge panels, inviting comparison to the three wise men or the three stooges, depending on whether you win or lose. First comes the Honorable Phillip Galanter, tall, thin, and Aryan, with slack jowls like Ed Meese used to have and blond hair thinning to gray.

He's followed by a wizened senior judge, the Honorable Morris Townsend, shuffling slowly along, and finally the Very Honorable and Terribly Handsome Chief Judge Armen Gregorian, my boss.

"Armen looks good up there, doesn't he?" Sarah says, crossing her legs under the skirt of her sleek slate-gray suit.

He sure as hell does. Towering over the two of them, Armen grins down at the crowd in an easy way. His complexion is tinged with olive; his oversized teeth remind me of an exotic JFK. There are precious few perks in working for the judicial branch, and a boss who looks like a sultan is one of them. I lean near Sarah's perfumed neck and whisper, "I got first dibs."

"In your dreams."

"But you're too young for him."

She smirks. "Too young? Is there such a thing?"

"Bitch." I elbow her in the ovary.

"Oyez! Oyez!" calls the crier. "All persons having business with the United States Court of Appeals for the Third Circuit are admonished to draw near and give their attention, for this court is now in session. God save the United States and this honorable court. Be seated, please."

The panel sits down and the first appeal begins. Ben takes notes on the argument by the appellant's lawyer, who had his civil case dismissed by the district court ten floors below us. The young lawyer has been granted ten minutes without questions from the judges to present his argument, but he's blowing them fast. Armen's forehead wrinkles with concern; he wants to cut to the chase, but this poor guy can't get out of the garage.

"A Third Circuit virgin," Ben says, with the superior snicker of someone who has never done it. I fail to see the humor. I know what it's like to stand before a judge when the words you memorized don't seem to come and the ones that do roll down backward through your gullet and tumble out your butt.

"I guess my time is up," the lawyer says, obviously relieved to see the Christmas light on the podium blink from yellow to red. He thinks the hard part's over, but he's dead wrong. The light turns green again. *Go!*

"Who wants the first question?" Armen says, looking over his colleagues on the panel. He flicks a silky black forelock out of his eyes; he always needs a haircut, it's part of his sex appeal. "Judge Galanter?"

"Counsel," Judge Galanter says quickly, "your appeal concerns the Racketeer Influenced and Corrupt Organizations Act, RICO, but I wonder if you understand why the statute at issue was enacted by Congress."

"It was passed because of organized crime, Your Honor."

"The statute was aimed at extortionists, murderers, and loan sharks. The typical organized criminals, correct?"

The young lawyer looks puzzled. "Yes, Judge Galanter."

"It prohibits a pattern of racketeering activity, the so-called predicate acts, does it not?"

"Yes, sir."

Armen shifts in his high-backed chair.

"But your client isn't suing mobsters under RICO, is he, counsel?" Galanter says.

"With all due respect, Your Honor, I think this appeal presents a matter of national importance. It involves the manipulation of—"

"Flower peddlers, isn't that right, counsel? Not mobsters, not extortionists, not killers. Florists. The ad says, *Nothing but the Best for Your Wedding or Bar Mitzvah.*" He chuckles, as does the gallery. They have to, he's an Article III judge, as in Article III of the Constitution; if you don't laugh, the FBI shows up at your door.

"Yes, the defendants are floral vendors."

Galanter's thin lips part in an approximation of a smile and he arches an eyebrow so blond it's almost invisible. "Floral vendors? Is that a term of art, counsel?"

The gallery laughs again.

"Florists," the lawyer concedes.

"Thank you. Now, carnations are the bulk of your client's business, is that correct?" Galanter flips through the appendix with assurance and reads aloud. "'Pink ones, red ones, even the sprayed ones,' according to your client's affidavit. Although I see sweetheart roses did well in February." He pauses to look significantly at Judge Townsend, but Townsend's eyes are closed; God knows which way he'll go on this case. He thinks people enter his dreams to have sex with him, so it's impossible to tell right now if he's pondering RICO law or watching lesbians frolic.

"They're a group of florists. A *network* of florists."

"Oh, I see, a *ring* of florists. Do you think Congress intended even a *ring* of florists to be covered by this racketeering statute?"

Armen hunches over his microphone. "Counsel, does it really matter what they sell?"

"Go get 'em, boss," I say under my breath.

"Sir?" says the lawyer. He grabs the side of the podium like a kid stowed away on a sinking ship.

"It wouldn't make sense to have a rule of law that turned on the occupation of the defendant, would it?"

"No, sir," says the lawyer, shaking his head.

Armen leans forward, his eyes dark as Turkish coffee. "In fact, after what the Supreme Court said in *Scheidler,* even a group of abortion protestors can be subject to RICO, isn't that right, Mr. Noble?"

Galanter glances over at Armen like a jockey on a Thoroughbred. "But Chief Justice Rehnquist made clear in *Scheidler* that there was a pattern of extortion, of federal crimes. Where's the federal crimes with the floral conspiracy? Florists wielding pruning shears? Gimme that money or I snip the orchid?" Galanter shudders comically and the gallery laughs on cue.

"But they do threaten society," the lawyer says, fumbling for the rigging. "Mr. Canavan signed a contract, and they didn't send him any orders. They intended to drive Canavan Flowers into bankruptcy. It was part of a plan."

"Your client did file for Chapter Eleven protection, didn't he?" Armen says.

Suddenly Judge Townsend emits a noisy snort that sounds like an ancient steamboat chugging to life. Armen and Galanter look over as Judge Townsend's heavy-lidded eyes creak open. "If I may, I have a question," he says, smacking his dry lips.

"Go right ahead," Armen says. Galanter forces a well-bred smile.

"Thank you, Chief Judge Gregorian," Judge Townsend says. He nods graciously. "Now, counselor, why are you letting my colleagues badger you?"

The smile on Galanter's face freezes in place. The gallery laughs uncertainly.

"Sir?" the lawyer says.

Judge Townsend snorts again and lists gently to the starboard side. "As I see it, the question with this new statute is always the same."

Ben whispers, "New? RICO was passed in the seventies."

"The question is always, How is this case different from a case of garden variety fraud? How is it different from other injuries to one's business, which we decide under the common law?" Judge Townsend waves his wrinkled hand in the air; it cuts a jagged swath. "In other words, have you got some precedent for us? A case to hang your hat on?"

The lawyer reads his notes. "Wait a minute, Your Honor."

Judge Townsend blinks once, then again. Galanter smooths back the few hairs he has left. The lawyers in the gallery glance at one another.

They're all thinking the same thing: Nobody tells the Third Circuit to wait a minute. The answers are supposed to roll off your tongue. The case is supposed to be at your fingertips. Better you should pee on the counsel table.

"Way to go, Einstein," Ben says.

"I know I have the case somewhere," says the attorney, nervously riffling through his legal pad. He should be nervous; the circuit court is the last stop before the Supreme Court, which takes fewer appeals each year. It's all those speaking engagements.

"Armen's upset," Sarah whispers, and I follow her eyes. Armen is looking down, worried about the appeal. The only sound in the tense courtroom is a frantic rustling as the lawyer ransacks the podium. A yellow page sails to the rich navy carpet.

The silence seems to intensify.

Galanter glares at the lawyer's bent head.

A sound shatters the silence—*tickticktickticktickticktick*—from the back of the courtroom.

The back rows of the gallery turn around. The sound is loud, unmistakable.

Tickticktickticktickticktick.

Row after row looks back in disbelief, then in alarm.

Tickticktickticktickticktick.

"It's a bomb!" one of the lawyers shouts.

"A bomb!" yells an older lawyer. "No!"

Tickticktickticktickticktick.

The crowded courtroom bursts into chaos. The gallery surges to its feet in confusion and fear. Lawyers grab their briefcases and files. People slam into each other in panic, trying to escape to the exit doors.

"No!" someone shouts. "Stay calm!"

I look wildly toward the back row where Artie was sitting. I can't see him at all. The mob at the back is pushing and shouting.

Ticktickticktickticktick.

Ben and other law clerks run for the judges' exit next to the dais. My heart begins to thunder. Time is slowed, stretched out.

"Artie's back there!" I shout.

Sarah grabs my arm. "Armen!"

I look back at the dais. Armen stands at the center, shielding his eyes from the overhead lights, squinting into the back row. Judge Townsend is stalled at his chair.

Galanter snatches Armen's gavel and pounds it on the dais: *boom boom boom!* "Order! Order, I say!" he bellows, red-faced. He slams the chief judge's gavel again and again. "Order!"

"Oh, my God," Armen says, when he realizes what's happening. "It can't be."

2

"Are you saying it was Shake and Bake?" I ask, incredulous.

"Yes. I'm busted. Totally," Artie says. He flops into his chair in the small law library that serves as the clerks' office, having been grilled behind closed doors by Armen and an assortment of bureaucrats. "It took the poor guy an hour to stop crying. He was worried he got Armen in trouble, can you believe that?"

"Yes," Ben says, typing nimbly at his computer keyboard.

"I don't get it," I say. "Did he have a bomb?"

"No. He had a shot clock."

"A what?"

"Actually, he *was* the shot clock."

"I still don't get it."

"Neither do I," Sarah says.

"I do, but I don't care," Ben says, gulping down his third cup of coffee. He gets in at seven and guzzles the stuff like a thirsty vampire. "The whole thing's absurd."

"No, it isn't," Artie says. "Not if you think like Shake and Bake."

"Like a paranoid schizophrenic?" I say.

"Look, Shake and Bake was watching the argument. He knew the lawyer had to answer a question and he thought time was running out, like in basketball. He figured the guy had twenty-four seconds to shoot. It got all crossed up in his head."

I try not to laugh. "So he starts ticking."

"Yeah, with his mouth. He was counting off the time." Artie yanks the knot on his cotton tie from side to side to loosen it.

"That's ridiculous," Sarah says.

"Not to a paranoid schizophrenic who loves basketball," I say, a quick study.

"Right, Grace." Artie nods and tosses the tie on the briefs scattered across his desk.

"Told you. Absurd," Ben says, tapping away.

"Is he really schizophrenic?" Sarah leans over the Diet Coke and soft pretzel that constitute her breakfast. These kids eat trash; it gives me the heebie-jeebies.

"I don't think so," Artie says, unbuttoning the

collar of his work shirt. "He's like a little kid. Harmless."

I smile. I own a little kid. They're not harmless.

"Why do you say he's harmless?" Sarah asks. "He's obviously not."

"Come on, Sar. He's fine. Shake and Bake can't even do his laundry. You think he can blow up a building?"

"I do, Weiss," says a dry voice at the door to the clerks' office. It's Eletha Staples, the judge's Secretary for Life, a willowy, elegant black woman. Prone to drama, Eletha pauses dramatically in the doorway.

"Yo," Artie says.

"Right, bro. Yo." Eletha rolls her eyes as she walks into the room, trailing expensive perfume. Her glossy hair is pulled back into a neat bun at the nape of a slim neck. In her trim camel suit she looks more like a judge than a secretary, and the day black women get to be federal appellate judges, she'll be mistaken for one. "Who you invitin' next, Charlie Manson?"

"That's not funny, El."

Eletha stops in the center of the office and puts a hand on her hip; a quintet of clawlike polka-dotted fingernails stand out on her otherwise classy look. "It's not funny, bro?"

"No."

"It's not funny when you invite a *crazy man* to court? It's not funny that some *nut boy* endangers Armen's life? Endangers the lives of us *all*?"

Artie fiddles glumly with his Magic Eight Ball, one of the many toys on his desk. "He'd never hurt any of us, he idolizes Armen. And he's not a nut boy."

"He ticks, Artie," I remind him.

Eletha looks crazed, but she crazes easily. "What are you tellin' me, he's not a nut? The man thinks he's a friggin' Timex! Why they let him in the courthouse I'll never know."

"They have to," Sarah says. "He has a right to access. It's in the Constitution."

"The hell it is," Ben says, without looking away from his monitor.

"He's not a nut." Artie pouts.

Eletha puts a hand to her chest and begins Lamaze breathing to calm herself. I first saw this routine three months ago when she had to interview me for my job, because Armen had gotten stuck in Washington. After she calmed down, we spent an hour swapping ex-husband stories. I touch her arm. "El, keep breathing. Don't push, it's too soon."

She looks down at me, her face suddenly grave. "That's not the worst of it. Did you hear?"

"Hear what?"

"They filed the appeal in the death penalty case this morning. *Hightower.* The death warrant expires in a week." Her words hang in the air for a moment.

"Oh, no." I sink deeper into the leather chair next to Artie's desk. I better not get this case. I'm a working mother now; I have enough guilt for an entire hemisphere.

"A week?" Ben says, shaking his neat head. "Of course Hightower waited until the last minute.

Wait till the bitter end to file and hope the warrant expires. It's a game with them."

Sarah looks over sharply. "It's only his first appeal."

"Fine. Let's make it his last."

"Ben, he even tried to kill himself. He thought he deserved to die."

"He did."

Eletha's soft brown eyes linger on Ben's face, but her thoughts are clearly elsewhere. "This case is gonna be a real bitch. The law clerk's gonna be up all night, Armen's gonna be up all night, and I'll be up all night. Last time, I didn't tell Malcolm why." Malcolm is Eletha's son, whose picture she keeps on her desk; he's an intelligent-looking boy with lightish skin and glasses. "Some things kids don't have to know."

I wonder how I'd tell Maddie. What would I say? Honey, Mommy works for a man who decides whether another man should live or die. No, Mommy's boss is not God, he just looks like him.

"Has Armen served on many death panels?" Sarah asks.

Eletha rubs her forehead. "Too many."

"Three," Ben says. "All dissents. The proverbial voice in the wilderness."

Eletha glances at him. "They were from Delaware, I think. None from Jersey. And we haven't executed in Pennsylvania since I don't know when."

"About thirty years." Ben pops the SAVE button with an index finger. "Elmo Smith, for the rape-murder of a Catholic high school girl. But I can't recall the method." He pauses just a nanosecond, his mind working as rapidly as the microprocessor. "Pennsylvania executes by lethal injection now, but then—"

"Christ, what difference does it make?" Sarah says, making tea on the spare desk. "Move to Texas, you can watch it on pay-per-view."

Ben snaps his fingers. "Electrocution, that's right!"

"Death penalty for twenty, Alex," Artie says, and Eletha starts to breathe in and out, in and out.

"The death penalty is revenge masquerading as justice," Sarah says, unwilling to let the grisly subject go. I like Sarah but am coming to understand that not letting anything go is an avocation of hers. It served her well last November; she worked on Armen's wife's campaign for the Senate, in which the feminist lawyer came from behind to win by a turned-up nose.

"When we talk about justice," Ben says, "we shirk thinking in legal terms."

"I'm impressed, Ben. Did you make that up all by yourself?"

"No. Oliver Wendell Holmes said it."

Sarah looks nonplussed.

"Played for the Knicks," Artie says. He launches the Magic Eight Ball on an imaginary trajectory through that great basketball hoop in the sky, that one all men can find when they don't have a real ball. The air guitar principle.

"It's irrelevant what happens at this level anyway," Ben says. "It's going up to the Court."

"And what'll that do to your chances, Safer?" Artie says.

Ben hits a key but says nothing.

"Chances for what?" I say.

"Didn't you know, Grace? Ben is waiting for a phone call from Justice Scalia. He's this close to a Supreme Court clerkship." Artie squints at his forefinger and thumb, held a half-inch apart. "Maybe even *this* close, am I right, Ben? *This* close?" He makes his fingers touch.

"Ask the Eight Ball," Sarah says.

"The Eight Ball! Excellent!" Artie shakes the ball and turns it upside down to read it. "Oh, my God, Ben," he says in mock horror. "*'Better not tell you now.'* Very mysterious."

I look at Ben, reading his monitor screen. "Ben, did you really get an interview with Scalia?"

"Yes," Ben replies, without looking away from the monitor.

"But Grace, Ben has a big problem," Artie says ominously. "If Armen decides *Hightower* and the guy don't fry, we got trouble. Big trouble, right, Ben?"

Ben types away. "Of course not, Weiss. I still have the credentials."

"You mean like clerking for Armen the Armenian? Husband of Senator Susan, another flamer?" Artie winks slyly at Sarah, and she smiles back. I wonder if they're sleeping together, and how Sarah squares it with her lust for Armen. Not to mention her alleged allegiance to Armen's wife.

"The chief has sent clerks to the Court," Ben says. "He's very well regarded by the Justices."

"By the *conservative* Justices?"

"Depends on what you mean by conservative."

"Anybody not on life support."

Ben's mouth twitches, and I can tell Artie's hit a nerve. I hold up my hand like a traffic cop. "That's enough outta you, Weiss. Don't make me come over there."

"Who else is on the panel in *Hightower?*" Sarah says.

Eletha looks at a piece of paper in her hands. She doesn't notice Ben reading the paper upside down, but I do; Ben spends more time reading upside down than right side up. "Here it is. Gregorian, Robbins, and Galanter."

"Awesome!" Artie says. "That means Hightower walks. Armen writes the opinion, Robbins joins it, and Galanter pounds sand. Two to one."

Sarah looks less certain. "Galanter's a Federalist, but Robbins can go either way on this one."

"What's a Federalist?" I ask.

"Fascists. Nazis."

"Republicans with boners," Artie adds.

Ben clears his throat. "It's a conservative organization, Grace. Of which I was an officer in law school, as a matter of fact."

Suddenly, the door to Armen's office opens and men talk in low, governmental tones as Armen walks them to the main door of chambers. Artie strains to listen and Ben inhales what's left of his coffee. Eletha turns around just in time to catch Bernice.

"Roarf! Roarf!" Bernice, a huge Bernese mountain dog, bounds through the door. Yes,

Armen brings his shaggy black doggie to work, all hundred pounds of her. He's the chief judge, so who's gonna tell him he can't? Me? You? *"Roarf!"*

"No! Don't jump up!" Eletha barks back. The sharp noise stops Bernice in her tracks. Her bushy black tail, white at the tip, switches back and forth; she sneezes with the vigor of a Clydesdale.

"Sit, Bernice. Sit!" Armen says, coming up behind the dog.

Bernice wiggles her wavy hindquarters in response. Her eyes roll around in a white mask that ends in rust-colored markings on her muzzle. Bushy rust eyebrows give her a permanently confused look; appearances are not always deceiving.

"She never sits, Armen," Eletha says. "I don't know why you even bother."

"She used to, she just forgets," Armen says. "Right, girl?" He scratches the plume of raggy hair behind Bernice's ears and looks at Artie. "So, Weiss, you shitting bricks?"

Artie sets the Eight Ball down. "Enough to build a house, coach. I'm really sorry."

"Can't you grovel better than that? I'm disappointed."

"*Really* sorry, coach. I am not worthy." Artie bends over and touches his forehead to the briefs on his desk. "It'll never happen again," he says, his voice muffled.

Armen smiles. "Good enough. Shake and Bake can come to the games, but he has to stay away from the courthouse. If he doesn't, the marshals will shoot him on sight. Plus I got you out of jail free, so you owe me a beer."

Artie looks up, relieved. "After the game next week. At Keeton's."

"Fine." Armen's gaze falls on the papers in Eletha's hands and his smile fades. "Is that *Hightower?*"

"Yes."

He takes the papers and begins to read the first page. His brow wrinkles deeply; I notice that the dark wells under his eyes look even darker today. He's given to occasional black moods; something will set him off and he'll brood for a day. It makes you want to comfort him. In bed.

"Chief," Ben says, "the defendant killed two sisters."

Armen seems not to hear him. His broad shoulders slump slightly as he reads.

"One was a little girl and one was a teenager, very popular in the town."

Armen looks up from the memo and his eyes find me. "It's yours, lady," he says.

I hear myself suck wind. "Mine?"

"You're Grace Rossi, right? It's got your name all over it."

"Me, on a death penalty case? But I'm part-time."

"I'll give you time off later, and don't whine."

"But I don't want to get involved," I whine.

He half smiles. "Get involved. Somebody's life is at stake."

"But why me?"

"I need a lawyer on this one."

Sarah freezes as she looks at Armen. I can almost hear the squeak of a hinge as her perfect mouth drops open.

3

Empty coffee cups dot the surface of Armen's conference table, along with sheaves of curly faxes, photocopied cases, and trial transcripts from the *Hightower* record. We worked straight through dinner and into the night, reading cases and talking through the opinion. Then Armen began to tap out an outline on his laptop and I picked up the habeas petition to check our facts.

It says that Thomas Hightower was seventeen when he cut school to go drinking with a fast crowd, which got him drunk and dared him to kiss the prettiest girl in school. Hightower went to her farm, where he found Sherri Gilpin in the shed. He asked her out, and she laughed at him.

"Date a nigger?" she said. Allegedly.

In a drunken rage, Hightower slapped her and she fell off balance, cracking her skull against a tractor. He tried to give her CPR, at which point her little sister Sally came in and began to cry. Hightower says he panicked. He couldn't leave witnesses; it would have killed his mother. So he throttled the child, then, full of shame, he got back into his car and drove himself into a tree. Enter the Commonwealth of Pennsylvania, which saved his life, reserving for itself the honor of putting him on trial. For death.

Hightower couldn't afford a lawyer, not that one in the small coal-mining town would represent him anyway. The county judge appointed a kid barely out of night law school to the case, and the jury convicted Hightower of capital murder. During the sentencing hearing, where the jury decides life or death, Hightower's lawyer argued from the wrong death penalty statute, one that had been ruled unconstitutional three years earlier by the Pennsylvania Supreme Court. Somehow he had missed that.

The obsolete death statute, the only one presented to this predominantly white jury, said nothing about the fact that a jury could consider Hightower's youth, his diminished capacity because of alcohol, his lack of a prior criminal record, and the remorse that he demonstrated by his suicide attempt as "mitigating circumstances" in deciding whether to impose the death penalty.

The jury took only fifteen minutes to reach its decision. Death.

I set the papers down and look out the huge windows that make up the fourth wall of the office. It's the dead of night. Orangey street-lamps stretch toward the Delaware River in rib-bons. White lights dot the suspension cables on the Ben Franklin Bridge. Traffic signals blink on and off: red, yellow, green. The lights remind me of jewels, twinkling in the black night. I watch them shimmer outside the window and turn the legal issues over in my mind.

The question is whether Hightower's lawyer was so ineffective that the trial was unfair. Strictly as a legal matter, Hightower probably deserves a new trial; what he deserves as a matter of justice is another matter. This is why I practiced com-mercial litigation. It has nothing to do with life or death; the questions are black and white, and the right answer is always green.

"Well," Armen says to himself. "Well, well, well." He stops typing and reads the last page of his draft. The office is quiet now that Bernice has stopped snoring. I feel like we're the only people awake, high in the night sky over the twinkly city.

"Well what?"

"I think we're going to save this kid's life. What do you think?"

The question takes me aback. "I don't know. I don't think of it that way."

"I do." He smiles wearily, wrinkling the crows' feet that make him look older than he is. "I wouldn't stop if I didn't think so."

"Was that your goal?"

"It had to be. His lawyer was incompetent. Anybody else would have gotten him life in prison, instead he's scheduled to die. They set him up." He leans back in the chair. Fatigue has stripped something from him: his defenses, maybe, or the professional distance between us. He seems open to me in a way he hasn't before.

"I didn't think of it as saving his life. I thought of it as a legal issue."

"I know that, Grace. That's why I wanted you on this case. You narrowed your focus to the legalities, divorced yourself from the morality of the thing."

It stings. "Do you fault me? It's a legal question, not a moral one."

"Really? Who said?"

"Holmes."

"Fuck Holmes," he says, stretching luxuriously in a blue oxford shirt. His shirtsleeves are bunched at his elbows; his tie is loose. He's so close I can pick up a trace of his aftershave. "It's both those things, Grace, law *and* morality. You can't separate law from justice. You shouldn't want to."

"But then it's your view of justice, and that varies from judge to judge."

"I can live with that, it's in my job description. Judges are supposed to judge. When I read the Eighth Amendment, I think the framers were telling us that government should not torture and kill. That's the ultimate evil, isn't it, and it's impossible to check." His face darkens.

"I don't understand," I say, but I do in part.

Armen's culture is written all over his olive-skinned features, as well as his chambers: the framed documents in a squiggly alphabet on the walls, the picture of Mount Ararat over his desk chair, the oddly ornate lamp bases and brocaded pillows.

"It started piecemeal with the Armenians," he says, leaning forward. "Our right to speak our own language was taken away. Then our right to worship as Christians. By 1915, they had taken our lives. We were starved, hanged, tortured. Beaten to death, most of us, with that." He points at a rough-hewn wooden cudgel mounted over the bookshelf.

"I didn't know."

"Not many do. Half my people were killed. Half a million of us, wiped out by the Turkish government. All my family, except for my mother." A flicker of pain furrows his brow.

"I'm sorry."

He shakes it off. "The point is, government cannot kill its own citizens, not with my help. I know Hightower did a terrible thing. He killed, but I won't kill *him* to prove it's wrong. He should be locked up forever so he never hurts another child. He will be, if I have any say in it." He seems to catch himself in mid-lecture; then his expression softens. "So thank you, for getting involved."

"Did I have a choice?"

"No." He relaxes in the leather chair. "You are involved, you know," he says quietly.

I see the city lights glowing softly behind him and feel, more than I can understand, that we aren't talking about the case anymore. "I don't know—"

"Yes, you do. I'm involved too, Grace. Very involved, as a matter of fact."

I can't believe what I'm hearing. I feel my heart start to pound softly. "We can't do anything about it."

"Yes, we can. Give me your hand." He holds out his hand to me.

I look at it, suspended between us, at once a question and an answer. This situation is supposed to be black and white, but it doesn't feel that way inside.

"Stop thinking. Take it."

So I do, and it feels strong and warm. He pulls me in to him, as naturally as if we've done this a million times before, and in a second I feel myself in his arms and his kiss, gentle on my mouth. Suddenly I hear a noise outside the office and push myself away from his chest. "Did you hear that?"

"What?"

"There was a noise. Maybe the door?"

"Everything's all right," he says. He kisses me again and shifts his weight up underneath me but I press him away.

"Wait. Stop. We can't."

"Why not?"

There are rules, aren't there? "You're married, for starters."

He smooths my hair back from my forehead and looks everywhere on my face. "Not anymore," he says. "My marriage is over."

It's a shock. "What? How?"

"It was over a long time ago. Susan asked me to stay with her until the election was over, and I did. She's coming in the morning to sign the papers. We file tomorrow."

"For divorce?"

"Yes."

"I can't believe it."

"It's true." He touches my face. "So you're not in love? Have I been reading you wrong?"

So much for hiding my emotions. "I don't know. I mean, I think about you, but it's been so long."

"How long?"

"Too long to admit."

"That's long enough, don't you think," he says, kissing me deeply. Before I can object I find myself responding, and then I don't want to object anymore. I lose myself in his kiss, in his warmth. His hands find their way to my breasts, caressing them as we kiss, arousing me. He begins to unfasten the buttons of my blouse, and I feel a skittishness rise, a sort of shame.

"You sure no one's out there, in the office?" I say.

"No one." He undoes the button above my breasts, exposing the string of pearls inside my blouse. I stop his hand and his eyes meet mine, uncomprehending. "I won't hurt you, Grace," he says softly. "Let me. Let me love you a little."

"But I—"

"Shhh. I dream about this, about doing this with you."

"Armen—"

"Let me. You have to." He smiles and moves my hands away, placing each one on the armrests of the heavy chair. "Keep your hands there. We're going to take this slow."

I feel myself breathing hard, excited and scared. "We can't do this, not here."

"Hush." He unfastens the next button, then the next. "Look at yourself, you're so beautiful."

I look down and see a flash of pearls tumbling between my breasts. The scalloped cup of a bra. My skirt hiked way up, past the opaque ivory at the top of my pantyhose. I can't stand it, being undone like this. I look away, out the window. I expect to see the night sky, but the wall of plate glass reflects a dark-haired man and a lighter-haired woman astride him.

Strangely, it's easier to bear this way, like in a mirror. I can watch it as if it were happening to someone else.

"It's all right now," he whispers.

I watch him slip the silk blouse from my shoulders, freeing one arm and the other, then reaching around and unhooking my bra. I feel my breath stop as he tugs my bra down slowly, as if he's unveiling something precious and pure. He takes a breast in each hand and teases the nipples, and I feel an exquisite tingle as each one contracts under his thumbs. I encircle his head, this head of too-long hair that I know so well, and he burrows happily between my breasts, nuzzling one and then the other.

I hear myself moan and wrap my legs more tightly around him. He responds, rocking me against the hardness growing in his lap, sucking at one nipple and then the other. I feel wetness where he's suckled and then a slight chill as he suddenly lifts me up and lays me gently back on his arms across the table. My legs lock around his waist and my hands reach for the edge of the table. My pearls fall to the side, the *Hightower* papers flutter to the floor, and God knows what else slides off the desk.

Poised over me, he stops suddenly. "You're not looking at me. Look at me, Grace."

I watch him in the reflection. I can't do what he's asking.

He turns my face to his, and his expression mingles concern and pleasure. "Why won't you look at me?"

"Is your marriage really over?"

"Yes."

"You swear it?"

"On my life." He bends over and kisses me gently, pressing between my legs. "Now let it go, Grace. Let go."

I close my eyes as my body responds to him. And then my heart.

4

The ringing of a telephone shatters a deep, lovely slumber. I hear it, half in and half out of sleep, not sure whether it's real.

PPPRRRRRRINNNGGG!

I open my eyes a crack and peer at the clock. Its digital numbers read 7:26 A.M.; I've been asleep for two hours. I have four whole minutes left. The phone call is a bad dream.

PPPRRRINNNGGG!

It's real, not a dream. Who the hell could be calling at this hour? Then I remember: Armen. I feel a rush of warmth and stumble to my bureau, cursing the fact that I don't have an extension close to the bed like everybody else in America. I wish I could just roll over and hear his voice.

"Honey?" says the voice on the line. It's not Armen, it's my mother. "Are you up?"

"Of course not. You know how late I got in, you were baby-sitting. What do you want?"

"I've been watching the TV news." I picture her parked in front of her ancient Zenith, with a glass mug of coffee in one hand and a skinny cigarette in the other.

"Mom, it's seven-thirty. Did you call to chat?" I flop backward onto my quilt.

"I have news."

I'm sure. You would not believe the things my mother considers news. Liz Taylor gained weight. Liz Taylor lost weight. "What, Ma?"

"Your boss, Judge Gregorian? He committed suicide this morning."

I sit bolt upright, as if I've been electrocuted. I can't speak.

"They found him at his townhouse in Society Hill. I didn't know he lived in Society Hill. They said his house is on the National Register of Historic Places."

I'm stunned.

"He was at his desk, reading papers in that death penalty case."

"How—"

"He shot himself."

No. I close my eyes to the mental picture forming like cancer in my brain.

"There was no suicide note," she continues. "They called somebody named Judge Galanter, who lives in Rosemont. This Galanter gets to be chief judge now, eh?"

I shake my head. There must be some mistake. "My God," is all I can say.

"Judge Galanter says the court will continue with its operations as before."

I think of Galanter, taking over. Then Armen, dead. This can't be happening.

"Galanter said the *Hightower* case will be reassigned to another judge. Wasn't that the case you stayed late on?"

"Who found him?"

"His wife, when she got in from Washington. She's the one who called the police."

"Susan found him? Did she say anything? Did they interview her?"

Her response is an abrupt laugh; I imagine a puff of smoke erupting from her mouth. "She's holding a press conference this morning."

Susan. A press conference. What is going on? Why would Armen do such a thing? I close my eyes, breathing him in, feeling him still. Just hours ago, he was with me. Inside me.

"Are you there?" my mother asks.

I want to say, I'm not sure.

I'm not sure where I am at all.

5

I pack Maddie off to school in record time and barrel down the expressway into Center City, rattling in my VW station wagon past far more able cars. KYW news radio confirms over and over that Armen committed suicide. I swallow the pain welling up inside and tromp on the gas.

I can't get to the courthouse doors because of the press, newly arrived to feast on the news. Reporters are everywhere, the TV newspeople waiting around in apricot-colored pancake. Cameramen thread black cables through a group of demonstrators, also new to the scene. There must be forty pickets, walking in a silent circle, saying nothing. I look up at their signs, screaming for justice against a searing blue sky: HIGHTOWER.

But I have to get inside.

"Would you like one?" asks an older man in a checked short-sleeved shirt. He holds a pink flyer in a hand missing a thumb; his face is weatherbeaten like a farmer's. "It tells about my daughters."

"Your daughters?" I look up in surprise.

He nods. "Do you have children?"

"Yes. A daughter."

"How old?"

"Six." I don't want to talk to him. I can't think about *Hightower* now. I want to get inside.

"Does she like Barney?"

"No, she likes Madeline. The doll."

The deep creases at his eyes soften into laugh lines. "My little one, Sally? She liked dolls. She had a Barbie, and Barbie's sister, too. What was the name of that sister doll?" He looks down at a pair of shiny brown shoes and scratches his head between grayish slats of hair. "My wife would know," he says, his voice trailing off.

"Skipper."

"Right!" He laughs thickly, a smoker. "That's right. Skipper. Skipper, that's the one."

I seize the moment. "Well, I should go."

"Sure thing. You hafta get to work." He thrusts the flyer into my hand. On it is a black-and-white photograph of two pretty girls sitting on a split wooden rail. The typed caption says SHERRI AND SALLY GILPIN. I glance at it, stunned for a second. I knew the way they died, but I didn't know the way they lived. The younger one, Sally, has a meandering part in her hair like Maddie's, a giveaway that she hated to have her hair brushed. I can't take my eyes from the little girl; she was strangled, the life choked out of her. What did Armen say last night? *We saved a life.*

"You better go, we don't want you to get fired on our account," says the man. "God bless you now."

I nod, rattled, and make my way through the crowd with difficulty. Several of the women in line look at me: solid, sturdy women, their faces plain, without makeup. I avoid them and push open the heavy glass doors to the bustling courthouse lobby. I slip the flyer into my purse and flash a laminated court ID at the marshals at the security desk in front of the elevator bank. Two minutes later, I plow through the heavy door to chambers.

Eletha is sitting at her desk, staring at a blue monitor with a stick-figure rendering of a courthouse made by one of the programmer's kids. Underneath the picture it says: ORDER IN THE COURT! WELCOME TO THE THIRD CIRCUIT COURT WORD PROCESSING SYSTEM! The door closes behind me, but Eletha doesn't seem to hear it.

"El?"

She swivels slowly in her chair. Her eyes are puffy, and she rises unsteadily when she sees me. "Grace."

I go over to her, and she almost collapses into my arms, her bony frame caving in like a rickety house. "It's okay, Eletha. It's gonna be okay," I say, feeling just the opposite.

I rub her back, and her body shakes with high-pitched, wrenching cries. "No, no, no," is all she says, over and over, and I hold her steady through her weeping. I feel oddly remote in the face of her obvious grief, and realize with a chill I'm acting like my mother did when my father disappeared; nothing has changed, pass the salt.

I ease Eletha into her chair and snatch her some tissues from a flowered box. "Here you go."

"This is terrible. Just terrible. Armen, God." She presses the Kleenex into her watery eyes.

"I know."

"I can't believe it."

Neither can I. I don't say anything.

"I was going to call you when I came in, but I couldn't." Her eyes brim over again.

"It's okay now."

"Susan called me. This morning. Then the police. Then Galanter. God, how I hate that man!"

"It was Susan who found Armen, right?"

"She came in from Washington and there he was."

"When did she come in, right before dawn?"

"I guess. I don't know." She blows her nose loudly.

"Who told Galanter?"

"I don't know, why?"

"I don't understand. I was with Armen until five."

"So you two worked late."

"Right." I avoid her eye; Eletha left at two o'clock. Then I think of the noise I heard, or thought I heard. What time was that? "Eletha, last night after you left, did you come back to the office?"

"No, why?"

"When I was with Armen, I thought I heard somebody out here."

"Who?"

"I don't know."

"Didn't they come into Armen's office?"

"No. Not that I saw."

She shakes her head; she's not wearing any makeup today. "The clerk's office, the staff attorneys, they got work to do on a death penalty case. Maybe it was one of them, dropping off papers."

Just then the chambers door opens and in walk Sarah and Artie. They both look like they've been crying; I recognize Sarah's anguished expression as the one I saw in the mirror this morning. She breaks away from Artie and storms into the room.

"Is Ben here?" she shouts, pounding past us to the law clerks' office, her short cardigan flying. "Where the fuck is Ben?"

"I don't know," I say. "Eletha, do you?"

"He hasn't called."

Sarah punches the doorjamb with a clenched fist. "Damn it! I want to see him, the little prick!"

"Sar, stop," Artie says. He walks numbly over to Eletha and puts his arm around her. "It's not going to bring Armen back."

Sarah strides to the phone on Eletha's desk and punches in seven numbers without looking at anyone. "I've been calling that asshole all morning. Pick it up, you little prick!"

"Relax, Sarah," I say.

Her blue eyes turn cold. "What do you mean, relax?" She slams down the phone.

"Look, we're all hurting."

"Ben's not, he caused it. He pressured Armen about *Hightower* so he could get that fucking clerkship. He even showed him that newspaper article, the one about victim's rights. He knew it would bother Armen. He didn't care how much."

"You're talkin' crazy," Eletha says, between sniffles.

Sarah looks from her to me. "Grace, you saw him last night. Was he upset?"

"No," I say, wanting to change the subject. "I thought I heard a noise—"

"What?" Sarah says. "What kind of noise?"

"I don't know, a noise. Like someone was here, outside his office. Maybe around three o'clock or later."

"Did you see anyone?"

"No."

"So what if you heard a noise?"

"Nothing," I say. "Unless it was you or Artie. Was it?"

Artie snorts. "At three? We were asleep." Then he catches himself. "Oh, shit."

Sarah glares at him. "Nice move, Weiss."

So it's true about them. I don't understand Sarah; sleeping with Artie, but crazy about Armen. And Artie and Armen are so close. *Were* so close.

"Oh, what's the difference now?" Artie says. "I don't care if everybody knows, it's not like we're doing anything wrong." He looks at me and Eletha, his eyes full of pain. "I love her, okay? We fuck like bunnies, okay? Is that okay with you?"

"Sure," I say. Eletha nods uncertainly.

"See, Sar, the world didn't end."

Sarah ignores him and presses REDIAL. "The important thing is to find Ben."

I walk away from the tense group. I want to see Armen's office before they do. Alone. I stop in the doorway, bracing myself. Still, I feel a sharp pang at the sight. My gaze wanders over the exotic brocade, the strange-looking documents, and the Armenian books in their paper dust jackets, frayed at the top. The place smells of him still; I can almost feel his presence. I can't believe he would kill himself. Why didn't I know? Why didn't I see it coming?

I enter the room and finger the papers on the conference table. Everything is the way I remember it, except that some of the *Hightower* papers are gone, the ones he was working on at home. The cases are scattered over the table; the laptop is at the edge. Even the dog hairs on the prayer rug are the same. It reminds me of Bernice. Where was she last night when he killed himself? Where was I, sound asleep?

Suddenly I hear a commotion in the outer office, then shouting. I rush to the door and see Artie shove Ben up against the wall, rattling a group portrait of the appeals court.

"Artie, stop it!" I shout, but Eletha's already on the spot. She steps in front of Ben, shielding him with her body.

"He deserves it!" Artie says, his chest heaving in a thick sweatshirt. He stands over Ben, who begins to *kack-kack-kack* in his old man cough, rubbing his head where it hit the wall.

"Back off!" Eletha says, in a voice resonant with authority. A sense of order returns for a moment; Eletha is in charge and we are in chambers. The king is dead, long live the queen. Then it passes.

"Where have you been?" Sarah shouts at Ben, who struggles to his feet, hiding almost comically behind Eletha.

"Go to hell, Sarah. I pulled an all-nighter, so I slept in. Do I need your permission?"

"You worked all night? On what?"

"*Germantown Savings.* I wanted to finish it."

"You didn't hear the phone?"

"No."

"The fuck you didn't!" Sarah looks like she's about to pick up where Artie left off and Eletha wilts between them, her strength spent.

"Okay, Sarah," I say, "cool it. You want to talk to Ben, do it when you're calmer."

Her eyes flash with anger. "Playing Mommy again?"

"Yes, it comes naturally. Now go to your room. Time out until the press conference." I point to the clerk's office.

"Press conference?" Eletha says. "Who's givin' a press conference?"

I check the clock above the chambers door. "Susan is, in fifteen minutes."

Eletha's eyes threaten to tear up again. "How can she? Before Armen's body is even cold."

"It's not like it's so easy for her," Sarah says defensively, "but she feels the need to explain. The public has the right to know."

I feel my heart beat faster. "She's going to explain why he committed suicide?"

"That's what she told me on the phone."

"It's his business, not the public's," Ben says, smoothing his tie.

Eletha looks as surprised as I do. "But how does she know? There was no note."

"She's his *wife*, Eletha," Sarah says.

His wife. The word digs at me inside. If he hadn't died, they'd have filed for divorce. Today.

We gather around the old plastic television in the law clerks' office, watching Senator Susan Waterman take her place at the podium. I suppress a twinge of jealousy and scan her face for a clue about what she's going to say. Her stoic expression reveals nothing. She looks like a wan version of her academic image; her straight dark-blond hair, unfashionably long, is swept into a loose top-knot, and her small, even features are pale, a tele-genic contrast to the inky blackness of a knit suit.

"Ladies and gentlemen," she says. She glances up from the podium, unaffected by the barrage of electronic flashes. "My husband, Chief Judge Armen Gregorian of the Third Circuit Court of Appeals, died this morning by his own hand, here in Philadelphia. He loved this city, even though it had not always been kind to him. Even though the press had not always been kind to him, and especially of late." She glares collectively at the press, which dubbed the fierce expression "Susan's stare" during her campaign.

"They're all pricks," Sarah says, but even she sounds spent.

Susan takes a sip of water. "My husband did not leave a note to explain his actions, but it is no mystery to me. Some are already saying he did it because of the press's criticism of his liberal views, but I assure you that was not the reason. Armen was made of sterner stuff." She manages a tight smile at the crowded room, having reprimanded and absolved them in one blow.

"I've heard others say it was because of the death penalty case he had to decide, and the stress and strain it may have caused him. It would break anyone, but not Armen Gregorian. He *was* made of sterner stuff." She lifts her head higher, in tacit tribute. Eletha, in the chair next to me, squeezes my hand.

"On the surface, my husband had everything to live for," Susan says. "He was the chief judge, and we had a wonderful, happy marriage that was a solid source of comfort and support to us both."

What is she saying? They were on the brink of divorce.

"But my husband was Armenian. The genocide of the Armenian people is called the forgotten genocide. Most of his family was murdered. His mother survived, only to commit suicide herself. This month—April—is when Armenians remember their tragic history." She looks around the room. "Like the Holocaust survivors who later died by their own hand, my husband was a victim of hate. Let us pause for a moment of silence to remember Armen Gregorian and to remember that the power of hate can destroy us if we do not fight against it." The camera lingers on her bowed head.

Sarah begins to sob, and Artie hugs her close.

I lean back in my chair, as if pressed there by a gigantic weight. Armen told me about the genocide, though he didn't tell me about his mother. But still, would he commit suicide because of it? That night? The genocide was on his mind, but so was *Hightower*. And me. I feel like crying, but the tears won't come.

Neither will Ben's. He looks knowingly at Sarah and Artie, cuddled together.

His dark eyes are bone dry.

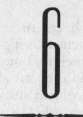

6

Judge Galanter's breath carries the harsh tang of Binaca. Cigar smoke clings to the fine wool of his double-breasted suit. His movements are deliberate and his speech formal, as if he were trying to control each syllable. I know as sure as he's standing before us, flushed slightly in front of Armen's desk, that Galanter has been drinking. It evokes another memory of my father, flitting like a ghost across my mind.

"You law clerks can stay on for a week or two," he says.

"We hadn't even thought about it," Artie snaps from the doorway.

"I'll attribute that crack to your extreme emotional distress, Mr. Weiss."

Artie looks away from Galanter, out the window. The courthouse flag flies at half mast, flapping in the wind that gusts off the Delaware River.

"Finish up the cases you're working on. Draft the bench memos as before and hand them in to me. Argued cases will have to be reargued." Galanter slides a gleaming Mont Blanc from his breast pocket and makes a check in a leather Filofax he's holding like a missal. I can imagine what it says.

Things to do: Take over. Before noon.

"Next order of business. The office will have to be packed up. How much time will you need, Eletha?"

Eletha sits at the end of the conference table, fuming. "I would have to talk to Susan about that," she says, crossing her slender arms across her chest.

"Senator Waterman? Already spoke with her. She said it's up to you. Box the stuff and ship it to the house, she'll go through it there. How long will it take you? I have to plan my own move."

"You mean you're takin' this office?" Eletha asks.

Galanter jerks his chin upward, as if the folds of his turkey neck were pinched in his collar. "Of course, it's the chief judge's. I'd like to be in in two weeks. By the way, I understand the staff attorneys need an extra secretary, so there's room for you there. Talk to Peter about that." He makes another check in his Filofax, and Eletha breathes in and out, in and out.

"Judge," I say. "I was wondering—"

"Of course. I forgot about you. They may need an extra staff attorney downstairs. You should apply. Part-time will be a problem, you'll have to step up to a normal work week."

"No. I wanted to ask about *Hightower.*"

He purses his thin lips. "I've reassigned it. The death warrant expires Monday, but we'll have it decided well in advance."

"Who was it reassigned to?"

"That information is strictly need-to-know. Did I mention the memorial service?" He shoots a questioning look at Ben, who's standing against the bookshelves. Ben shakes his head discreetly.

"Not a high priority," Artie says.

Galanter points at Artie with his pen. "Don't test me, young man. I've just about had it with your lack of respect."

"Respect?" Artie explodes. "Who are you to talk about respect? Armen just died and you can't wait to take his office. Can't wait!"

"Artie," Sarah says nervously.

"Listen, you," Galanter says, raising his voice. "This court has to maintain operations. We have a public trust."

"Fuck you!" Artie shouts, almost in tears. He storms out of the room into his office and slams the door.

"I've never seen such conduct in a law clerk! Ever!" Galanter says.

"Judge Galanter." I start talking, almost reflexively. "Artie and Armen were close. This is hard for him. For us all." I hear an involuntary catch in my voice, but Galanter's gaze is fixed in the direction of the clerks' office. I feel a shiver of fear inside, from somewhere deep, but press it away. "You were saying, Judge, about the memorial service?"

Galanter looks down at me, still lost in his own anger. "What did you say?"

"The memorial service."

"The memorial service? Oh, yes." He exhales sharply, regaining control, and returns the pen to his breast pocket. "Memorial service. The day after tomorrow, Thursday. In the ceremonial courtroom. The time's not fixed yet."

"Have you heard about the funeral arrangements?"

"No idea. Senator Waterman said she'd call about that. Eletha, get me that memo I sent you."

Eletha doesn't move a muscle. "Memo? What memo, Judge?"

Galanter hasn't drunk enough to miss the challenge in her manner. He tilts his head ever so slightly. "The one about the new sitting schedule. I sent it this morning, on E-mail."

"I was busy this morning."

"So was I. Get it now," he says, staccato.

Eletha leaves the room. In a second she's slamming her desk drawers unnecessarily.

Galanter hands me some papers from his book. "Xerox these for me and come right back."

I take the papers and leave the office. When I open the door to the hallway, Eletha's giving the finger to the wall.

I read the papers on the way to the Xerox machine. It's a complete sitting schedule, with

Armen's initials crossed out next to his cases and a new judge's written in. All of Armen's cases, reassigned so fast it'd make your head spin.

READY TO COPY, the photocopier says. I open the heavy lid, slap the paper onto the glass, and hit the button. The light from the machine rolls calcium white across my face.

Suicide? I don't understand. They were going to file for divorce, if what Armen said was true. I feel a pang of doubt; would Armen lie? Of course not. Afterward we talked for a long time, holding each other on the couch. He was an honest man, a wonderful man.

READY TO COPY. I hit the button. You don't kill yourself just because you're Armenian. Armen was a survivor. And he hated guns, was against keeping them in the house. Where did he get the gun?

READY TO COPY, says the machine again, but I'm not ready to copy. So much has happened. We found and lost each other in one night. I stare at the glass over the shadowy innards of the machine; all I see is my own confused reflection. What was that noise last night, and does it matter?

I turn around and look down the hall, but it's empty. There are only two occupied judges' chambers on this whole floor, ours and Galanter's; the rest are vacant, the chambers of judges who sit nearer their homes in Wilmington and northern New Jersey. Only eleven people work on the entire floor.

Now it's ten.

A boxy file cabinet sits against the wall next to the judges' elevator. A few paces to the left is the door to the law clerks' office. To the right, down the hall, are Galanter's chambers.

Everything looks perfectly normal.

I step away from the machine and peer at the government-spec brown carpet. There's nothing on the rug, no trace of anything. I straighten up, feeling stupid. What am I looking for, muddy footprints? Clothing fibers? What am I thinking? I shake my head and turn back to the Xerox machine.

ADD PAPER, it says. The words blink red, like the old pinball machines that go tilt.

Damn it. Why am I the only one who refills this thing? I look in the cabinet next to the machine for a ream of paper, but it's empty except for the torn wrapper. The law clerks never pick up after themselves. I slam the cabinet door and walk down the hallway back to chambers.

Bbbzzzzzz goes the security camera, as I tramp angrily by.

Then it hits me. I do an about-face and look up at the camera. It's black and boxy, and looks back at me like a mechanical vulture perched above the judges' elevator.

The camera's on all the time, monitored by the federal marshals. It saw everything that happened in the hall last night and probably recorded it, like at ATM machines.

It knows if anyone came into chambers and saw Armen and me together. And it knows who they are.

7

His breast pocket bears a plastic plate that says R. ARRINGTON over the shiny five-star badge of the marshal service. His frame is brawny in its official blue blazer, and his dark skin is slightly pitted up close. "Lunchtime!" I say to him, making an overstuffed tuna hoagie do the cha-cha with a chilly bottle of Snapple lemonade. "All this can be yours."

He does not look impressed. "No can do, Grace."

The hoagie and the lemonade jump up and down in frustration. "All I want is two minutes. I look at the monitors, then I'm outta there."

"There's twenty monitors, Grace," he says,

sighing deeply. Maryellen, the cashier in the building's snack shop, cocks her head in our direction. She may be blind, but she's not deaf. I decide to be more quiet.

"Come on, Ray. You said only one monitor shows our hallway. How long can it take to look at a monitor?"

He folds his thick arms. "Maybe if you tell me why this matters."

I glance at the jurors behind us buying newspapers, gum, and fountain soda. The ice machine spits chunks into a tall paper cup, and a juror plays mix-and-match to find the right size lid. He'll never find it; I never can, and I have a J.D. "Let's just say I want to check security."

"Come clean, Rossi."

I consider this. Ray is one of the few marshals who liked Armen; he's also one of the few African Americans, which I suspect is no coincidence. "Tell you what. Get me in. If it pays off, I'll tell you why."

"What am I supposed to tell the marshals?"

"What marshals? You're the marshal."

"I'm a CSO, technically. A court security officer. I mean the marshals watching the monitors."

"Tell 'em I'm checking security, that I'm the administrative law clerk to the chief judge."

"Grace." His somber expression reminds me of something I'd rather not dwell on. Armen is gone.

"Forget it, I'll tell them something. I'll handle it. Just get me in, I'll owe you. Big-time."

Suddenly he snaps his fingers. "I know what you can do for me."

"Anything."

"You can introduce me to your fine friend, the lovely Eletha Staples."

"Eletha? Don't you know her?"

"I've been workin' here as long as she has, but she won't give me the time of day. She seein' anybody?"

I think of Leon, Eletha's boyfriend, who gives her nothing but grief. "No."

"Hot dog!" He rubs his hands together; it makes a dry sound. "Lunch. I'll start with lunch, take it nice and easy. Can you set it up?"

"Deal." I set the tuna hoagie and Snapple on the counter in front of Maryellen. At the last minute, Ray tosses in two packs of chocolate Tastykakes.

"What are you having today, Grace?" Maryellen says. Her cloudy eyes veer wildly around the room.

"Thanksgiving dinner," I say to her and she laughs.

After we leave the snack bar, Ray leads me through a labyrinth of hallways to the core of a secured part of the courthouse. It would have been impossible to find this myself, and when I reach the barred entrance I understand why.

It's a prison.

Sixteen floors from where I work, in the same building. It gives me the creeps. The sign on the barred door says: ONLY COUNSEL MAY VISIT PRISONERS.

We head down another hall, past a room with a number of empty desks in it, and open a door onto a small room, brightly lit by a ceiling of fluorescents. A wall of TV screens dominates the room, giving it a futuristic feel. There must be twenty-five black-and-white TV screens here, trained everywhere throughout the courthouse.

The monitors in the left bank flash on the stairwells at each floor of the building, and the large screens in the middle offer an ever-changing peek into the courtrooms. In 12-A there's a young woman crying on the witness stand. In 13-A an older man is being sentenced. In 14-A a little boy is testifying.

"It's like a soap opera, huh, Worrell?" Ray says amiably to the stony-faced marshal watching the screens. He's a stocky middle-aged man in a black T-shirt that says UNITED STATES MARSHAL SERVICE. It looks more like a get-up for Hell's Angels, but I do not remark this aloud.

"Ugh," the man says, his attention focused on the TV pictures of prison cells on the far right. Each cell is numbered and occupied by a man in street clothes, probably awaiting trial. They sit slumped or asleep in their cells; one is a black teenager in an oversized sweatshirt, just a kid. I think of Hightower.

"This is Grace Rossi, Worrell. She's a lawyer, works for the appeals court. She wants to see—"

"I want to see the monitors," I say with faux authority. "It's a security check for the new chief judge."

Worrell begins to laugh at one of the prisoners, a Muslim crouched over in prayer. "Say it loud, brother. You're gonna need it." Ray looks sideways at the monitor.

"Where's the screen for the eighteenth floor?" I ask.

"That one." He points to one of the screens. The bottom of the screen reads 16-B. In the high-resolution picture, a young secretary pauses to tug up her slip. Worrell chuckles. "They forget Big Brother's watching."

Of course they forget; I did. So did whoever came into our chambers, if anyone. I watch the picture flicker to 17-B. It's a view of the hallway outside the judges' elevator on the seventeenth floor. On the wall hangs a fake parchment copy of the Constitution. Our floor is next.

"Yeow!" Ray hoots as soon as the scene changes. Eletha is photocopying at the Xerox machine, her back to the camera. Her skirt clings softly to her curves, and with her back turned you can't see how haggard she looks today. "Now ain't that pretty?" he says, in a tone men usually reserve for touchdown passes and vintage Corvettes.

Worrell grunts. "She's all right."

Ray gives him a solid shove. "Listen to you, 'She's *all right*.' Shit, man! She's more than all right, she's *fine*. And she's mine, all mine. Right, Grace? Grace?"

"Right," I say, preoccupied by the scene on the TV screen, which shows Eletha walking down the hall and into chambers. Bingo. The camera would have seen whoever came into chambers last night, wherever they came from. "Where's the tape?"

Worrell looks at me blankly. "What tape?"

"The tape. The tape of what the camera saw last night."

"We don't tape."

"What?"

"There's no tape, lady."

"I don't understand." I look at Ray for confirmation.

"I coulda told you that, Grace," he says.

I don't believe this. "At the MAC machine they tape. Even in the Seven-Eleven they tape."

"Seven-Eleven's got the money. This is the U.S. government. You're lucky we got the goddamn judges."

Ray looks embarrassed. "Downstairs we tape. The monitors at the security desk, they tape the stairwell and the judges' garage. Just not here."

"But somebody watches the monitors at night, don't they?"

Worrell leans back in the creaky chair, plainly amused. "Guess again."

"Maybe we should go," Ray says.

"Hold on. There's no night shift?" I hear myself sounding like an outraged customer.

"We got a fella walks around the halls," Worrell says, "but that's it. One marshal. The government don't have the money for somebody to watch TV all night." His face slackens as he returns to the screens.

"All right. Who was the marshal last night, walking the halls?"

"McLean, I think."

"McLean? Is he the big one with the mustache?" The Mutt of the Mutt-and-Jeff marshals I see in the mornings.

Worrell nods. "Don't you guys got some work to do?"

"Let's go, Grace," Ray says.

"Sure. Thanks," I say, disappointed. So much for the short answer. We start toward the door but Worrell erupts into raucous laughter.

"Holy shit, what a case this one is."

Ray glances at the monitor, then scowls. "I'd love a piece of that guy. He's not crazy, he knows just what he's doin.' Jerkin' us around."

I look back. One of the prisoners is smack in the middle of cell seven, standing on his head. "Jesus."

"What a country," Worrell says. "That jerk's gettin' a nice bed for the night, and you know who's gonna pay for it? You and me. The taxpayers. For him they got the money. For us, no. You talk to your boss about that, okay, lady?"

But I don't answer. I recognize the man in the cell. "Ray, let's go."

"**S**hake and Bake is in jail?" Artie says, shocked. "Show me where, Grace."

"You can't visit him."

"What do you mean I can't visit him?"

Eletha looks over wearily, dead on her feet against the bookcase in the law clerks' office. "That lunatic is the last thing you should be worried about today."

"Grace," Sarah calls from her desk, "what were you doing in the security office?"

"I wanted to see the cameras."

"What cameras?"

"You know, the ones in the hallways. I wanted to see who's on the other side."

"Why?"

"I was curious. I wanted to know if they saw anything peculiar."

"Is this about the noise?" Sarah asks.

Ben looks up from the newspaper accounts of Armen's death. "What noise?"

"I heard a noise last night, so I wanted to see the tapes, only—"

"Tapes?" Sarah asks. "You mean of what they see in the cameras?" She flushes slightly, and I play a hunch I didn't even know I had.

"Yes. They tape everything, for security reasons. Like at Seven-Eleven."

"They do?"

"Sure." I look at Eletha. "Right, El? They tape from those cameras."

"If you say so," Eletha says, playing along. "They keep the tapes?"

Thanks, El. "Yep, in a vault. They said they'd show me tomorrow."

Ben presses a button on his computer keyboard. The modem sings a computer song as he logs on to Lexis, the legal research database. "Surprised the government has the money."

"Safer, what the fuck are you doing?" Artie asks. "Are you working? *Today?*"

"I'm going on Nexis, that okay with you?"

"What's Nexis?" Eletha asks, as Sarah suddenly busies herself making a full-fledged tea ceremony out of a single bag of Constant Comment. She has to be the one I heard last night, and she should never play poker.

"Anybody gonna answer me? What's Nexis?"

Eletha plops into a chair like a much heavier woman. Her chin falls into her hand. "Forget it. Who gives a shit?"

"Nexis is a database of newspapers," I say. "It has magazines, newspapers, wire services. Everything."

"How do you like that?" Ben says, in his own world as he reads his computer screen. "We're under HOTTOP. *Hightower* and the Chief."

"Christ, Safer!" Artie says.

"I need a translation," Eletha says.

"HOTTOP stands for hot topics in the news," I say, the words sour in my mouth. Without thinking twice, I cross to Ben's computer and press the power switch to OFF. The powerful unit crackles in protest, then fizzles out. "Show some respect, Ben. A man is dead." I feel a wrenching inside my chest and turn my back on Ben's surprised expression.

"Way to go, Grace!" Artie says, bursting into applause.

"She's right," Eletha says. She stands up and smooths out her skirt. "I don't even know what we're still doin' here. We should all go home. The packing can wait."

"I can't believe he's gone," Sarah says, standing at the coffeemaker. The only sound is the hot water spurting into the glass pot. Sarah removes the pot a little too soon and the last drops dance across the searing griddle like St. Vitus.

"Let's not get maudlin, please," Ben says.

Artie looks as if he's about to snap, then his brow knits in alarm. "Wait a minute. Grace, does Shake and Bake know about Armen?"

"I have no idea."

"Oh, fuck. I have to get in to see him. There's no telling what he'll do when he hears. Where's the prison?"

"On the second floor, but they won't let you in."

"The hell they won't. He has a right to counsel, doesn't he? I'm counsel." Artie bounds over to the coat rack and tears Ben's jacket from a wooden hanger, leaving it swinging.

"That's my best jacket, Weiss," Ben says.

"I know, dude. Thanks." He yanks the jacket over his chest. "Sar, lend me your briefcase."

"You really want to do this?" Sarah hands him a flowered canvas briefcase but Artie pushes it back at her.

"Give me a pad instead. Where'd you say they're taking him, Grace?"

"Courtroom Fourteen-A, before Katzmann. They're trying to charge him with trespassing on federal property."

Artie shakes his head. "I tell ya, these kids today, in and out of trouble. Where did I go wrong, Mom?"

"Don't ask me, pal."

"I gave him everything. Summers in Montauk, winters in Miami Beach." He gives the jacket a reckless tug and Ben flinches.

"Will you at least take it easy?" Ben says.

Eletha covers her eyes. "I didn't see this. This is not happening."

"How do I look, Mom?" Artie says to me. He sticks out his arms, and the sleeves ride up to his elbows. "Hot?"

"Smokin'."

"Excellent." He sticks a legal pad under his arm and runs out of the clerks' office. I hear the heavy pounding of his feet as he heads for the outer door. My eyes meet Sarah's, but she looks down into her steaming mug of tea.

"You okay, Sar?" I ask her. Flush her out. Isn't that what detectives do?

"Sure." She takes a quick sip of tea, avoiding my gaze. "Who's *Hightower* been reassigned to, Ben?" she asks.

"What makes you think I know?"

"You know Galanter's clerks. The buzz-cut boys."

The telephone rings at Eletha's desk. "Shit," she says. "Thing's been ringing all day." Before I can offer to get it, she kicks off her heels and is padding to her desk.

Ben flicks on the power switch, animating the machine. "Grace, hate me if you must, but I'm logging on again."

"Tell us who got *Hightower*, Safer," Sarah says, but I hold up my hand.

"Sarah, think a minute. Who's even more conservative than Galanter?"

"Adolf Hitler."

"On our court, I mean."

"Judge Foudy."

"Right. And Galanter would pick somebody to vote with him, now that Armen's gone. He'd want to stack the deck. Change the result."

She blinks. "Could he do that?"

"Sure. He's the chief judge. In an emergency, he picks the panels."

Ben pounds the keys. "I neither confirm nor deny."

He doesn't have to, I know it. Galanter has shifted the majority to himself, blocking Hightower in. No matter which way Robbins goes, it'll be two votes to one for death. Poor Armen; he didn't save Hightower's life after all. I stand up, wanting suddenly to be alone.

"Look at this item," Ben says, his voice tinged with sarcasm. "What a nice gesture from Senator Susan, and how like a Democrat."

"What?" Sarah says, and I stop at the doorway.

"From *The Washington Post*. Says here that Susan tried to donate Bernice to a group called Service Dogs for the Handicapped. I can almost hear the wheelchairs plowing into each other, can't you?" He laughs so hard he coughs: *kack-kack-kack*.

"Very funny," Sarah says.

"Bernice is gone?" I say, surprised to feel a twinge inside.

"Gone but not forgotten," Ben says, recovering enough to hit another key. "They didn't want her, evidently. They only take puppies."

"So where is she?" I ask from the doorway, only half wanting to know.

Ben hits the key again. "It doesn't say."

"I know," Eletha says. She walks into the room, waving a yellow Post-it on her finger. "They just called."

"Who did?"

She holds the paper in front of my face. On it is a phone number I don't recognize. "I voted for Susan, but I'll never forgive myself."

"She's too big, Mom," Maddie says, shuddering in her nightgown. "Look at her *teeth*."

Bernice strains against her red collar, which still says A. GREGORIAN; her wagging tail swats my thigh with each beat.

"But I'm holding her, honey. She won't hurt you, she can't. Just come over and let her sniff you. She's all clean now." I bathed Bernice right after I bathed Maddie, using green flea shampoo they sold me at the dog pound, along with a leash, two steel bowls, and a thirty-dollar trowel for shoveling a megaton of dogshit.

"*Rrronononr,*" Bernice grumbles, a guttural

noise that makes Maddie's blue eyes widen in fear.

"What's that?"

"She's talking to you, honey. She wants you to love her."

"But I don't love her. I don't even like her." Maddie tugs anxiously at the end of a damp strand of hair; her hair looks brown when it's wet, more like my mother's original russet color than her own blazing red.

"Aw, can't you just give her a little pat on the head? Her hair's washed too." I scratch Bernice's newly coiffed crown and she looks back gratefully, her tongue lolling out. "See? Look how happy she is to be with us."

"But why did *we* have to take her?"

"Because nobody else would. They all have apartments that don't allow pets. We're the only ones with a house who could have a pet."

"They could move."

"No. Now come closer."

She doesn't budge. "Why couldn't you just leave her there? In the dog pound."

"You know what would happen to her. You saw *Lady and the Tramp*."

"They don't do that right away, Mom. They wait about six or five weeks."

"No, they don't wait that long."

"Somebody else could have adopted her."

"I don't think anybody would have. You should have seen her in the cage." I flash on the scene at the pound; Bernice penned by herself, barking frantically next to a streetwise pit bull. "Nobody would have taken her, Maddie. Most people like puppies, not dogs."

"I like puppies. Little puppies."

I sigh. I got my second wind when I washed Bernice, but the day's awful events and my own fatigue are catching up with me.

"It's not *my* fault, Mom." Maddie pouts. "She's scary."

"I know, you're being very brave. How about you go up to bed now? You look tired."

"I'm not tired. You always say I'm tired when I'm not."

"All right, you're not tired, but I am. Go up to bed, and I'll be right up."

She makes a wide arc around Bernice, then scurries upstairs, and I take the disappointed dog into the kitchen and put her behind an old plastic baby gate. She whimpers behind the fence, but I don't look back. I reach Maddie's room just as she turns off the light and hops into bed. "She's so big, Mom," she says, a small voice in the dark.

I sit down at the edge of the narrow bunk bed and let my weariness wash over me. I smooth Maddie's damp bangs back over the uneven part in her hair. It reminds me of Sally Gilpin, and I feel grateful to have my daughter with me, how-ever terrified she is of big dogs. That much is right in the world. "I understand, baby."

"Where will she sleep?" Maddie says, digging in her mouth with a finger, worrying a loose tooth from its moorings.

A good question, only one of the hundred I haven't answered. "I have it all figured out."

"Mom, look," she says with difficulty, owing to the fist in her mouth. Her eyes glitter in the dim light from the hallway. Huge round eyes, like Sam's; my color but his shape. Across the bridge of her nose is a constellation of tiny freckles too faint to see in the dark.

"Look at what?"

"Look." She moves her hand, pointing at one of her front teeth, which has been wrenched to the left.

"Gross, Maddie. It's not ready. Put it back the way it was, please."

"Everyone else has their teeth out. My whole class."

"But you're younger, remember? Because of when your birthday is."

"*Duh*, Mom."

"*Duh*, Mads."

She punches the tooth back into place with a red-polished fingernail. "It doesn't even hurt when I do that tooth thing. I like to stick my tongue up in the top." Which is exactly what she does next.

"Stop, Maddie."

"You know how there's like the top of your teeth? And you can stick your tongue in the top and wiggle it around?"

"Kind of."

"Well, I like to stick my tongue in there and make like buck teeth."

"Terrific. Just do it with your tongue, not your finger, okay? And don't show it to me or I'll barf."

"Why can't I use my finger? It works better."

"You'll give yourself an infection."

"No, I won't."

"Fine. Don't blame me when your mouth explodes."

She giggles.

"You think that's funny?"

She nods and giggles again, so I reach under the covers and tickle her under her nightgown. "No. No tickling!" she says.

"But you love to be tickled."

"No, I hate it. Madeline likes it. You can tickle her." She fishes under the thin blanket and locates her Madeline doll, which she shoves at my chest. "Tickle her."

I look down at the soft rag doll with its wide-brimmed yellow felt hat. Madeline has a face like a dinner plate, with wide-set black dots for eyes and a smile stitched in bumpy red thread. Her orange yarn hair is the same color as Maddie's, but we didn't name Maddie after the Ludwig Bemelmans books, we named her after Sam's grandmother. When I gave Maddie the doll at age three, they became inseparable. "You really do look like Madeline, you know?" I say. "Except for the hat."

"No, I don't. She looks like me. I look like myself."

I laugh. "You're right." I lean over and give her a quick kiss. Her breath smells of peanut butter. "Did you brush?" I ask, second-rate sleuth that I am.

"I don't have to brush if I don't want to."

"Oh, really? Who said?"

"Daddy. He told me it was *my decision*." Her

tone elides into the adolescent sneer that comes prematurely to six-year-old girls.

"Don't be fresh."

"Don't be fresh. Don't be fresh. Daddy says you can break the rules sometimes."

"Oh, he does, does he?" Easy for Sam to say. After his highly suspect charitable deductions, fidelity was the second rule he broke. Sam is a high-powered lawyer who lost interest in me at about the same time I became a mother and quit being a high-powered lawyer myself; ironically, I thought that was just when I was getting interesting.

"Gretchen says that if your tooth comes out too soon, you have to wait a long time for a new tooth to grow." She twists a hank of Madeline's yarn hair around her finger.

"Is Gretchen a girl in your class?"

"Gretchen knows about bugs and gerbils. She knows about why it's a hamster and not a gerbil. She has three teeth out. Madeline likes her."

"Then she must be nice."

"She is. She has long hair, really long. Down to here." She makes a chop at her upper arm. "She wears a jumper."

Like Madeline. "Do you eat lunch with her?"

"Sometimes. Not usually. Usually I'm alone."

"Why?"

"I don't know that much people, so nobody ever sits next to me."

I try to remember what I read in that parenting book. Talk so your kid will listen, listen so your kid will talk; it's catchy, but it means nothing. "What can we do about that?"

"I don't know." She shrugs.

I forget what the book says to do when they shrug. "Would you like to have Gretchen over? Maybe one of the days I'm off from work?"

"She won't come."

"You don't know that unless you ask."

"But I don't know her exactly as a best friend, okay?"

"But, honey, that's how you get to know some-one."

"Mom, I already told you!" She turns away.

I am at a loss. There is no chapter on your child having no friends. I even spied on her at recess last month after I went food shopping. The other first graders swung from monkey bars and chased each other; Maddie played by herself, digging with a stick in the hard dirt. Her Madeline doll was propped up against a nearby tree. I found myself thinking, If she's digging a grave for the doll, I'm phoning a shrink. Instead I telephoned her teacher that night.

"She'll be fine," she said. "Give her time."

"But it's March already. I'm doing everything I can. I help out in the classroom. I did the plant sale and the bake sale."

"Have you set up any play dates for her?"

"Every time I suggest that, she bursts into tears."

"Keep at it."

"But isn't there anything else I can do?"

"Let it run its course. She's on the young side."

"But she was fine last year, in kindergarten. She was even younger."

"Weren't you home then?"

Ouch. Then my alimony ran out and almost all my savings; with child support, I can swing part-time. "Yes, I only work three days a week, and she has her grandmother in the afternoon. It's not like she's with a stranger."

"She's just having some trouble with the adjustment."

Well, *duh,* I thought to myself.

But I didn't say it.

Bernice's ears prick up at the sound of a soft knock at the front door and she takes off, barking away, back paws skidding on the hardwood floor. In a minute, there's the chatter of a key in the lock; it has to be Ricki Steinmetz, my best friend. She's the only one with a key besides my mother.

"Rick, wait!" I shout, but it's too late.

The door swings open and Bernice bounds onto Ricki's shoulders. *"Aaaiieee!"* Ricki screams in surprise.

"Bernice, no!" I yank the dog from Ricki's beige linen suit, leaving distinct rake marks in the shoulder pads, and hustle Ricki and Bernice inside before my neighbors call the landlord.

"Is that a *dog?*" Ricki says, backing up.

I hold a finger to my lips and listen upstairs to hear if Bernice's barking woke Maddie. Ricki understands and shuts up, her mouth setting into a disapproving dash of burgundy lipstick. There's no sound from Maddie's room. Bernice chuffs loudly on Ricki's cordovan mules.

Ricki gasps. "Did you see that? She threw up on my shoes!"

"She just sneezed."

"These are Joan and David!"

"Come in the kitchen, would you?" I take Bernice by the collar and walk her like Quasimodo into the kitchen. "What are you doing here? It's almost nine o'clock."

Ricki snatches a paper napkin from the holder on the dining room table and follows me into the kitchen. "Didn't your mother tell you I called? I wanted to come over and see how you were, after what happened," she says, wiping her shoe. Ricki is a family therapist who takes clothing as seriously as codependency. She still looks put together even after a day of seeing clients; her white silk T-shirt remains unwrinkled, her lips lined. In fact, she'd look perfect if she didn't have those rake marks on her shoulders and that goober on her shoes.

"It'll dry."

"Disgusting." She slips on the shoe. "It's the judge's dog, isn't it?"

"Yep."

"Tell me you're taking it to the pound."

"Nope. I own it. Her."

She stands stock-still. "You're kidding me."

"Don't start with the dog. I heard it from my mother, I heard it from my daughter. You came over to be supportive, so start being supportive." I sit down on one of the pine stools at the counter in my makeshift eat-in kitchen, and Bernice stands beside me, tail wagging. I scratch her head.

"Sorry. You want some coffee, on you?"

"I'll make it." I start to get up, but Ricki presses me onto the stool with a firm hand.

"Sit!" she says.

Instantly, Bernice plops her curly-coated rump onto the floor.

"Wow," I say, astonished. "I never saw her do that."

Bernice pants happily, her long tongue unrolling like a rug.

"Cute," Ricki says.

"And pedigreed, too. When can I drop her off?"

"No way." She opens the freezer.

"But you have more room than I do. You need a Swiss dog. Think of the boys, if they get lost in the mall."

"I'm ignoring you." She rummages through the boxes of frozen vegetables. "Where's the coffee?"

"On the door." I give up and watch my new dog lie down at the foot of my stool, shifting once, then again, to get comfortable on the tile floor. She needs a dog bed, but I'll be damned if I'll buy that, too.

"What happened to that cappuccino decaf I gave you?" Ricki shouts from inside the freezer. Icy clouds billow around her chic wedge of thick brown hair.

"It's gone. Use the Chock Full O' Nuts."

"You don't have flavored?"

"I have coffee-flavored. Now close the door."

She grabs a can and shuts the door. "I'm going to understand your crummy mood because you're entitled to it. You have a good reason to feel crummy."

"Is this the supportive part?"

"Yes. I'm validating you."

"Like parking, you stamp my ticket?"

"Just like that." She pries the plastic lid off the can and spoons the coffee into the basket, then pours the water into the coffeemaker. I watch her as if I've never seen this done, my brain stuck in a sort of stasis. The red light on the Krups blinks on: a machine, highly reliable and predictable. People are not machines, and so they do unpredictable things. Things that strike like a bolt from the heavens, stunning you where you stand.

"You okay?" Ricki asks.

I watch the coffee dribble into the glass pot. "I still can't believe it."

"I know." Ricki puts her arm around me, but I don't feel her touch, not really. A spring storm howls outside, rattling the loose storm windows. These things seem like they're happening around me, and not really to me. "It's a shock," she says.

I think of Armen. His hand in my hair. How easily he lifted me to the couch. The weight of his body, the strength of it. He was lovely. "It's just not possible."

"I know," she says, stroking my hair.

He was happy. I know he was. "He didn't even own a gun."

"I read it was registered to his wife."

Susan. She's the one who found him. He was going to tell her about us. "She put Bernice in a *dog pound,* Rick. What kind of a woman does that to her husband's pet?"

Ricki glances at Bernice, comatose on the floor. "I can see it."

"They had a terrible marriage, no matter what she says. They were going to divorce."

"How do you know all this?"

"He told me."

"He told you about his marriage? Since when?"

"And Sarah, one of the law clerks, worked on Susan's campaign. I think she came by chambers late at night. She got nervous when I told her about the tapes."

"Tapes?"

"It was a bluff, but it worked." I hear myself sounding slightly hyper. "Then there's Galanter."

"Galawho?" Ricki steps away from me, concerned.

"Judge Galanter, who becomes chief now, for the next seven years. He'd never have gotten to be chief if Armen hadn't died. He would have been too old to be eligible, past sixty-five. I wonder if he drinks."

"A judge, drinking? A federal appellate judge?"

"What, it's confined to the trades?" I experience it again, as a flash of insight: the fighting, a woman's fists pounding futilely against a man's bulky shoulders. My mother and my father. I can't remember any more than that. I was six when he left.

"Grace, you're losing it." She looks at me like I'm crazy, and maybe I am. I feel it welling up inside of me.

"Is it possible that he didn't commit suicide? Is it possible that he was murdered?"

"What?" she says.

I tell her the whole story, about Armen and me. She looks drained when I'm done, but still caring, and I imagine that's what she looks like after a session with one of her flakier clients. She sets down her empty coffee mug with finality. "I'm worried about you, Grace. You've lost a man you cared for, and not for the first time. There was Sam."

"What's Sam have to do with it?"

"It's a loss."

"No, it isn't. It's not a loss when you lose someone who doesn't want you. Happily ever after, just not together."

Ricki crosses her arms. "You don't mean that."

"I sure do. You may not think my life turned out so great, but I do. I'm okay. At least I was until this happened."

"Maybe Armen's death is kicking up a lot of stuff for you."

"What stuff?"

"Abandonment. Loss. Think of your father."

"My father?" I almost laugh. I hate it when she turns into a shrink. "How do you guys make these connections? My father was a drunk. Armen was wonderful."

"But they both left you. It makes sense that you're having trouble accepting it."

He left you. It hurts to hear her say it; that much is true. "I don't think that's it. I can accept that he's gone, Ricki. What I can't accept right now is that he committed suicide. At least I can't accept it without question, like the rest of the world. I don't understand it, okay? Not yet, anyway."

She holds up two neatly manicured hands. "Okay. Okay. I'll shut up. After all, you're the cop here."

"What'd you say?"

"You heard me."

But she's right. I did, and it gives me an idea.

10

EXECUTIVE PARKING LOT, says the sign on the steel racks of Samsonite briefcases. It's the only spark of humor in the grim police station, from the aging alcoholic asleep in the lobby to the battleship-gray paint peeling off the cinder-block walls. Detective Ruscinjki blends in here, with his gray hair and gray eyes. He folds his furry arms behind an ancient typewriter in the bustling Central Detectives' office and looks up at me. "You sure you're not with the media?" he asks.

"No."

A black detective in shirtsleeves and shoulder holster walks by, ignoring us.

He looks unconvinced. "We got lots of calls from the media on this case. Print media. Electronic media. They'd say anything to get past the desk, anything to get the gory details."

"I'm not a reporter. I told you, I worked for Judge Gregorian. I have court ID if you want."

He leans back in his chair at a long table in the common room. "All right, Miss Rossi, so you're not with the media. You're not his lawyer, either, or a member of the family. That means I tell you what I tell the reporters. The case is closed. We have no reason to believe that the judge's death was anything other than a suicide." A lineup of battered file cabinets sits behind him, solid as the stone wall he's putting up for my benefit. Or detriment.

"I was just wondering how you can be so sure. Is there some physical evidence you found?"

"Not that I intend to discuss with you. Trust me, it was a suicide. I saw it."

I feel my mouth open. "What? You *saw* Armen?"

He frowns, confused for a moment. "The judge? I was on the squad Monday night, I got the call. That's why you asked the desk man for me, isn't it?"

"I didn't ask anybody for you. I just said I needed to talk to one of the detectives about Judge Gregorian."

He takes one look at me and seems to sense there was something between Armen and me; he's not a detective for nothing. "I'm sorry," he says, softening. "Sit down."

So I do, in a stiff-backed metal chair catty-corner to him.

"Listen to me," he says, leaning on the typewriter. "I've been a detective for nine years now, spent twelve years on the force before that. I don't rule it a suicide unless I'm one hundred percent. On this one, I was one hundred percent. So was the ME."

"ME?"

"Medical examiner. He was there himself, since the judge was so prominent, husband of the senator and all. They'll have the toxicology reports in a month, and the autopsy results. But I tell you, we agreed on the scene, him and me."

A medical examiner; an autopsy. I can't even think about it, not now anyway. "What was the evidence?"

He shakes his head. "I couldn't tell you that even if I wanted to."

"I read a lot about it in the newspapers. They seemed to have plenty of information."

"An important man, a case like this, the papers will know a lot. We may have a leak or two, there's nothin' I can do about that. But none of it comes from me."

"I read in the paper that the gunshot wound was to the right temple. Armen—the judge—was right-handed. Is that the type of evidence you look for?"

"One of the things."

"The papers said the gun was his wife's."

"She kept it in the desk. Felt very bad he used it that way. Cried a river."

"The paper also said the doors and windows were locked. So that's something you look for too, right? In a suicide."

"Yes. Generally."

"In the *Daily News* they said it was a contact wound. What does that mean? Like you said, 'generally'?"

"Miss Rossi, I'm not going to tell you about this case. I can't."

"Just generally, not in this case. Does it mean a wound where the gun makes contact?"

Ruscinjki purses his lips; they're as flat as the rest of his features, and his receding hairline is a gentle gray roll, like a wave.

"How can you tell that it made contact?"

"I can't say—"

"I'm just asking a question. Not in this case or anything. Hypothetically."

"Hypothetically?" A faint smile appears.

"Yes. If I were to say to you, How can you tell if something is a contact wound, what would you say?"

"How we know it's a contact wound is the gunpowder residue. If it's a contact shot it sprays out like a little star. A shot from a coupla inches away, the gunpowder sprays all over."

I try not to think about the gunpowder star. "Okay. What else do you see with a typical suicide? Educate me." I imagine I'm taking a deposition of a reluctant witness, and I'm not far wrong.

"Gunpowder residue on the hand, and blow-back."

"Blowback?"

"Blood on the hand that held the gun. Blood on the gun, too."

I try not to wince. "Okay. Anything else?"

"Cadaverous spasm."

"And that is?"

"The body's reaction to the pain of the blast, the shock of it."

"How does the body react? Generally?"

"The hand grips around the gun and stays that way. After death."

"Is there anything else?"

"No. That's mostly all of it."

"I see. Now. If you don't have this type of evidence, the three things you mentioned, the case is not one hundred percent. Is that right?"

"Right. In a case where there's no note."

I almost forgot. "Is it odd there was no note? I mean, in the typical case do you see a note?"

"Most times there is a note. Most suicides lately are your AIDS people, people who know they're going to die. They leave a note. They prepare."

"So if there's not a note, does that tell you it's not a suicide?"

"Not at all. It doesn't tell me anything, one way or the other. Lots of suicides leave their notes way in advance—depression, preoccupation, withdrawal." His tone grows thoughtful, more relaxed; he'd rather talk psychology than pathology. So would I.

"But Judge Gregorian wasn't depressed."

"According to the secretary, he did become depressed about this time of year. Something about Armenians." He brushes dust off the typewriter keys. "The press was all over him because of that death penalty appeal. Not that I'm talking about the actual case." The sly smile reappears, then fades.

"But he seemed to handle that fine."

"The senator said his mother committed suicide. It runs in families, you know."

"But it's not inherited."

"They get the idea. All of a sudden it becomes a possibility. It's like kids in high school, they come in clusters." He looks sad for a moment. "People kill themselves all the time, for lots of reasons we can't understand. Who can understand something like that, anyway?"

I consider this and say nothing, sickened by the image of Armen slumped over, his lifeblood seeping out. A lethal black star on his temple. His own blood spattered on his hand.

"The judge had a watchdog, too. A good watchdog."

Bernice. "What about his dog? Did you see her that night?"

He laughs. "I would say so, it tried to take my arm off. We had to lock it in the bathroom, wouldn't let us near him. I read the wife donated it to the Boys Club."

So much for his detective work; Bernice is in my wagon out front, she fussed so much I decided to take her with me to work. "So you figure that in, right? The dog would have attacked a stranger."

"Yeah. Sure."

"But not someone she knew."

He shrugs. "So?"

"So if he was killed, the killer was someone he knew."

"He wasn't killed. All the evidence is consistent with him killing himself."

"It's only consistent with him putting a gun to his right temple. What if someone made him do it?"

He shakes his head. "There would be signs of a struggle, or a forced entry, and there aren't any."

"But it's possible."

"I doubt it."

"But is it possible? Hypothetically?"

He gets up with an audible sigh, pushing down on his thighs like a much older man. "You know, there are support groups."

Support groups. Therapy. He sounds like Ricki.

"Listen, Miss Rossi. You may never understand it. Doesn't mean it didn't happen."

I meet his cool eye. He's a detective, an experienced one. Maybe he is right about Armen. Still, maybe he's not.

I leave the police station and walk to my wagon, parked at a meter across the street. Bernice has escaped from the cargo area and is nestled officially in the driver's seat, but she doesn't notice me coming toward her. She's watching a thick-set man get into a black boxy car a couple down the line.

Odd, he looks like someone I saw yesterday in my neighborhood.

I watch the car pull out quickly. A new car, American-made. The license plate is from Virginia.

Strange.

"*Roarf!*" Bernice says, startling me.

"Get back, beast," I say to her through the car window.

You're no fun, say her eyes.

Christ. I fish in my blazer pocket for my car keys, but they come out with a folded strip of legal paper. I figure it's an old shopping list until I open it up:

Grace—

This is only the beginning for us. I love you.

Armen

P.S. I hope you find this before your dry cleaner.

I look at the note in disbelief. I read it again. Armen.

I love you. My God. I feel a wrenching inside my chest.

It's his handwriting; it always looked like he was writing in Armenian, even when he wasn't. How did this get here? When did he write it?

Of course.

The last time I wore this jacket was Monday, the night we were together. It was slung over the back of my chair.

I check the other pockets, but they're empty. When did Armen leave this note? Then I remember. I used his bathroom before we left. My jacket was at the conference table.

This is only the beginning for us.

I shake my head. Not the sentiment of a man intending to kill himself. Not at all.

"*Roarf!*" Bernice barks again, trying to stand in the seat. Her slobber has smeared up the window.

I look back at the police station and consider

running back inside. No. I'd have to tell the detective everything, and he'd find a way to dismiss it anyway. He's one hundred percent, he said.

I look down at the note in my hand, feeling a surge of pain inside, and with it, a certainty. Armen didn't commit suicide. He was murdered. I know it now. I'm holding proof positive. Exhibit A.

Unaccountably, I think of the black car. I look down the street, but it's long gone.

Someone's life is at stake, Armen had said. *Get involved.*

I put the note back in my pocket and slip my car key in the door. There's going to be an investigation, but it'll have to be my own. Because I'm involved, starting now.

As soon as I can get into the driver's seat.

The intercom buzzes on my telephone as soon as I get to my desk in the vacant clerks' office of the judge who lives in North Jersey. It's lined with case reports and lawbooks, and furnished in a cheap utilitarian way, with a wooden desk, side table, and chair. "Yes?"

"Grace? I've been calling you at home, it's your day off, isn't it?" It's Sarah. My heart gives a little jump.

"Yes, but I'll be in every day for a while, and today I have to look at that marshals' tape."

"That's what I wanted to talk to you about. I'll be right over."

My heart pounds as we hang up. Jesus, is she going to confess to murder? What will I do? I open my desk drawer, and a gleaming pair of scissors glints from a logjam of yellow pencils. I put the scissors near my right hand on the desktop, feeling idiotic for arming myself against a baby lawyer from Yale.

"Knock knock," Sarah says. She leans confidently against the doorjamb. A filmy skirt billows around her freckled ankles; a melon sweater complements her hair.

"That was fast."

"We need to talk, you and I."

I let my hand linger near the scissors. "I'm listening."

She slides into the hard leather chair across from my desk and crosses her long legs in the drapey skirt. "You might as well say it. You know I'm on the tape."

"I haven't seen it yet, so I don't know that. Why don't you tell me what I'm going to see?"

She tosses her hair back. "I have a better idea. Why don't you tell me what I saw that night in Armen's office? On the conference table and the couch, as I recall."

I feel myself stop breathing. *I love you.* "What you saw was none of your business. You were spying."

"You were fucking your boss."

I rise to my feet involuntarily behind the desk. "What were you doing there?"

She doesn't bat an eye. "What's the difference what *I* was doing there? You were *fucking* him, Grace."

The mouth on this child. "Stop saying that."

"You two were having an affair, I knew it all along. That's why he wanted you on *Hightower*. When he told you he wouldn't marry you, you threatened to blackmail him. Tell the papers, ruin his reputation. You and Ben put so much pressure on him that he killed himself the same night."

I look at her in astonishment. "That's ridiculous, all of it. Where did you get *that* from?"

"I figured it out."

Typical Yale grad; totally impractical—or smart enough to know that the best defense is a good offense. "It's crazy."

"You should be ashamed of yourself," she says. Her voice rises in anger, but I can't tell if it's an act or not.

"Wait a minute, Sarah, what were you doing in chambers in the middle of the night? You were supposed to be in bed with Artie."

"I knew Armen would be working late. I was bringing him a sandwich."

"You left Artie to bring another man something to eat?"

"Artie wouldn't mind. He loves Armen."

"So you told him?"

She looks uncertain. "Not exactly."

"Of course you didn't. You didn't care if Armen was hungry, Sarah, you knew I'd be working late with him, and you wanted to see if anything was happening that shouldn't be. If he was cheating on Susan, your friend."

"Are you kidding?" She laughs abruptly. "I knew their marriage was over."

Part of it is true, leaving me dumbfounded. "How do you know that?"

"I practically ran her campaign, remember? I'll be her chief aide after this job. She tells me everything."

"Then why were you so worried about the tapes?"

"Because I knew I was on them."

It doesn't square. "So why is that a problem, if you have nothing to hide? A tape of you with a sandwich, so what?"

Her blue eyes freeze like ice. "You don't know what you're talking about. What are you accusing me of?"

I don't even know, but she's getting angrier, so I spin a plausible argument out of the meager facts I've been dealt, making something out of nothing, like any good lawyer. "All right, how's this? You come to the office and see Armen and me on the couch. You're so enraged you can't sleep. You go to his house, and he lets you in. Even Bernice is happy to see you, so she doesn't make a fuss."

"Ridiculous."

My hand inches over to the scissors. "You scream at him, lose control, like you did the other morning with Ben. He tells you he loves me and you go even crazier."

"Why would I do all that?"

"Because you're in love with him."

Sarah's mouth drops open, and before I can stop her she's lunging right at me. I feel the sting of a hard slap across my cheek and stagger backward, the scissors slipping from my hand. She comes at me again, her face contorted with uncontrollable rage. I know that expression, have seen it before on someone else, and for the first time in my life I realize I've been slapped before, with that much force. I slide down against the bookshelf, then am caught by strong arms. My father's. Sarah's.

"Grace!" Sarah yells. "Oh, God, are you all right?"

Grace, are you all right? Are you all right?

The room is spinning, and fear runs cold in my stomach. "No, no," I hear myself saying.

"God, Grace, I'm so sorry! Here, wait," I hear Sarah saying, as if through a fog. The next thing I feel is a warm splash on my face. Wetness dribbles down my cheeks and onto my blouse. Sarah comes into hazy focus as a familiar odor brings me around. "Are you okay? Are you conscious?" she asks.

I wipe my face, then smell my wet hand. "Is this *coffee?*"

"Yes. Here, sit up." She helps me to a sitting position against the bookshelf and kneels on the rug opposite me.

"Why did you throw coffee at me?" Dazed, I watch as a full cup sets into a brown Rorschach blotch on my white blouse.

"I thought you were going to pass out. It was the only thing around. Not that you didn't deserve it," she adds, a trace of resentment wreathing her voice.

"I deserved it?"

"You shouldn't have said I loved him."

"You did, didn't you?" I wipe my cheeks on my sleeve; the blouse is a goner anyway.

"Don't say that, it would hurt Artie so much. And what you said, about me killing Armen, that was awful."

"I didn't say you killed him."

"You were about to." Her eyes well up as suddenly as Maddie's. In all her bravado, inside she is a child. A sheltered, spoiled child. "I would never kill Armen. I would never kill anyone. It's inconceivable."

I consider this. "I do think Armen was murdered," I say, hearing it out loud; it sounds right and horrible, at the same time.

"Do you really?" She blinks back her tears.

"You know Susan, right? If she came in from Washington and he told her about me, could she have killed him, in a jealous rage? A crime of passion?"

"Never. Never in a million years. She's not like that, emotional like that." She shakes her head.

"I want to talk to her."

"She's leaving for a fact-finding mission."

"Fact-finding? When?"

"Any day now, she's not sure."

"Where?"

"Eastern Europe, Bosnia. Investigating the genocide there."

A regular genocide hobbyist, that woman. "Don't you think it's odd for her to leave the country right now?"

"No. I think it's good for her. She needs to get away."

Suddenly I hear Bernice barking loudly, a fierce, threatening bark, one I haven't heard before. Someone shouts in the hallway; then a louder voice, Eletha's, screams, "No! No!"

"What's that?" Sarah says, alarmed.

"Trouble." I scramble to my feet. Sarah's right behind me as we tear toward chambers.

11

"Bernice, no!" I shout, but she pays even less attention than usual. Driven by instinct, her brown eyes lock onto her quarry, whose pin-striped back is quite literally against the wall.

"Somebody get this animal!" Galanter bellows, jowls flapping, arms splayed out like the Antichrist. A half cigar smolders between his fingers.

"Bernice, no!" I shout again, but her glistening black lips retract to display a lethal set of canines, only three feet from Galanter's belt buckle. She growls, and I feel a bolt of fear inside. She has the power to tear him to pieces and, apparently, good cause.

"Rossi, control this animal! Now!" Galanter sputters, his face a hot red.

"Just relax, Judge," I say, approaching Bernice slowly from behind. I have no idea if she'll bite me if I try to stop her.

I call to her softly, but she growls again and drops her head to crotch height. Galanter's blue eyes flare open in fear, and Artie begins to laugh.

"Hold still, dude," he says. "You got nothing to lose. She won't even find it."

"You're out of a job, mister!" Galanter says.

"Tell me about it," Artie says. "Grace, be careful now."

"Bernice won't hurt me. Will you, Bernice? You wouldn't hurt your mommy." I reach her glossy hindquarters with my fingertips and stroke my way up her back to her collar.

She growls again, baring more of her canines.

"She's going to jump!" Galanter shouts.

"No, she won't." My hand inches up to Bernice's neck and I grab the red leather collar securely in my hand. "Don't move yet, Judge."

"Hold her!" Galanter screams, slipping away from in front of Bernice.

"No, wait!" I yell, as Bernice lurches after the fleeing judge. My arms almost tear loose from their sockets and my heels skid along the carpet. Sarah throws her arms around my waist as Bernice thrashes in my grip, torquing her enormous body left and right in desperation. Her frantic barking reverberates in the tight corridor. I bury my face in a mountain of fur and hold on for dear life.

"SuperJew to the rescue!" Artie shouts. He tackles Bernice in midair, and she yelps in pain and frustration.

Galanter scrambles down the hall, pant legs flapping. He reaches his chambers and slams the door.

I release my grip on the dog, and so do Artie and Sarah. Bernice explodes out of the pileup and races to Galanter's chambers. She leaps onto the closed door and barks wildly.

"Jesus." I collapse next to Sarah and Artie, both flat on their backs on the carpet. I can't catch my breath; the coffee stain heaves up and down. Bernice has never acted that way before, and you don't have to be Oliver Wendell Holmes to figure out why.

"Can you believe that?" Eletha says.

"It's his aftershave," Artie says. "Or his personality."

Sarah rolls over and looks at me grimly. "What do you think, Grace?"

What do I think? I think I may not be able to complete my fact-finding mission on Susan, but I know where to find Galanter. I think the new chief judge will be needing an assistant. With experience.

"How do you know all this?" I ask Ben at the end of the day, in Armen's darkening office.

"That's what I've been wonderin' too," Eletha says, without looking up from the folders she's been filing. On the cardboard box it says DEAD FILES. "Why does Mr. Safer here know every damn thing before I do?"

"One of Judge Galanter's clerks told me, the only one who's still speaking to us after what Bernice did." Ben casts a cold eye at the dog, sleeping soundly where Armen's area rug used to be.

"But how can they hold phone argument in *Hightower?*" I ask. "You use the phone for status conferences, little things like that. Not for argument on a death case."

"Why not?" He crosses his arms, his oxford shirt a crisp white.

"Death is different, that's why not."

He looks up at the ceiling, searching the recessed lights like other people gaze at the stars. "Where have I heard that before?"

"Anthony Amsterdam, when he argued before the Supreme Court in *Gregg v. Georgia,*" Eletha says. "'Death is final. Death is irremediable. Death is unknowable; it goes beyond this world.'"

"How did you know that, Eletha?" Ben says with obvious surprise.

"Oh, I been workin' in de big house for a while now, Mr. Ben." She laughs naughtily. "It was in one of Armen's articles. I typed it and I never forgot it." Her smile fades and she returns to the box. "Hand those folders to me, Grace, the ones in front of you."

I slide the case files and appendices along the smooth tabletop. "Ben, when are they going to hold this phone argument?"

"Tonight at seven." He checks his watch. "An hour and a half."

"After the close of business?" Curiouser and curiouser.

"They have to do it tonight, to leave time for the Supreme Court to decide the appeal. It's Hightower's fault. He caused it by waiting until the last minute."

Now I understand. "It doesn't have anything to do with the timing or the Supreme Court. Galanter doesn't want argument during regular business hours because that would be public."

"Not necessarily."

"No? You think the newspapers would let the panel hold a closed argument in this case? The first death case here in *decades*? They'd be upstairs with motion papers before you could say First Amendment."

"As is their wont, but—"

"Galanter won't have that, so he calls a phone conference when the evening news is over. When the newspapers are sold out. Everybody will be watching *Home Improvement*."

"You've become quite the cynic, Grace." Ben unrolls a shirtsleeve and twists the cuff button closed expertly. "In fact, I heard the most outlandish thing about you today."

"What?"

"It's so absurd I can barely bring myself to repeat it." He sets to work on the other shirtsleeve, unfolding one three-inch panel after the next. "I heard you think the chief was murdered."

Eletha looks over at me in surprise.

"I do. Call me crazy."

"You're crazy," Eletha says. She lets the file slip into the box, where it lands with a *tick*.

"I thought you had more sense than that." Ben

fastens the button at the cuff, then holds both arms out and inspects them. "Well, I have to go. I'll leave you to your conspiracy theories."

"I didn't say it was a conspiracy."

Ben gasps in a theatrical way. "Maybe it is. Maybe the entire federal judiciary is in on it. Maybe they all conspired to kill him because he was—tall!" He turns on his heels, laughing, and walks out of the room. I watch him head into the clerks' office where he turns off his computer, then the lights. I listen for the sound of the door closing as he leaves. I know Eletha well enough to know she's waiting too.

"What the fuck you doin'?" she says, as soon as the chambers door clicks shut.

"Don't be shy, Eletha."

"Are you serious about this?"

"Yes."

"Is that what was goin' on with those marshal tapes yesterday?"

"Yep."

"They don't tape, do they?"

"Nope."

She shakes her head. "So what are you up to?"

"It doesn't make sense that he would kill himself."

"What are you sayin'?"

So I tell her, leaving out the most important part, the part about Armen and me. When I'm finished, she leans on the file box and looks directly at me. "Look, Grace, I knew he was in love with you. I knew about it before you did. He told me."

I feel my face redden. "You did? He did?"

"Mm-hm." She nods. "I have to admit, I told him not to get involved because you two work together. You know what he said? He told me he didn't give a good goddamn."

I smile. It warms me inside.

"So I know why you're thinkin' what you're thinkin'."

"Then why'd you tell me I was crazy?"

"Because Ben was here."

"What a good liar you are. Jeez, Eletha."

"Thank you, thank you." She curtsies prettily, then straightens up, rubbing her lower back. "Ow. Damn, I'm gettin' old."

"So what do you think? You knew him longer than any of us. Would he commit suicide?"

She sighs. "I worked for Armen for thirteen years, but I can't figure it out. It's hard to believe I wouldn't have seen something like that comin'. Like a sign."

"But the police say you said—"

"How do you know what the police say?"

"I went there this morning. They're sure it's a suicide. The detective was quoting you, things you said."

An angry frown contorts her features. "They didn't listen to me. That white cop askin' me those questions? He knew what he thought and he didn't want to hear anything different."

"I wanted to ask them about Susan. It was her gun."

"I can't get over what she did to Bernice. Dang, that woman's cold!"

"Do you think she would've—"

"Possible. It's possible. I wouldn't put it past her." She nods.

"And today with Galanter, that was wild."

"You mean Bernice? She shoulda bit it off. I'd put it down the garbage disposal myself."

I smile. "Has Bernice ever done that before?"

"Are you kidding? That dog is a doll baby." She shakes her head. "So you workin' with the police or something? They gonna reopen the case?"

"No. I'm on my own. Single Moms, Inc."

"You're talkin' about murder? Accusing a senator? Galanter? Shit, Grace."

"Not accusing, just asking questions. Developing theories. Being a lawyer."

She sighs and stretches backward with a tiny grunt. "Oh, my back."

"You all right?"

"It hurts. The lifting doesn't help."

I feel a pang of guilt. She's been packing by herself since Armen died; the office is littered with boxes, some taped closed, some still open. A lifetime of paper stored away; his whole career. It makes me sad, and it has to be hard on her, too. "I should have helped you. I'm sorry."

"Nah, s'all right. It's a lot of stuff, though. He saved everything, I swear." She points to the back of the office, to the long mahogany credenza behind Armen's desk. "We got all the personal stuff back there, the articles and stuff. Then we got the academic stuff and old case files against the side wall."

"Why don't you go home? I'll finish the box."

"Why you pushin' me out, girlfriend? You wanna look around?"

"I wasn't thinking of that, but it's a good idea."

She picks her sweater off the back of the chair. "All right, don't stay too late. Tomorrow, baby." She knocks hard on the wood, and Bernice wakes up with a startled bark. We both laugh.

"Dog almost ate a judge," I say.

"Smartest thing she ever did."

"Second smartest."

She pauses at the doorway and smiles softly. She knows the first: loving Armen. I suppress a stab of pain as I listen to her lock up her desk and gather her handbag and newspaper.

"By the way, El, have I got a man for you," I call out to her.

"You know I'm seein' Leon."

"Time for a change," I say, but she's out the door. It closes harshly, accentuating the stillness of the suddenly empty office.

I look around at the boxes and files filling the room. The brocade throws are folded into neat squares and stacked on a chair for packing. I never asked Armen where he got them or even what they were. Most of the other Armenian artifacts have been wrapped in bubble paper. I step between the boxes to his desk and find myself running my finger along its surface, leaving a wake in the dust like a light snow. I laugh to myself. A wonderful man, but not a neat man.

I look at Armen's chair and try to imagine him sitting in it again. It's so hard to believe he's gone. Murdered. It tears at me inside. Maybe there are clues here. Something. Anything.

I look over from the chair to the credenza beyond. None of its doors are open; Eletha hasn't started on it yet. What had she said was in there? The personal stuff. I walk around the desk and kneel on the carpet in front of the cabinet.

You were raised better, says my mother's voice, stopping my hand on the gold-toned knob.

"No, I wasn't," I say. I slide open the thin door and take the first paper off the top of the stack. Its typeface is faded and old-fashioned, from the days of Smith-Coronas.

TOWARD AN ARMENIAN IDENTITY
by Armen Gregorian

I brush the dust away. He wasn't a judge yet; it doesn't say if it was published. I sit down and skim the short article. Well-written, heartfelt. I reach for the next paper in the cabinet, but as I slide it out, a pack of old check registers falls to the carpet, bound by a dirty rubber band. I slip one out, skimming the entries: Food Fare $33.00, Harvard Coop $11.27, Haig $6.00 (for Chinese food). Judging from the sums, it was a long time ago, though Armen didn't bother to date the entries or keep a running tab of the balance.

Typical. It would have driven me crazy over time, but time is something we didn't have. Time was taken from us. From him.

I feel a lump in my throat and slip the register hastily back under the rubber band. I shove it next to another checkbook. It looks newer than the other papers in the cabinet, so I pull that one out.

It's a maroon plastic checkbook, fake alligator on the front and back. At the lower right corner it says PHILADELPHIA CASH RESERVE in gilt-stamped script. The checkbook looks brand new. I snap it open, anxious without knowing why.

The balance is staggering: $650,000. I had no idea. I look at the name and address and hear myself gasp.

Greg Armen. The address is an apartment in West Philadelphia.

What apartment is this? Armen lived in Society Hill, in a townhouse he owned with Susan. I look again at the name on the checks. Greg Armen. Obviously an alias. But why?

I hear my mother's voice inside my head: Come on, kid. A judge with a secret bank account? A false address? An alias?

A bribe.

Impossible. I push the voice away and flip through the checkbook. There are no entries since the initial one, which is undated.

Was Armen involved in something? Does it have anything to do with his death?

I swallow hard and think twice before committing theft. Well, once maybe. Then I take the checkbook and close the cabinet.

12

Only an hour later I have crossed the threshold into another world. A scented, serene world, where the colors are chalky washes of pastels and the air carries the scent of primrose. Is it heaven? In a way. It's the Laura Ashley shop at the King of Prussia mall. I called Ricki to discuss the checkbook and she agreed to meet me here. I trail in reluctantly behind her, holding her bags like a pack animal. "So what do you think?"

"I told you what I think. I think you should go straight to the police. Show them the note from Armen and the checkbook." She plucks a frilly blouse off the rack and holds it against her chest. "You like?"

"For you or for me?"

"I don't need blouses, you do. That coffee stain is so attractive."

I tug my blazer over the brown blotch. "I have enough blouses."

"No you don't. You have the yellow one you wear over and and over, and the blue." She slips the blouse back onto the rack. "But it is a lot of money."

"The blouse or the bank account?"

"The blouse."

"So's the account."

"I wonder if he declared it, the crook."

"Don't say that." I look around the small store, but it's empty. Nobody can afford this stuff, not even in King of Prussia. "He's not a crook."

"You sound like Richard Nixon."

I set the bags down beside the rack. "I bet it has something to do with his murder."

"Murder? You're losing it, Grace. I told you. The checkbook doesn't mean he was murdered. Maybe he committed suicide in regret over taking a bribe." She snatches a blouse from the rack and her hazel eyes come alive; it's off-white, with billowy sleeves and a Peter Pan collar. She hoists it proudly into the air. "This is perfect."

"For what? Punting on the Thames?"

Ricki puts the blouse back onto the rack. "You have a bad attitude, you know that?"

"But we don't know it's a bribe, Rick. All we know is that it's a checking account of some kind."

"A boatload of money under an alias? Come on." Her concentration refocuses, laserlike, on the next ruffled blouse on the rack. She picks it up and appraises it. "This is nice."

"What about the note?"

"What about the blouse?"

"Where am I going to wear it, Rick? Tara?" She slaps it back onto the rack. "Maybe we'll have better luck with the dresses." She turns smartly away and heads over to a lineup of dresses whose skirts are so voluminous they puff out like parachutes. Ricki extracts one with an expertise born of practice and waves it at me from across the store. "Very appropriate, don't you think?" she says.

I pick up the bags and follow her. "No feathers? I want feathers. And a headpiece."

A young saleswoman, more like a saleschild, perks up from behind a counter littered with fragrant notecards and stationery. She looks like Alice in Wonderland in a black velvet headband and a white pinafore. "That's one of our most popular styles," she says.

"I hate it," I whisper.

Ricki looks daggers at me. "Give it a chance, Sherlock."

"No."

The saleschild's face falls.

Ricki slaps the dress back in place. "You are so stubborn. So stubborn."

"Rick, listen."

"You said you wanted me to help you."

"This isn't what I meant."

"Why do I bother? You call me up and I come. My one night without clients and here I am. I should have gone food shopping. There's no milk in the house." She puts her hands on her hips and glares at me.

There's no milk in the house. The all-time low watermark of motherhood.

I put my hands on my hips and we face off at opposite ends of the dress rack, the High Noon of Mothers. No milk in the house, and Ricki is the most organized of women; it must gnaw at her conscience like an overdue library book. I feel the first pang of guilt, which means she's quicker on the draw. "Give me the goddamn dress," I say.

"Good." She plucks it from the rack and pushes it at me.

"I'm not promising anything."

"Fine."

The saleschild comes over. "Can I help you?" she says brightly. Too brightly for minimum wage.

"Yes," Ricki says. "My friend needs dresses. With her eyes, I think a royal blue would be nice."

"Rick, I'm standing here. I can speak."

The saleschild looks from Ricki to me.

"I don't want anything fancy," I say.

"Not fancy?" The saleschild looks puzzled; fancy is all they sell. They have a monopoly in fancy.

"She doesn't mean fancy," Ricki says, "she means fussy."

"No, I mean fancy. Empire waistline, hem to the floor. I'm too old for puffed sleeves."

"Fussy," Ricki says again.

The saleschild looks at Ricki, then at me. The poor girl's getting dizzy. I hand her the dress for balance.

"Where are the business-y dresses?" Ricki asks.

"I'm out of a job, Rick."

"Then you need interview clothes."

"Follow me," says the saleschild. She pads in ballet slippers to a rack of dresses and takes three from the rack. Any one of them would work at my coronation, but Ricki badgers me to try one on. We squeeze together into the flowered dressing room. Ricki always comes into dressing rooms with me; she doesn't realize this was okay when we were in high school but now that we're almost forty, is a bit odd.

"Are we having fun yet?" I mutter, stepping into the billowing dress.

"Let me zip it up for you," Ricki says.

"It's the least you can do."

She zips the dress more roughly than necessary and I regard myself in the mirror. The style makes me look tall and thin, which must be some sort of optical illusion. Still, all I can see is that my eyes look too small and my nose looks too big; my father's Sicilian blood, acid-etched into my features. I look terrible.

"You look stunning!" Ricki says from behind me.

"Uncanny. That's just what I was thinking."

"The neckline is so pretty."

I look down at my chest and catch sight of the scalloped bra, barely covered by the dress. It reminds me of Armen, of that night. *This is the beginning for us. I love you.* "What about the note he wrote me, Rick?"

But she's busy picking up a flowered scarf and tossing it around my neck. She's caught brain fever from the shopping, like early man, blood-lusting after the kill. She found the right dress, now the whole village can eat. "Here, if you're not in love with the neckline."

"Rick, what do you think about the note?"

"What note?" She drapes the scarf to the left, then squinches up her nose.

"The one I found in my pocket."

She rearranges the scarf over my shoulder. "Are we talking about that again?"

"Yes."

"I'm trying to take your mind off your official police duties, but you're not letting me."

"Just tell me where the note fits in, huh? Is that the act of a man who would kill himself a few hours later? You're a shrink, you tell me. You must have handled suicide in your practice."

"Only one, thank God." She crosses herself quickly even though she's Jewish.

"But depressed people, right? You must see tons of depressed people."

"Oh, they ship 'em in."

"Rick, will you help me? You may actually know something here."

"Why, thank you."

"You know what I mean."

She ties the scarf around my neck. "Okay, so you're asking me? Professionally?"

"Yes."

She pats the knot and steps back, squinting at my costume like a movie director. "I think your friend the judge was a very interesting personality, and I think his behavior was totally consistent with suicide. Even the note."

"But how?"

"Let me ask you this. How well did you know this man?"

"Armen? I knew him well."

"You worked for him for three months. Part-time."

"We worked closely together. I knew him well."

"Think about it," she says. "You didn't know he loved you. You didn't know he was sitting on a pile of money. You didn't know he had an apartment."

"But I knew what mattered, what kind of man he was. Everybody knew that. And what's this have to do with psychology anyway?"

"Everything. He was a very important judge, a powerful judge, and the husband of a United States senator. On top of that, he's a *macher* in the Armenian community. A hero, right?"

"Yes." I feel vaguely like I'm being led where I don't want to go.

"So people like that, they're managing constantly under the pressure to live up to very high standards. The standards of others, of the community. It's tough to keep that veneer perfect, to keep up appearances. They begin to keep secrets, like he did, and pretty soon what they know about themselves grows further and further away from what the world thinks of them. In the right circumstances, a person like that falls apart. The veneer cracks, and so do they."

"But it wasn't a veneer. He really was—"

"Perfect?"

I feel it inside. "Yes. In a way. He believed in things. He cared, really cared, and he fought hard."

"Don't you think you're idealizing him, Grace?"

"No, I'm not idealizing him." My throat tightens, but it could be the scarf. "Take this frigging thing off. I feel like a boy scout in drag."

She avoids my eye and unties the scarf. "You worked for him for a short time. You had a business relationship with him until one night. Now you're charging around, going to the police, ransacking his office for clues."

"I wasn't ransacking."

"You're acting like it was a fifteen-year relationship, like he was your husband. But he wasn't. In fact, he was somebody else's."

Ouch. "That's beside the point. The man was murdered, Ricki."

"You don't know that. It's not your job to investigate it, even if it *is* true. If you were my client, I'd ask you why you're doing all this. What would happen if you didn't?"

"His killer would go free."

"And what's the matter with that?"

I look wildly around the frilly dressing room. "What's the matter with murder? It's very bad manners, for starters."

"Don't be snide, I mean it."

"But what kind of question is that, What's the

matter with murder?" I hear my voice growing louder.

"No, the question is, Why does it matter if his killer goes free?"

I hold back my snidehood. "It's terrible. It's *unfair.*"

"Then it's the unfairness that strikes you."

"Yes, of course."

She purses her lips. "You're a person who's been treated unfairly. By your father, then by Sam. You had a baby, he wanted out. He broke the contract."

I feel a churning inside. "Yeah, so?"

"So maybe it's not *this* unfairness you're fighting about, maybe it's unfairnesses in your past. Ones you can't do anything about."

"Oh please, Ricki."

"Think about it. Keep an open mind."

"The man is dead, Rick. Am I just supposed to ignore that?"

She folds her arms calmly, like she always does when I get upset. Therapists never have emotions; that's why they want to hear ours. "How long have we known each other?" she asks.

I boil over. "Too damn long."

"Well, that's a very nice thing to say."

"If you wouldn't analyze me at every turn—"

"You asked me to."

"I asked you to analyze *him,* not me."

"Why do you need me to analyze him if you know him so goddamn well? Hmm?"

I have no immediate answer. The word *uncle* comes immediately to mind, but I push it away.

"Well?" A triumphant smile steals across her face. "I should've been a lawyer, right?"

Right. Or a personal shopper.

The red-lighted numbers on the clock radio say 4:13 A.M.; they're oddly disjointed, constructed like toothpicks laid end to end. It flips to 4:14.

The house sleeps silently. The dishwasher stopped cranking at 1:10, leaving only the clothes dryer in the basement. A wet bathroom rug thudded against the sides of the drum, keeping me awake until 2:23. Since then I have no excuse except for my own feelings, tumbling as crazily as the rug in the dryer. The fury, grief, and confusion cycle: it comes right after spin-dry.

Maddie's in the next room, her door closed against Bernice, who sleeps in my bed like a mountain range bordering my right side and curling under my feet. This must be why they call them mountain dogs. I shove her over, but she doesn't budge. My thoughts circle back to Armen.

He said he loved me, but there's obviously much he didn't say. A secret bank account. An alias. I sit up and shake two powdery generic aspirins from the bottle, then swallow them with some flat seltzer from a bottle on my night table. I flop back in bed and stare up at the white ceiling with its cracked paint, trying to put away my emotions.

But I'm having less success than usual. Anxiety makes my chest feel tight. I wonder vaguely if they have a drug for that, and then I remember that they do.

Alcohol.

The thought warms me like brandy. I throw off the covers, slip on a terry bathrobe, and tiptoe down the creaky stair. Bernice looks up but doesn't follow; she won't go in the kitchen now unless she's dragged into it.

I flick on the kitchen light and dim it down, then open up the tall kitchen cabinet that was built into the wall sixty years ago. My landlord let me strip the old paint away, and underneath was a fine bare pine, which I scrubbed and pickled white. I love this cabinet, a true old-fashioned larder, which finds room for every grocery I buy on its five shelves. The liquor is at the top, like a penthouse above the stories of oversized cereal boxes, cans of soup, and baked beans.

I grab a stool, climb up on it, and pull down a thick shot glass, one of the multitude my mother gave me a long time ago. Half I threw out and half I stowed in the basement until Maddie found them. I eventually had to sneak them away from her, finding something unseemly about a child's tea party with shot glasses and a steel jigger. I hid them up here, where they line up like pawns guarding the liquor bottles.

I peer at the dusty bottles and try to make a decision. What shall I treat myself to? It's all left over from my wedding, the last time I had more than two drinks. Alcohol goes right to my head, but that's suddenly what I want.

A bottle of Crown Royal stands like a king

behind the pawns. The lattice blown into its glass catches even the dim light. I pick the bottle up by its gold plastic crown and climb down from the shelf.

I am going to get drunk. This strikes me as a daring and powerful act, something a man would do. I am going to have myself a drink, yessir, I am going to tie one on. I put the bottle on the counter and crack open the cap, which sticks slightly. The bottle's almost full. I take a whiff.

Fragrant. Sweet. Tangy. Strong.

I remember this smell, and it brings a memory down on my head. My parents fighting again, shouting. My father, lurching out the door. My mother, crying alone. A bottle of Crown Royal sitting in the center of a kitchen table, eye level with me: It's so majestic, glinting like gold. A regal beacon in a world where Daddy is gone and the future is a mystery.

I pour myself a shot.

13

My head buzzes with liquor from the night before; my stomach gurgles like a polluted stream. Getting drunk isn't as manly as I thought it would be. At least not the next morning.

You don't have to be hung over to be seeing double. Even triple. There are judges everywhere in the grand ceremonial courtroom: circuit judges, district judges, bankruptcy judges, magistrate judges. They gather like ravens in ebony robes on either side of the dais and in the reserved section in front of it. Twenty representative judges from the circuit and district courts fill the dais in two tiers. Crows on the power lines.

The audience, relegated to the back rows, is standing room only. Lawyers, academics, and reporters clog the courtroom. Standing in the back are older men in shabby overcoats, the courtroom junkies dressed up. Shake and Bake isn't here, but one of them, in a dark overcoat, looks familiar. Thick and bulky, like a thug. I try to think where I've seen him before.

Outside the police station? Maybe the man in the black car with Virginia plates.

I crane my neck to see him better, but he disappears behind a group of Armen's closest friends, the Armenian men in his dinner club; they cleave together, olive-skinned and outnumbered. Susan has been doing what she can to cut them and everybody else out, flying Armen's body to Washington for a funeral tomorrow. Meanwhile she sits dry-eyed in the front row, sucking up all the attention by saying nothing, like a vacuum.

Does she know about Greg Armen?

It makes me sick to my stomach. Everything does.

Ben has joined Galanter's clerks, up front. Artie sits with Eletha, comforting her before the service begins, but he looks like he needs comforting himself. He's more unkempt than usual, his hair uncombed and his rep tie wrinkled. Sarah is next to me in the row behind them; she and Artie don't exchange a word during the ceremony. Is there trouble in Paradise? I haven't been paying attention.

Chief Judge Galanter begins the memorial service from the coveted center seat. His statement is ruthlessly generic, and over as soon as it starts.

A few of the other judges make short speeches, their words shaky, their sentences halting. They mourn, but it's a peculiar sort of mourning, characterized by bewilderment. One of their own, a suicide. Only Judge Robbins says the word, his eyes red-rimmed behind rimless spectacles. I close my mind until the service is over, hoping my head will stop thundering.

When it's over the judges adjourn to the robing room, and some of Armen's Armenian friends linger near the dais, waiting for a chance to talk to Susan. At the periphery of the crowd are reporters, interested in the same thing. Susan doesn't seem to mind talking to anyone and doesn't shed a tear. Her own husband's memorial service. What had the detective said? *Cried a river?*

A wild-haired reporter with a day's stubble gets close to her and says, "Senator, just clear up one thing for me. Senator, over here."

She looks up, but her smile vanishes when she seems to recognize him. "One question, Sandy. That's it."

"Is it true that you and the judge were having marital problems?"

Shocked, the well-wishers turn and look at him.

Susan's mouth sets into a thin line. "I'm fine. Thanks for asking." Instantly, a tall, preppy aide in expensive eyeglasses takes her elbow and hustles her through the crowd to the robing room door.

"Have some decency!" an older lawyer says to the reporter, who takes off through the crowd after Susan. Two marshals, Mutt and Jeff, head after him; the big one, McLean, takes the lead.

"What an asshole," Sarah says, but I watch the reporter until I lose him in the crowd. "Let's go."

Sarah and I bobble together in the mass of people leaving the ceremony. I whisper to her, "How do you think he knew?"

"Lucky guess. He's been hustling since the campaign, trying to get a real job."

I consider this, but it hurts my head to think. I keep seeing the checkbook, hidden now in my underwear drawer.

We pour out of the courtroom doors into the marble walkway that connects the north half of the federal building to the courthouse. I let the crowd carry me past the plant-filled atrium on the right, which the court employees use to smoke in. A hunchbacked man sweeps up the discarded cigarette butts with a broom.

"You'd think we could find him something better to do," says a man's voice beside Sarah. The wild-haired reporter. Up close, he looks sweaty and his curls are permed. "Remember me, Miss Whittemore?"

"What happened to the marshals?" Sarah says, and picks up the pace next to me.

"I'm Sandy Faber. I write for a lot of newspapers in the city."

"Where do you get off asking a question like that?" Sarah says, barreling ahead.

The reporter falls into her brisk stride. "Did I upset your client, Miss Whittemore?"

"I don't have any clients, and you don't fool me for one minute. You're the one who wrote that victim's rights story. You called Armen a killer."

"I didn't call him a killer, I merely quoted—"

"I don't want to hear it."

The reporter scrambles over to me and grabs my arm. "Ms. Rossi, it'll just take a minute. I know you cared about the judge."

"We all did," I say, wresting my arm back.

"Somebody didn't. The person who killed him."

It stuns me in my tracks, but Sarah reacts instantly. "How dare you!" she says. "You want me to call the marshals?"

"Take a look at your co-counsel here, Miss Whittemore. She's not so sure it's a suicide either."

I feel my gorge rising, only partly from the alcohol. I look past the crowd for the ladies' room and spot it at the end of the gleaming hall. "I have to go."

"Grace, are you all right?" Sarah asks.

I wave her off. "See you upstairs."

"Ms. Rossi?" calls the reporter, who takes off after me, opening his skinny steno pad as we walk. "You were close to Judge Gregorian, weren't you?"

Does he suspect anything about me and Armen? I hurry past the crowd. The rapid motion makes me seasick. I'll never drink again; I don't know how my father stood it.

"Did you know that the judge and his wife were having marital problems?"

I try to ignore him and make my way through the crowd to the ladies' room. I zigzag left and right, like a sunfish trying to tack in a hurricane.

"Can you shed some light on that, Ms. Rossi? Ms. Rossi?"

I reach the door and pull its stainless steel handle with all my might, but the reporter stops it with his hand. He's breathing heavily; he smells like cigarettes.

"Grace, are you gonna let somebody get away with murder?"

I look into his face with its sheen of sweat. I feel a stab of confusion and nausea. I yank on the door. "I have to go."

"Is that the way it's gonna be? Is it?" he calls after me, as the heavy door closes between us.

I lurch into an empty stall, lock it, and drop on to the seat until the wave of nausea passes. I hang my head, examining the speckles in the floor tile; gray, black, and white fragments tumble together like a kaleidoscope. Between each tile is a steel line where the grout would be, but it wiggles from time to time. I right myself and wrestle with the oversized dispenser for a square of toilet paper.

Are you gonna let somebody get away with murder?

I wipe my face with the thin square and decide to stay there until the earthquake stops. I listen to other women flush the toilets, wash their hands, and leave. I wait until all the hands are washed and all the women have gone. In time, the voices outside the bathroom diminish, then disappear altogether.

I think of the checkbook. I think of Armen. I'm not sure if I can't move or won't. I stay a long, long time at the bottom of the tall, glistening courthouse, sitting on the john in silence, thinking about my murdered lover. The judge with the alias.

What does that reporter know?

I hear the bathroom door open.

Shit. Who's coming into my bathroom? I feel intruded upon. I hate to share a public bathroom with the public, especially when my stomach is barely parallel to the floor.

Whoever it is walks farther into the bathroom. There's no sound of pumps on the floor; she must be wearing flats. I lean over and squint through the slit where the door meets the jamb, but I can't see anybody.

I know someone is there, but she's not going into a stall. She doesn't turn on the water, either, or strike a match for an illicit smoke. Maybe she came in to fix her makeup or brush her hair. I listen for the sounds, but nobody's fumbling in a handbag.

Still, someone is there. I heard the door. I feel a presence. I squint through the slits but see nothing.

Then I hear the faintest sound, of human breathing.

Someone is standing right in front of my door.

Panic floods my throat. I rise involuntarily.

There's a shuffling outside the stall as the presence moves closer in response. I lean next to the door, every nerve taut, straining to listen.

I hear the breathing, louder now.

I look underneath the door to my stall.

Planted there is a pair of large black shoes.

A man's.

14

"Who's there?" I shout, terrified.

"Are you all right?" says the man. Concerned, professional. "You've been in there awhile."

"Is that you, Faber?"

"No, I'm a special agent with the FBI."

"In a ladies' room?" My voice clatters off the tile walls. "Go away or I'll scream, I mean it! Right now!"

"Wait, relax. I swear to you, I *am* an FBI agent. Our office is here in the building. Seventh floor."

"Anybody would know that. It's on the directory."

"I'm with the agency for ten years now. I trained at Quantico. Eighteen months, not counting in-service training."

"Quantico, Virginia?" I think of the man at the memorial service, the car with the Virginia plates.

"Yes. Listen, I don't have much time. Here's my ID." A hand materializes above the shoes, carrying a card-size plastic wallet.

I start to reach for it, then draw back. What if he grabs my wrist? "Drop it. Near the toilet. Now." I sound ridiculous, even to myself.

"All right, all right." He tosses the wallet into the stall like a Frisbee; it banks against the toilet and settles at my feet. I'm not close enough to the door for his hand to reach under, so I pick it up. My hands have stopped trembling. So has my stomach. I open the billfold like a tiny book. On one leaf is a photo of Tom Cruise and on the other is a Pennsylvania driver's license.

"What is this, a joke? Where's your FBI badge?"

"I can't carry my creds, I'm undercover."

"Sure you are. You a friend of Tom's, too?"

"It goes with my cover. Look at the license, at least you'll see who I am."

I look at the driver's license. His features are nondescript in the state-sponsored mug shot, and it says that he's six feet one, 185 pounds. His hair is dark brown, eyes blue. It could be the man with the Virginia plates, but I had only a glimpse of him. "What's your name?" I ask.

"It's right on the license."

"Maybe you stole the license. What's your name?"

"Oh, a test. I get it. Abe Lincoln."

"You think this is funny? You scared the shit out of me. If this is standard FBI procedure—"

"It isn't, believe me. They'd have my ass. I

wouldn't do it unless I were absolutely desperate."

That rings true. "So what's your name, desperate?"

"Thaddeus Colwin."

I strain to read the name on the driver's license. Thaddeus Colwin III. "Thaddeus?"

"It's Quaker."

"A Quaker cop?"

"A good cop, a bad Quaker. Call me Winn anyway. Thaddeus is my father."

"Wait a minute, if you're undercover, why are you carrying around your real license?"

"I knew I'd be contacting you after the service, and I knew you'd bust my chops."

"How'd you know that?"

"You're a lawyer. Duh."

Hmmm. "Do you have kids?"

"No, and my favorite color is yellow. This is getting kind of personal, isn't it? We just met."

A comedian. "What's your address?"

He sighs. "Twenty-one thirty-three Adams Street, Philadelphia. Pennsylvania."

"Social security number?"

"What?"

"Tell me your social security number or I scream."

"What is it with you?" he says, amused no longer.

"I'm somebody's mother, that's what it is with me. If you kill me, my daughter's stuck with a dog. For a father."

"166-28-2810."

It matches the driver's license. Maybe he *is* for real. "What do you want anyway?"

"Can you come out? I need to talk to you. I don't have much time. Somebody could've seen me come in here."

"Why do I have to come out? Why can't we talk like this?"

A huge sigh. "Artie told me you were like this."

"Artie? Artie who?"

"Weiss. The law clerk."

"You know Artie? How?"

"We play ball."

"Where?"

"At the Y. Now I have three minutes left. Will you please open the goddamn door?"

"Where did Artie go to school, if you know him so well?"

"That's a no-brainer, it's the first thing he tells anybody. Now open the door, I'm backing up against the wall. See?"

I look through the slit but see only the dark edge of a coat. "Go over to the sink and turn the water on. Keep pressing on the faucet top, so I know you're at the other end of the room, away from the door."

"Very clever. You go to Harvard too?" I hear the sound of footsteps, then the water being turned on.

"Are you pushing the top?"

"What?" he shouts. "You know I can't hear you when the water's running."

I'm beginning to hate this guy. I open the thumbscrew and peek out of the door. I freeze on the spot. I can't believe my eyes.

It's Shake and Bake. He's standing at the faucet in

the ladies' room, complete with beard, cellophane rain bonnet, and black raincoat.

My God. A paranoid schizophrenic. I slam the door closed and bolt it. He must have stolen the driver's license. "Get out! You're not supposed to be in the courthouse! I'm going to scream!"

"Fuck!" I hear him shout. I look through the crack and watch him release the faucet in disgust, then slap it. "Fucking fuck!"

"You're not allowed in here!"

He turns toward the closed door. "It *is* me, I'm with the FBI," he says, in a voice as cultivated as someone named Thaddeus Colwin III would have. "Look, I ran the water, didn't I? Would a crazed killer do that? Open the door. Please."

"You? Shake and Bake? A federal agent?" I watch him through the crack.

"Open the door," he says. He slips the rain bonnet off the back of his head like a major leaguer after a strikeout. "Please."

"If you're an FBI agent, why did you make that scene at the oral argument, with the bomb?"

"It was part of my ingenious master plan."

I can't tell if he's kidding. "What plan?"

"Trust me, I'm smarter than I look."

"Smart? It got you banished from the courthouse."

"But it got me in good with the reporters, and that's very useful to me right now. Please come out. We don't have much time."

"We?"

"*Please.*"

I open the door a bit. "So you're a federal agent or a schizophrenic impersonating a Quaker."

His expression settles into businesslike lines behind the grimy beard. "You were close to Armen, right?"

I can't get over the incongruity of such an educated voice coming out of a bag man. "A reporter just asked me that."

"Were you close to him?"

"Wait a minute. Does Artie know about you?"

"No. No one does, except you."

"Why me?"

"Because I need you."

"What for?"

His eyes look slightly bloodshot in the harsh overhead lights. "This is confidential. All of it."

"Fine. What?"

"Are you going to work for Judge Galanter?"

"Possibly. How did you know that?"

"You told Sarah, Sarah told Artie, Artie told me."

"They teach you that at Quantico? Whisper down the lane?"

"Hey, whatever works. It's the only rule in this game." He breaks into a crooked grin, but I don't like his insouciance. Or his scummy teeth.

"You know, Artie really likes you. He worried about you when you were in jail."

"I know."

"He risked his career pretending to be your lawyer."

He purses his authentically parched lips. "Don't worry about me and Artie, okay? I have a job to do, he'll understand."

"Oh, I see. Manly men, ye be. So what's the story?"

"I'm undercover in an investigation supervised by the Justice Department. I can't tell you the details, I shouldn't even be meeting with you myself. All I can tell you is that it concerns charges of official corruption."

I feel my nausea resurge. "Corruption?"

"In the judiciary."

I think of the checkbook nestled in my Carter's at home. Armen's checkbook. "What kind of corruption?"

"Bribery, obstruction of justice."

Oh, God. "A federal appellate judge? Those are impeachable offenses."

"They're also crimes, so I couldn't care less if he loses his job. I need you to help me look for certain evidence."

"What's the matter with a search warrant?"

"I don't have enough for probable cause, not yet." His face grows tense. "What time is it anyway? I can't wear a watch on this job."

I glance at my wrist. "Noon."

"Shit. I have to be at the shelter, otherwise they run out of sandwiches. If you'd come out of the goddamn stall earlier—"

"What kind of evidence are you talking about?" I say, but he's busy yanking out the bottom of a ratty T-shirt so that it shows under his faded WHITE WATER KINGDOM sweatshirt.

"Do I look pathetic enough? I only made seven bucks yesterday. All this bullshit about not encouraging us."

"Tell me more about the investigation. Is Galanter the only suspect?"

"No, and that's all you need to know. Don't tell anybody we talked. Give me back Tom Cruise." He slips on his rain bonnet and ties it under his chin like a babushka. "After all, I'm the Rain Man."

"I get it." I hand him the wallet, which he slips into a pocket sewn into the folds of his trousers. "What if I want to call you?"

"You can't. I'm homeless, remember?" He pushes his pants down around his hips and starts to leave the bathroom. "I have to go. I'll explain it all later."

"Do you think Armen was murdered?"

His face falls suddenly behind its hobo's mask. "Why do you ask?"

"Why don't you answer?"

"Maybe."

I feel my heart pounding. "Do you think it has to do with your investigation?"

"Maybe."

I think of Armen, lying face forward on his desk. Did he really take money for a case? There are so many questions, and only one thing is clear. It hurts inside.

"I miss him too," the agent says. Then he opens the ladies' room door and slouches out.

Maddie's gone outside to play, and my mother hands me her dinner dish for rinsing. The child left more peas than I thought. Puckered now, they careen randomly on the surface of the dish. "Let's talk about Dad," I say, taking the plate.

"Let's not," my mother says. She walks back into the dining room without meeting my eye. I watch her receding form, soft and shapeless in a pink acrylic sweatsuit. The back says NUMBER ONE GRANDMA. She bought it for herself.

"Why not?" I call after her.

"It's not that time of year yet."

At least she's in a good mood. "What do you mean?" I maneuver Maddie's plate into the wire dishwasher rack. Bernice, standing at her now-customary place at the dishwasher door, sniffs the plate, disappointed to find it clean already.

"You're early," my mother says, returning with my messy plate of waxy mashed potatoes. "You usually don't start with those questions till Christmas." Her mouth is a tight smile; wrinkles radiate like tiny scars from the edges of her lips.

"I could be late, did you ever think of it that way? I mean, is the glass half empty or half full?" I take the plate and she turns silently on her heel. "Depends on your perspective, Ma, right?" I watch the water splash harmlessly off an insoluble potato mound, then stow the dish in the rack to let Bernice finish the job.

My mother comes back as Bernice is in mid-meal. "Don't let the dog do that, Grace! It's unsanitary. We eat off those dishes. Shoo, shoo!" She bangs a glass down on the counter and takes a swipe at Bernice, who backs up, confused.

"It's all right, Ma. It's going into the dishwasher."

"They're not even cheap dishes, they're expensive dishes. It's unhealthy. The germs."

"The hot water kills the germs."

Her frown deepens as she eyes Bernice, who's licking her chops sheepishly. "When I sit at your table, I don't like to think I'm eating off a dog dish."

"It's not like I feed her from the dish."

"It's the same thing. You're lucky my mother can't see this. You know what she would do? She would set your place at the table with the dog's dish."

She never talks about her childhood. "Your mother would do that?"

"She sure would. My mother was spiteful. She'd explain it to you this way. If your dish is good enough to feed the animal, then you don't mind eating out of the dog's dish. Believe me, Grace, she would." She shakes her head and walks into the dining room. "It's so common."

I would remind her that we're common, that she manicured nails to support us, but this is family history long since revised; she tells people she was in the beauty industry, whatever that is. "Is the table clear, Ma?" Bernice trots back to the dishwasher, but I wave her off.

"One left." She comes back in and hands me her own plate. It doesn't need rinsing; you would never know anybody ate off it.

"Tell me about my father."

Her frown is replaced by a cynical smile. "What do you have to know? He had dark hair, he wore it slicked back. He was Sicilian, he might as well have been black. He was younger than me, so I should have known. End of story."

"Do you miss him ever?"

Her smile, weak to start out with, now fades completely. "No."

"Were you ever happy?"

"No."

"Not even before he started drinking?"

"He always drank. He drank from the beginning."

"So tell me—"

"There's nothing to tell."

"Tell me about his drinking, then. It's hard to remember."

"Good. It's better you don't." She does an about-face and heads out of the room. I brace myself as she returns with another glass.

"I remember that he drank Crown Royal."

Her face reddens but her expression remains rigid. She sets the glass down. "He drank everything. Beer. Wine. Whiskey. Cough syrup." She pushes back a steel-colored curl. "You know all this. Why do we have to go over and over it?"

"I remembered something about Crown Royal. It used to come in a purple sack with gold letters."

Her eyelids flutter. "It still does. You know that from now, not before."

"He gave me the sacks for purses," I say, the sentence popping out of my mouth of its own force, a memory I didn't know I had until this very moment. "For dress-up." I scan her face for verification, but it's a perfect blank. "Remember?"

"No."

"The purses? The gold braid on the side?"

"No."

"There was a drawstring."

She turns to go, but I grab her arm. My grasp is rougher than I intended, and in the half second she looks back I catch a fleeting expression on her face. This one I can read: fear. She's afraid I'm going to hit her. Suddenly I understand.

"Did he hit you, Mom?" I ask, horrified. Out-raged.

"Why are you doing this?" Her forehead creases with anxiety. She tries to wrench her arm free but I hold her tighter, almost involuntarily.

"I have to know. Did he hit you?"

"It's *my business.*" She yanks her arm from my grasp and backs unsteadily away from me toward the refrigerator door. Behind her is a jumble of crayon rainbows and happy-face suns. Maddie's drawings. "*My* business."

"It's my business, too!"

"No, it isn't."

"Mom, there's no shame in it. It's not your fault."

"None of this is your concern."

"I knew he left us, I never knew why. Is that why? Did you throw him out because he beat you? I'm not blaming you, I just want to know."

"Stop! Stop it right now!" She holds up a veined hand, her finger pads curled over like the tines on a hand rake. Years of nicotine, the doctor told her.

"Ma—"

"You let me be!" She hurries out of the room but I follow her, almost panicky. To make it better, to make it worse, I don't even know.

"Ma, it's just that I've been wondering—"

She whirls around and silences me with a crooked index finger. Her face, for the first time in my memory, is full of pain, and she fights for control. "Let it drop. What's done is done. Going over it doesn't do me any good, doesn't do anybody any good."

"Did he hit *me* too, Ma?"

"What are you talking about?"

"Something happened the other day at the office, and I remembered."

Her chest heaves like a boxer's under the silly sweatshirt. "Grace Deasey—"

"Grace Deasey *Rossi*, Mom. I had a father, and I would like to know what he did to me. That *is* my business."

She snatches her purse from a chair and almost runs to the front door. "You're out of your mind. You'll drive me out of mine if I let you. But I won't let you."

"Ma—"

"No," she says simply and walks out.

NUMBER ONE GRANDMA winks at me as the door slams closed behind her.

16

"Let's do it," Eletha says grimly as we encounter the first wave of reporters along the wall of the outer lobby to the courthouse.

"Grace! Grace Rossi!" one of them shouts.

Shocked, I turn toward the voice. It's the reporter from the day before, Sandy Faber. He's wearing the same sport jacket and more stubble. "Remember what I said, Ms. Rossi?"

"Which judge does she work for?" one of the women reporters asks. He ignores her, so she shouts at me. "Who do you work for, Ms. Rossi? Do you have any comment on *Hightower*? Why did it take so long to get the transcripts of the oral argument?"

"Holy shit," I hear Eletha mutter beside me.

I push forward away from the reporters, but the lunchtime crowd is barely trickling out the narrow courthouse doors.

"Come on, Ms. Rossi!" Faber shouts. "You gonna talk to me? Come on. Gimme a break here."

The heads of three other reporters snap in my direction. I feel Eletha's hand on my forearm.

"Who do you work for, Judge Meyerson? Judge Redd?" the woman shouts at me. "I can find out, you know."

"No comment," I say.

"Aw," the woman says, "just tell me who you work for. It's Simmons, right? That's who? Simmons?"

I feel Eletha's talons dig into my arm; she seems shaken. I press ahead, pushing in line for the first time in my life as a good girl. It works. The crowd surges forward, and Eletha and I squeeze out the door and into the crowd outside the courthouse.

"You all right?" I say to Eletha, but she can't hear me over the Hightower supporters to our left. *"No justice, no peace!"* they chant. Their signs read: DEATH PENALTY = GENOCIDE OF AFRICAN AMERICANS! ABOLISH THE DEATH PENALTY! SUPREME COURT ADMITS "DISCREPANCY CORRELATES WITH RACE!"

"Let's just get out of here," Eletha says.

"I'm trying, El." One of the signs is a picture of a young black teenager with smooth clear skin and a shy smile. He wears a red varsity football jacket. Hightower. The sound of the chanting resounds in my head.

At the front line of the swelling Hightower contingent is a prominent black city councilman and members of the black clergy. An older black woman standing next to one of the clergymen catches my eye; she's heavyset but dignified in an old-fashioned cotton dress, a calm eye at the center of a media hurricane. I recognize her from TV: Hightower's mother, Mrs. Stevens.

"Are you surprised by the amount of support that's being shown for your son?" a TV reporter says to her, thrusting a bubble-headed microphone in front of her face.

Mrs. Stevens looks startled, then the black councilman steps closer to the microphone, obstructing her from view. "We are going to hold a round-the-clock vigil to protest the death penalty, to show that it has always been racist in this country," the councilman says. "The Baldus study shows that African Americans are more likely to receive the death penalty than whites."

"Push, Grace," Eletha says.

"Okay, okay," I say. I force my way past the man in front of me, but find myself face-to-face with Mr. Gilpin, who's standing in my path. Even in the midst of the hubbub, his face relaxes into a smile.

"Hello there, my friend," he says, loud enough to be heard over the din. "Is this pretty lady a friend of yours?"

A tall black man in an X baseball cap chants over his shoulder, and behind him is the TV reporter and the black councilman. Gilpin acts like none of this is happening, as if it's a squabble over a suburban fence, not an incipient race war.

"Mr. Gilpin, this is Eletha Staples," I say.

Eletha extends a hand reluctantly. "Hello, Mr. Gilpin."

"Call me Bill, Eletha. You girls goin' out to lunch?"

"No justice, no peace!" booms a clear voice behind him, and the crowd begins to shove me aside.

"We'd better go, we're blocking the way," I say. I edge forward, but Eletha gets jammed between one of the Hightower supporters and a TV technician.

Gilpin grabs her arm and pulls her lightly to her feet. "Are you all right?" he says.

"Get me out of here, please. I hate crowds." She places a hand to her chest and starts breathing in and out. I'm worried she's going to hyperventilate and Gilpin must see it too, because in one swift movement he scoops us up by the elbows and drives through the mob. He deposits us at the curb and brushes back a pomaded hank of hair. "I played football in high school," he says.

Eletha tugs a handkerchief from the sleeve of her sweater and dabs at her forehead. "Thanks a lot."

Gilpin's eyes skim the crowd unhappily. "We started this, I know. But it'll be over soon."

Which is when it occurs to me. The politics of the new Hightower panel is all over the newspapers; Galanter and Foudy aren't closet conservatives. Gilpin must realize that Hightower's going to lose, and he's about to see his daughters' murder avenged. I wonder if Gilpin is happy that Armen was killed. Suddenly I like him less. "We'd better be going," I say.

He nods. "Sure enough."

"Thanks again," Eletha says, recovering.

We cross Market Street and the chanting trails off into the noontime traffic, making me suddenly aware of Eletha's stone silence. She chugs along the sidewalk like a locomotive and I tense up, feeling like a curtain has fallen between us: white on one side, black on the other. We come to the corner of Sixth and Chestnut and she squints up at the light. An executive takes a second look at her, then stares right at my breasts. My tension, pent up, bubbles over. "They're a B-cup, okay?" I spit at him. "Any other questions?"

The man hurries past us, and Eletha bursts into startled laughter. "I can't believe you said that!" she says.

"Neither can I. It felt great. Absolutely great." I laugh, suddenly lighthearted. "I've been wanting to do that all my life."

"So have I."

I meet her eye. "Are you mad at me, girlfriend?"

She shakes her head, still smiling. "I'm getting over it." The traffic light turns green and we cross Chestnut.

"It's not my fault I'm white."

She laughs again. "It's not that. It's that I can't believe you're messin' with Gilpin. You know better than that."

"I'm not messin' with him. He talked to me the first day."

"You shoulda walked away."

"I couldn't walk away, he's a person."

She holds up a hand. "I don't want to know he's a person, and I don't want to know Hightower's a person. These are names on a caption, not people. If you start thinkin' they're people, you won't be able to do your job. Look what happened to Armen."

"What?" We stop in front of Meyer's Deli, the only place she'll eat; Eletha's not Jewish, but she practically keeps kosher. "What do you mean by that, about Armen?"

She looks warily at the lunchtime crowd. "Let's talk inside, okay?"

We head into the noisy deli, with its old-time octagonal tile floor and embossed tin roof. Meyer's is always mobbed, but the line moves quickly because everybody inhales their food; the clientele consists almost exclusively of hyperactive trial lawyers. The hostess accosts us at the door and hustles us to an orange plastic booth against the wall. Our waitress, Marlene, appears at our table from nowhere. "You havin' the tuna fish?" she says to me, already writing down #12 on her pad.

"Only if you call me 'honey,'" I tell her. "I want someone to call me 'honey,' and not just for my body."

Eletha smiles. "Do what she says, Mar. She just attacked a man on the street."

"Okay, honey," Marlene says mirthlessly. She tears off the check and puts it face down, like we're at the Ritz-Carlton. "You havin' the white-fish on bagel, Eletha?" she says, scribbling on the order pad.

"Yes," Eletha says.

"What's goin' on at the courthouse, girls?" Marlene says. She rips Eletha's check off the pad and slaps it face down on the table. "They gonna kill that kid?"

Jesus. "We have no comment," I say.

Marlene scowls as she slips the ballpoint into her apron pocket. "I'm sick of the whole thing anyway," she says and vanishes.

Eletha leans forward. "So. I've been thinkin' about what you said, about Armen. About him being murdered."

"What?"

"Just accept that he's gone, Grace. That's hard enough. Anything else is a waste of time."

"I don't understand. You don't think he was murdered?"

"I'm not so sure."

Now I really don't understand. "Since when? That's not what you said yesterday."

"I know what I said. But last night I tried to quit school, and they told me Armen paid already, in advance."

"What are you talking about? You go to school?"

"Night school, at the community college. I got two more years left, and I've had it up to here." She draws a line across her throat.

Marlene materializes with our food. "Enjoy," she barks and takes off again.

"Eletha, I didn't know you went to school."

"I thought Armen might've told you." She picks up a bagel half and spackles it with whitefish salad.

"He didn't, but why didn't you?"

"It's a secret." She bites into her sandwich, but I'm still too surprised to start mine. "In case I flunk out."

"You won't flunk out."

"You never know. The whole damn thing was Armen's idea. Now he's gone."

"But I think it's wonderful, Eletha."

"You don't have to do it, girl. Three nights a week I get home at eleven o'clock. I gotta take two buses, then transfer to the subway. Malcolm's in bed, I don't even get to see him. If I'm lucky, I got an hour left to fight with Leon. I figured if I got an associate's degree, maybe I could transfer the credits and go on to college, then who knows."

"Maybe to law school?"

She smiles. "Maybe."

"That sounds great. I think it's great."

She puts down her sandwich. "Nah, it was a pipe dream. The only reason I didn't quit was Armen. He'd have been on my case forever, like he was till I quit smoking. That man was too much. He paid my tuition for me, clear through to graduation."

"But why does he pay it at all, if I can ask?"

"I couldn't afford to, so we had an agreement. He lent me the money and I paid him back in installments. When they told me it was all paid off, I started thinkin'. Maybe it *was* a suicide. Maybe he was fixing it so I couldn't quit after he was gone."

It can't be. "Maybe he just wanted you not to worry about it."

She shakes her head. "I feel like quitting anyway."

"Don't. He wouldn't want you to."

"I know that." She bites into her sandwich.

"El, can I ask you a question?"

She nods, her mouth full.

"How much money are we talking about for your tuition?"

"Couple thousand a semester."

"Where would Armen get that kind of money?"

"He makes a fine livin', hundred thirty thousand a year, and he saved like a fiend. He never spent a dime, that man."

It doesn't make sense. Why would Armen save if he had over half a million dollars? "He was a saver?"

"Always. But he was cheap, they all are."

"Who's they? Judges?"

"Armenians. You should see, when they'd have a dinner, I'd be countin' dimes on my desk. Who had the iced tea, who had the wine. I'm serious."

"That's racist, El."

"I know. But it's true." She laughs.

"Did his family have money?"

"No. Susan's did, but he didn't."

"So how much did he have saved, do you think?"

"Maybe fifty–sixty thousand. He told me not to worry about it, he'd take care of Malcolm's college. I worried plenty, but I don't make enough to save shit. Why?"

I look down at a half-eaten pickle. "Just curious."

We split up after lunch because Eletha has to run an errand; she promises me she'll take the back entrance into the building, because there's no demonstration there. As I reach the court-house, I consider doing the same myself. The mob has grown. People spill out past the curb and into the street, filling the gaps between the TV vans and squad cars. The police ring the crowd, trying vainly to keep it out of Market Street.

I cross against the traffic light, which turns out to be advisory anyway. A gaper block stalls traffic up and down the street. As I get closer to the courthouse, I see that something seems to be happening. The chanting stops suddenly; the crowd noise surges. Reporters and TV cameras rush to the door. I pick up my pace. It looks like breaking news, maybe the panel decision. My pulse quickens as I reach the edge of the crowd. I look for the hot orange cones that mark the walkway into the courthouse, but they've been scattered.

"What's going on?" I say, but am shoved into a woman in front of me. I turn around to see who's pushing. A cameraman stands there, and a lawyer with a trial bag.

"Sorry," says the lawyer, sweating profusely behind horn-rimmed glasses. "It's this person behind me."

"No!" someone screams at the head of the crowd, and then there's more shouting and pushing. The mob's moving out of control. I feel a sharp elbow in my back. It knocks me off balance.

"There's a decision!" someone shouts up front; then there's more yelling, even screaming. I feel panic rising in my throat as the crowd swells toward the door, carrying me with it, almost off my feet.

Suddenly there's a painful whack at the back of my head. I feel faint, dizzy. Everything gets fuzzy. My arms flutter, groping for anything to stay upright.

Gunshots ring out like distant firecrackers, and there's screaming and shouting, also far away. Strong hands catch me from behind. Someone says in my ear, "This is a warning. Let the judge rest in peace."

The words and the pain melt together.

And then slip beyond me.

17

I wake up on a green plastic couch in a room I've never seen before. My head hurts, but I can see everyone clearly. Standing over me are Eletha and the law clerks. Behind them are a few marshals I don't know, and the big mustachioed one, Al McLean, who was on duty the night Armen was killed. I'd been meaning to talk to him. His shrimpy sidekick, Jeff, sits silently in a chair nearby.

"Auntie Em, Auntie Em," Artie says, but nobody laughs.

"Hey, baby," Eletha says soothingly. She sits on the couch beside me.

"What happened?"

"You got caught in a riot, child. I shoulda walked back with you."

"Fifteen people were wounded," says Ben, from over Eletha's shoulder. "They ran out of ambulances, that's why you're here."

"Where?"

"Our lounge," McLean says, which explains the odor of stale cigarettes.

"I still say she should go to a hospital," Eletha says loudly, in McLean's direction. It takes me only a second to picture the fuss she must have made before I woke up.

"Somebody had a gun," Sarah says. "Two people were shot. Demonstrators."

The gunshots I heard. "Are they okay? Are they dead?"

"I don't know. Nobody knows."

Then I think of the warning just before I blacked out; it sends a chill through me. Was the person who warned me also the shooter? "Did they catch who did it?"

"No. No suspects, either. They don't know if it was a demonstrator or just some nut."

"And *Hightower,* the panel affirmed?"

"Names on a caption, Grace," Eletha says.

My head begins to pound dully. "Which means Hightower dies."

"Not so fast," Sarah says. "Robbins dissented. It'll be appealed to the Supremes."

"*Finis est,*" Ben says with satisfaction. "All they have to do is find a vein."

"Ben, stop it," Sarah snaps.

Eletha helps me to a sitting position. "You need to see a doctor, honey."

Behind her, Sarah says to Ben, "Don't be so fucking cocky. I didn't think it was such a good opinion. Galanter blew the ineffectiveness issue. Nothing Hightower's lawyer said to that jury could have made up for the failure—"

"Please, you two!" Eletha says, half turning toward them both. "This not the time or the place. Grace is hurt, and all you can do is argue!"

I squeeze her arm to calm her. "I'm fine, El. I just got a bump, that's all." My fingertips root through my hair to find the Easter egg on the right side. *Let the judge rest in peace.* I must be on the right track because somebody's worried about it. But who? I didn't recognize the voice. It sounded like a man, but it could just as easily have been a woman speaking low.

"You might have a concussion," Eletha says.

"I feel fine." I struggle to sit up.

"I told you she don't need no hospital," McLean says. Jeff watches from the chair.

"You shouldn't be sitting up," Eletha says.

"Fine. I'll stand." And I do, to stop her from worrying. The room spins a minute, and Artie steadies me with a strong arm.

"Grace!" Eletha shouts.

"Eletha, please. You're giving me a headache." I cover my ears and Artie laughs.

"She's okay, El," he says. "I got her."

"Somebody warned me out there," I say, slightly woozy.

"What do you mean?" Artie says.

I stop myself; I shouldn't say anything, not yet. "I thought I heard somebody warn me to be careful. I guess about the crowd."

"Did you see him?"

"No." I shake my head, and the fuzziness isn't hard to fake. "I guess it was nothing."

Eletha reaches out for my other arm. "You should go to the hospital. You look white."

"I am white."

"Excellent!" Artie says, laughing, and I convince Eletha that I'll survive if she lets me leave the marshals' lounge. I don't feel especially comfortable around McLean or Jeff anyway.

The courthouse lobby is almost vacant, like it was before the *Hightower* case started. No reporters or gawkers are in sight, just a handful of lawyers and witnesses, watched over by a platoon of marshals. "Where are all the reporters?" I ask, as we walk through the lobby.

"They cleared the building," Ben says.

"She picked up on that, dude," Artie says. "The mayor filed for a restraining order to block the press from in front of the courthouse. The DOJ applied for one inside."

"They won't get it," Sarah says.

"Yes, they will," Ben says. "It's within the police power. They'll get it because of the shootings."

We reach the elevators and the marshals make us walk through the metal detectors, even though Eletha threatens their life. Or maybe because she threatens their life. "You okay?" asks Ray, when I emerge on the other side.

"Sure. Thanks."

"Good." He looks relieved. Relieved enough to wave to Eletha.

We ride up in the elevator in silence. The law clerks seem uneasy, and I feel stone scared. People have been shot; it may or may not have to do with the warning. But the warning was real; it came from a killer, maybe Armen's killer.

"You'd better go home, if you're not going to a hospital," Eletha says as we step off the elevator.

"Maybe I will," I say. Ben is the first to find his keys, and he unlocks the exterior door.

Eletha pulls me by the arm, and we troop down the hall together. "First we'll get some ice on that bump, like the nurse said," she says. We push open the door to chambers, and standing in the middle of the room is Senator Susan Waterman.

I blink my eyes once, then again. She's still there.

Bernice, the dog who's been driving my station wagon, stands disloyally at her side.

"What are you doing here?" Sarah shouts, letting out a squeal of delight that reverberates in my brain. She rushes over to Susan and gives her a warm hug. "I thought you were in Bosnia!"

"I delayed the trip. We leave tonight."

Ben tightens his tie. "Senator Waterman," he says, extending a stiff hand, "please accept my condolences."

Susan breaks her clinch with Sarah. "Thank you, and I'm pleased to finally meet you," she says to Ben, pumping his hand so vigorously that her silver bangles jingle. Ben seems to forget that he's a Republican for a minute as he takes in the aura of power that envelops the woman. It's undeniable, despite the offhand way she wields it. "My husband told me so much about you, Jim."

Ben withdraws his hand. "I'm Ben. Ben Safer, Senator."

Her clear blue eyes focus on Artie. Tiny parentheses at the corners of her lips deepen into a smile. "Then *you* must be Jim," she says, vaguely off balance.

"Artie Weiss, Senator. I'm sorry about Armen." He can barely say it; he must still be hurting.

"Good God, I'm zero for two," she says with a light laugh. "Wait, I know. You're the basketball player."

"Right. I think Jim was one of last year's clerks," Artie says uncomfortably.

"Of course." She shakes his hand and then looks at Eletha. "You look wonderful, Eletha. How are you?" She extends a hand.

Eletha shakes it, obviously underwhelmed. She complained all morning about the funeral arrangements, or lack therof.

"Fine," she says. "How was the funeral?"

A flicker of pain crosses Susan's face; the first sign of grief I've seen. "Beautiful. I'm sorry you couldn't be there, El," she says, then her gaze focuses on me, direct and strong. "You must be Grace. My husband spoke about you all the time."

I bet he did. Did you kill him for it? "I'm sorry—"

"Thank you." She extends a hand and squeezes mine hard; I squeeze back just as hard. We have both proved our manhood. "And thank you for adopting Bernice. I was so surprised to see her here, I called the refuge and they told me. I couldn't possibly keep her, with my schedule."

I'm sure. "She's fine with me."

"Grace got caught in that mess down there," Eletha says. "Hit on the head. I keep telling her she should go home."

"By all means you should. I'll lend you Michael, he'll put you in a cab." She gestures to the tall aide with the expensive glasses, standing by Eletha's desk. I remember him from the memorial service.

"I feel fine, I really do."

"Nonsense." She marches me over to Eletha's chair and plops me down in front of the monitor. "El, would you get us some ice for this bump?"

"I was about to."

Bernice trots over to me and burrows under my hand, trying to make up for her inconstancy. Her brown eyes roll up at me like marbles. "Good dog," I say, softening, and pat her head.

Eletha returns with some ice wrapped in a paper towel and hands it to Susan, who brandishes it like Nurse Ratchett. "Where's the bump?" Susan says.

"In the back."

"Remember when Malcolm fell off his bike, Eletha?" Susan asks. She probes my head with a large hand and presses the ice into my noggin—not exactly a mother's touch. "He needed stitches, didn't he?"

"Twelve of 'em."

"Twelve stitches, can you imagine? Poor kid. He was four, right?"

"Five," Eletha says.

"I think that's enough ice," I say.

"Be still," she says. I want to hit her.

"Did you hear what happened out front?" Sarah asks. "Two shootings? You weren't down there, were you?"

"Of course not," Susan says, over my head. "I was up here, waiting for you."

"I didn't know you were coming in."

"I should have called, but I was en route and the shuttle was a mess. I came to pick up a few boxes. Are those all the boxes, Eletha, in the office?"

"For the most part. I still haven't packed all the case files yet."

"I was looking for some of the older things, his personal things, but I couldn't find them."

"What things?" Eletha asks. "The personal stuff is still in the credenza."

I think of the checkbook; I found it in the credenza. Is that what Susan is looking for?

"I looked, but all I found were school papers," Susan says.

"I think I'm done with the ice, Susan." I take her hand and move it away. "What are you looking for exactly? Maybe I saw it." I watch her face.

She looks down, mildly surprised. "Oh, maybe you have. Memorabilia, mostly. Pictures from our honeymoon, things like that. Special, personal things. I guess you haven't seen anything like that."

Is this a code? "No, I haven't seen anything special. Or personal."

She leans over me with the wrapped cube. "More ice?" We have ways of making you talk.

"No, thanks." I take the ice and toss it into the wastecan, then rise unsteadily, feeling her aide hovering at my shoulder. Is he the one who hit me? I wonder what his voice sounds like.

"Are you sure you're well enough to stand, Grace?" she asks.

Boy, she's good. I can't tell if what's beneath her smooth exterior is evil or just a smooth interior. "Sure. Thanks."

"Well, I'd better get ready. I'm holding a press conference before we go."

"Press conference?" Sarah says.

"Since I'm in town, considering what happened. Then we go. In two hours, isn't that right, Michael?"

The aide checks his Rolex and nods, apparently mute, at least in my presence. I need to hear his voice. I say, "You look so familar, Michael. Did you go to Penn?"

He shakes his head but doesn't say a thing. A man of few words.

"Where did you go to college?"

"Brown," he says quickly. Too quickly for me to hear his voice.

"Where are you from? Maybe that's where I know you."

"Maine."

"Oh? Where in Maine? My ex used to like Blue Hill in the summers."

"Bath."

It's still not enough. "Oh. Well, what's your last name? You looks so much like someone—"

"Robb."

Eletha shoots me a quizzical look and I give up; I'm out of questions and Michael's out of syllables. "I guess it was somebody else."

"Guess so," Susan says, with a faint smile.

18

ernice rests her chin on the top of the plastic gate like Kilroy over the fence. My mother shifts the ice pack on my head. "How's that?" she says.

"Ma, will you stop? I'm fine."

"You're not fine," she says, practically hissing. Her breath is a mixture of denture cream and stale cigarettes. She hasn't mentioned our skirmish last night; we're both pretending it didn't happen. "You shouldn't have been there."

"I had to eat, Ma. If I didn't eat you'd be yelling, 'Why didn't you eat?'" Of course, I didn't tell her about the warning. It's been worrying me since it happened, but I still can't remember any more than I already have. From the local news, it looked like the shooting had to do with *Hightower,* so the person who warned me wasn't the shooter. I hope.

"Here's the lady," Maddie says. Her eyes are fixed on the portable TV on the pine hutch. The national news comes on, and the first story begins with a miniature head shot of Susan, floating to the right of a graying Tom Brokaw. "She looks like she's in the movies, Mom. She's pretty."

"I heard she's ugly in person," my mother says.

"She's not." Especially for a killer. But by now she's in the air, heading out of my jurisdiction with monosyllabic Michael.

"Look, Mom," Maddie says. "She's gonna talk again." She points to the television, and I focus on the screen as the news runs part of Susan's speech.

"What happened in Philadelphia today, only a block from Independence Hall, makes a mockery of the Constitution. The framers envisioned that the First Amendment would create open, free, and robust debate. They did not anticipate that words would be replaced by gunfire and thoughts drowned in human blood."

"I don't like that part," Maddie says solemnly.

"Me neither," I say, absorbed by Susan's tiny image. Her star is on the rise, her career jump-started by her husband's death. The papers keep talking about her strength under fire; presidential timber, says the *New York Times.*

"I am happy to announce that the condition of the two shooting victims is now stable. However, we should use this near-tragedy to consider how we, as citizens of a free and democratic country, can exchange ideas through peaceful means, without resort to violence."

"What she's saying, Mom?"

"Nothing."

My mother laughs. "So what else is new? She's a politician."

The ice pack shifts on my head, and I seize the moment to grab it away. "I'm fine now, thanks. Please go sit down."

"I'm trying to help you."

"I know. I said thank you." I drop the melting ice pack next to the spaghetti bowl.

"Shhh!" Maddie says, staring at Susan.

"Was that a Chanel suit she had on?" my mother says, as she takes her place at the dinner table.

The broadcast cuts to scenes outside the courthouse: film of Mrs. Gilpin crying in the arms of a friend and her husband looking on with relief and happiness. He says to a woman reporter, "Now we can see justice done. Now we can close the book."

In the background is Mrs. Stevens, but Gilpin doesn't seem to make the connection that she's about to endure the same pain he had. The camera cuts to her, standing next to the black councilman. "How do you feel, Mrs. Stevens?" comes a shotgunned question, a reporter's drive-by.

"How do you think she feels, you jerk?" I say to the TV.

"I don't understand, Mom," Maddie says, but I hold up a finger.

On the TV, Mrs. Stevens swallows visibly. "I think my boy done wrong, but I don't think he deserves to die. He's still young, and the young—"

"Justice was not done here!" the councilman interrupts. "Thomas did not have a fair trial! We will appeal to the Supreme Court without delay, because time is running out. Meanwhile, two African Americans were shot here today, showing support for their young brother. . . ."

The camera focuses on Mrs. Stevens's numb expression, then a commercial for Rice-A-Roni comes on.

"So Senator Waterman makes the national news," my mother says, arching an eyebrow plucked into a gray pencil line.

"She calls these things press conferences, but she never takes any questions." I get up stiffly and turn off the TV.

"Aw, can we leave it on?" Maddie asks.

"No, honey, not during dinner."

"But we just watched during dinner."

"That was special." I sit down.

"I don't see what the big deal is," my mother says, half to herself.

Of course she doesn't. When I was a kid, we ate dinner on spindly trays in front of a console television. At least Walter Cronkite didn't hit us. "We've already discussed this, Mom."

Maddie resettles sullenly on top of the Donnelley Directory. "Grandma lets me watch TV during snack."

"I think it was a Chanel suit," my mother says quickly, chopping her spaghetti into bite-size pieces. She refuses to twirl it: too Italian. "Did you see?"

"See what?"

"The buttons. That's how you know it's Chanel."

"I didn't see."

"How's your head?"

"Full of important thoughts."

She frowns. "I still say you should report what happened. You were attacked."

"It's not worth it."

Maddie shifts on the phone book. "Are they gonna catch the guy that did it, Mom?"

"I don't think so, babe."

"Why not?"

"They don't know who did it."

"Serves them right." My mother snorts. "They're the ones with all the guns—"

"Wait a minute. That's enough," I say, and she quiets; we have a specific understanding. I wouldn't let her baby-sit for Maddie unless she agreed to suspend her two favorite activities: racism and smoking.

"What, Mom?" Maddie asks, confused. "What happened to the guy?"

"They think he ran away, honey."

"Where did he run to?"

"Somewhere in the city. Not near here."

Maddie nods knowingly and digs into her salad. "It's dangerous out there."

"What?" I laugh. "Where did you get that?"

"Don't you know?" she says, with a mouthful of iceberg lettuce.

"Finish chewing and then talk, okay?"

She chews the lettuce like a little hamster.

"Don't let her do that," my mother says, but I wave her off.

"How's that tooth, monster girl? Ready for the Tooth Fairy?"

Maddie swallows her food. "Almost ready. There's only one of those thread things. Wanna see?"

"No. Please."

Her face grows serious. "There are bad people, Mom, didn't you know that?"

"Really?"

"Uh-huh."

"What are you watching in the afternoons, *Dragnet* reruns?"

"Care Bears!" Maddie says, and grins at my mother. My mother winks back, and I decide to let them have their secrets.

"All right, so tell me how school was."

"Okay." She shrugs, shoulders knobby as bedposts in her white blouse.

"Did you have art?"

"Yeah."

"Yes. Did you make anything?"

"Yes."

"What did you make?"

"A picture."

"What is this, a deposition? What was it a picture of?"

She perks up slightly. "Trees. You stick little sponges in the paint and then on the paper. It makes fake leaves for the trees. It's scenery. It's for our play."

"You're going to be in a play?"

Maddie nods and sips her milk, leaving a tomato-sauce stain on the rim of the glass and a milk mustache on her upper lip. Then she grabs her napkin in a professional way and wipes her mouth.

"What's the play about?"

"Spring."

"That sounds nice. Is it a musical?"

She rolls her eyes. "No, Mom. That's in the olden days. We don't do anything as dumb as that."

"What a relief. Jeez."

Maddie squints at me to see if I'm kidding. I squint back, and we squint at each other like moles for a minute.

"Maddie told me some good news today, Grace," my mother says. She turns to Maddie. "Tell your mother how you made a new friend."

"You made a friend?" It's too much to hope for.

Maddie beams. "At recess."

"Terrific!" I feel my heart leap up. "I propose a toast. To Maddie and her new friend." I hoist my glass in the air, and so does my mother. The heavy tumblers clink loudly.

"She won't tell me any more about it," my mother says. "She says she's only allowed to tell you."

"Oh, a secret! So you played with this friend at recess? What did you play?"

"Digging."

"Like with Madeline?" I think of the day I watched her near the edge of the playground.

"Yep. He likes Madeline."

"Oh, he's a boy, huh? Is he cute?"

She wrinkles her nose. "Kind of. He's big."

"How big? Like a second grader?"

"No, bigger than that. Almost as big as Daddy."

My mother laughs. "That means fifth grade."

"What's his name?"

"It's a secret. He's my secret friend."

I wonder if he's imaginary. "But he's real, right? Not like Madeline. A real boy."

She looks confused. "He's a man, Mommy, not a boy. He helped me and Madeline dig a hole. He's strong."

"What? A man?"

My mother puts down her fork in surprise. "Not a stranger!"

"Maddie knows not to talk to strangers." I turn to Maddie. "Right, honey? He's not a stranger, is he?"

Her face flushes red. "He *knows* you and that's not a stranger."

"Who is he?"

"He said it's a secret. I told you. He knows you and your work. He knows your judge and the lady on the TV. That's not a *stranger*."

"What did he look like, Maddie?" my mother says, her voice thin with anxiety. "Tell Grandma."

Maddie looks from my mother to me, becoming uncertain. "I didn't do anything bad, Mom. He said he was my friend, and you said make a friend."

"Of course you didn't do anything bad," I say as calmly as I can. "Which recess did he play with you, Mads? Recess in the morning or recess after lunch?"

"He knows things. He said it's good to be careful, like you say. He said, Tell Mommy too."

I feel my gut tense up. "Tell me to be careful?"

"Maddie, what are you talking about?" my mother says. "How could you—"

"Ma!" I snap at her. "Let me talk to her."

My sudden anger makes Maddie's lower lip buckle. "Mom, I didn't do anything wrong." Her eyes well up with tears.

"It's all right, baby," I say. I scoop her out of her seat and she burrows into my neck. I think of the man and my skin crawls. Is this for real, and does it have anything to do with this afternoon? "Can you remember what he looks like, Maddie?"

"No," she sobs.

"That's okay. It's all right, now." I hug Maddie close and catch sight of my mother over the top of my daughter's tousled red head. Her face has gone gray and drawn with fear; her gnarled fingers shake as she reaches for her water glass. "You okay, Ma?" I ask her.

She looks up, startled. "Fine," she says.

Later, after we've cleaned up and Maddie's safely in bed, my mother makes coffee in silence while I call the principal at Maddie's school and tell him what happened during a recess that's allegedly supervised. He reminds me that the back field is huge, that there are only two playground aides for 350 children, and that Maddie was playing at the far end. I suggest politely that he hire more aides, then show my fine upbringing by not threatening grievous bodily harm, although I let him know a lawsuit is always an interesting alternative. Then I call Maddie's teacher, who mentions that Maddie has a vivid imagination. Not that vivid, I say to her, before I hang up.

I call the police in my tiny borough to report

the incident; they seem happy to leave their game of checkers to come over and do real police work, like on TV. One even has braces on his teeth. My mother lubricates them with hot coffee and I give them free legal advice, so they promise to cruise around the house tonight and the playground tomorrow and the next day. I decide not to tell them about Armen's murder or what happened to me at the courthouse; it's out of their distinctly suburban league.

But I'm getting the message the killer is sending, loud and clear. Someone is using everything they can—including my six-year-old—to warn me off, but it won't work. It only makes me want to fight back harder. Where do they get off threatening my child? They haven't met up with the fury of a single mother. Especially one who's run out of alimony.

19

The phone rings after the police leave. "Grace." It's a man's voice, almost in a whisper. "It's Winn."

"Who?"

"Winn. Shake and Bake. Get down here fast."

"What? It's eleven o'clock at night."

"Please. I can't talk long."

"Listen, you, somebody tried to grab my daughter today. And somebody hit me from behind."

"Are you all right?" He sounds stricken, but not as stricken as I am and only half as stricken as my mother.

"She's fine, we both are."

"Was she hurt?"

"No, but only because she was at school. I can't have this, Winn."

"I'll protect her. I'll get somebody on her."

"Who, kindergarten cop?"

"I'll make him a teacher. A janitor."

"That's not the point."

"I can't talk now, just come down here. It's Artie. He needs help."

"Artie? Where?"

"Northern Liberties."

Not one of Philadelphia's showcase neighborhoods. "What are you doing there?"

"We're at Keeton's. On the corner, at Third. There's a sign."

"Is Artie okay? In danger?"

"Nothing like that, but come now." He hangs up.

I hang up slowly, looking at the phone. I hate to leave Maddie tonight, after what happened to her, nor am I excited about driving around, after what happened to me. On the other hand, it might help to talk to Winn, and Artie's in trouble. There's a caffeinated couple of cops driving circles around my house and a bulldog of a grandmother seething in the living room; my daughter has never been safer. I decide to go, mumbling an excuse to my mother, like in high school.

I drive into town with an eye on the rearview mirror, and no one appears to be following me. I reach the warehouse district in a half hour. The streets are wider here than they are in the rest of Philly and almost deserted. Trash mars the sidewalk, and the homeless beg from the traffic on the expressway ramp. One man, apparently crazy, is draped in a blanket despite the warm, breezy night. I look away until I remember that it's an apparently crazy man I'm looking for. I look back, but it's not Winn.

I drive around the block, past a graffiti mural on an electrical wholesale store, until I find a ratty tavern. An old-time window of thick glass block is stuck into a dingy brick facade. Over the black-painted door a pink neon sign glows KE TON'S. Artie is lying in front, passed out under a dim streetlight. Winn is propped up against the lamppost, fuzzy-faced and dressed in a raincoat, looking oddly like a degenerate Paddington Bear. I pull up to the curb and get out of the wagon.

Winn smiles vacantly when he spots me. "Harvard's sick, Miss Rossi."

I kneel over Artie. There's stubble on his formerly handsome face, and his clothes are a mess. But then they always are. "Artie? You okay?"

Artie opens one eye, then covers his startled face with his hands. "It's alive! Make it go away, Grace. It's heinous!"

Winn smiles. "Harvard drank too much."

"I figured."

"I figured you figured." Winn claps his hands. "I figured you figured I figured you figured."

"He's crazy as a fuckin' loon, Grace," Artie says, his eyes still closed. "Sarah was right."

"Bye-bye, Sarah," Winn says.

Artie looks up at me, his mouth curving down in Pagliacci's exaggerated frown. "Sarah went bye-bye, Grace."

"I'm sorry, Artie."

"She was in love with Armen, she admitted it." His eyes fill up with drunken tears. "She never loved me."

Poor kid. "I'm sorry."

"I knew it all along, Grace. She thinks I'm stupid, but I'm not." He licks his dry lips. "I knew from the way she looked at him."

I grab the folds of Artie's denim jacket; it occurs to me that I have picked up a drunk before. This drunk budges only an inch.

"Armen was my friend, Grace. He was my friend."

"I know, Artie."

"I was right! I am a genius! I made law review!" he rails into the night, then his head lolls to one side. A piece of wax paper rolls over him like urban tumbleweed.

I struggle to move him but can't. "Would you help me, Shake and Bake?"

"No." Winn wags his head back and forth, ersatz autistic before my eyes. "I'm busy."

"That's funny, Shakie." My lower back begins to ache; I'm too old for this and in no mood. I straighten up and glare at Winn. "Now get up and help Mommy."

Artie's eyes fly open suddenly, like a corpse reanimated. "Look, Grace! Look what I got!" He starts to unbutton his fly.

Oh, Christ. "I know what you got, Artie. Keep it in your pants."

"No, no, Gracie! Something totally awesome! Look!"

I look down. Artie's work shirt is yanked up to

his neck. Directly north of his stomach, between two rather erect nipples, sits a basketball, regulation size. Its surface is brown and pebbled, and in the center, in familiar script, it says *Wilson*. "What is that?" I say, aghast.

"I got a tat! Isn't it so *excellent*?"

"A tat?"

"Artie has a tat-toooo," Winn says, singsong.

"No pain no gain," Artie mumbles. "Today I am a man."

"I got one, too," Winn says, getting up. He brushes off his soiled pants, which does nothing to improve them. "Two tats. One for Harvard, one for me."

"Terrific."

"*Barukh attah Adonai*," Artie says, "*Eloheinu meleckh ha-olam*. Let's light the candles!" He waves his hand in the air, then it flops back against the cracked sidewalk.

"Want to see my tattoo?" Winn asks, standing a little too close for comfort. He smells like cheap beer and body odor.

"Keep your shirt on, Shakie," I say.

"Grace's being mean to me, Artie," Winn says, pouting.

"Don't be mean to him," Artie says, eyes closed, from the pavement.

I look at Winn, unamused.

"Two points," says Winn. "For me."

Artie caterwauls in the shower while Winn sits forward on the beat-up couch in Artie's apartment, quizzing me about what happened to Maddie and me. He looks uneasy when I finish the story and takes off his rain bonnet to run his fingers through his greasy hair. "This is too dangerous for you, for your daughter. I never should have gotten you involved in it."

"So why did you?" I sit back on a folding chair in front of a secondhand coffee table.

"I had no choice. I had nothing on the leads I was running and I know something's there."

"What do you think's going on? You said Galanter's not the only judge involved." I sip a Coke to hide my anxiety.

"Everybody dance now!" Artie sings in the shower, to C + C Music Factory.

Winn glances at the bathroom door, then leans close enough to give me another whiff of his rich stench. "Allegedly involved. I'm not sure yet, but I think Galanter's in on it and maybe Townsend."

I feel stunned. And no Armen. "A conspiracy?"

"It happened before, in this circuit, in the nineteen forties. Judges Buffington and Davis, together they sold a group of cases. One of 'em was working with a Second Circuit judge, too, who took half a mil. You could buy a lot of justice for that much money back then."

I think of the $650,000. "But that was then."

"Last year, Judge Aguilar in California told a Teamster who was embezzling union funds about one of our wiretaps on him. And Judge Collins, my personal favorite, took a hundred thou to give a drug dealer a lesser sentence. Both federal judges. Collins even collected his salary during the six years he spent in jail."

"This a hobby of yours, judicial misconduct?"

"It's what I do. All I do, in fact."

"Like a specialty?"

He nods. "It's fun, it's brainwork, and it's mostly bloodless."

"The Quaker part."

"In a way. I like taking these guys down. They've had every advantage, every privilege, and still they go bad. They're hypocrites. They've got no excuse except greed."

It doesn't sound like Armen.

"Now it's Galanter's turn. It's a scandal, Grace. It'll blow the courthouse wide open."

My heart sinks. For the court and for Armen, when they find out about the bank account.

"You still upset about today? You look kind of sick."

I chug some Coke. "Just the gal for undercover work."

"You're not working undercover anymore. I want you out of it. Clear."

"Why?"

"You need to ask, after today?"

"You're assuming I want to get out. Tell me what you think is going on."

"You remember the case that was argued Monday, the one I blew up? *Canavan?*"

"The racketeering case, with the florists."

"Yes. The Mob *was* behind it. The lawyer just couldn't figure out how."

I force out the words. "The Mob?"

"I believe they got to the judges and paid somebody off to make it come out their way, either Galanter or Townsend or both. Artie told me the judges vote right after the cases are argued, and I needed more time to gather evidence. So I had to make sure the argument didn't happen. *Ticktick-ticktick*."

I put down my Coke and look at him with wonder. "They did postpone that argument."

"Of course they did, and I got more time to watch everybody play the game. I told you I'm smarter than I look."

I feel my pulse quicken. If Winn is right, the $650,000 couldn't have been a bribe for *Canavan*. Armen would have voted to reverse, sending the defendants to jail: clearly not the desired outcome from the Mob's point of view. "I don't understand something. Does this have anything to do with Armen's death?"

"I think so. He may have been killed to prevent him from voting in *Canavan*."

"My God. Who killed him?"

"Somebody they paid to do it. Some scumbag."

"Or Galanter."

"What?" He rears back slightly. "That's not how these cases work."

"Maybe this one did. There was no break in, and Bernice wouldn't have let just anybody in." I tell him how Bernice attacked Galanter, getting excited as I speak; it renews my determination to work for him.

"Where's the *Canavan* case now?" We both hear Artie turn off the water in the shower; Winn looks worriedly at the bathroom door. "Has it been scheduled for argument again?"

"I don't know, it was Sarah's case. It'll probably be listed with the next sitting, a month from now. What is it you want me to do, when I work for Galanter?"

"Do you have the job already?"

"No, but I'll get it."

"Don't. I told you, I want you out."

"I'm going ahead, so you might as well tell me what I'm looking for. I want to find out if Galanter killed Armen."

He rubs his gritty forehead. "I knew this was going to happen. I must've been crazy to—"

"All I need is for you to protect Maddie at school. I'll be with her the whole weekend. Plus I have the local police."

"You what?"

"I want you to park a car right across from the school field. Here's her picture." I fish one out of my wallet and hand it to him. "It's not a new one, she's actually cuter than that."

"Freckles. I like freckles." He smiles at the picture and slips it into his pocket. "I'll have her watched, but I still want you to bow out. Quit now, I'll handle Galanter. You're too exposed. I don't like it, Grace."

"Tell me what I'm looking for. Where do I start, the *Canavan* record?"

He looks directly at me. "Are you really going to do this?"

I think of Armen. He loved me; he was murdered. And he didn't take any goddamn bribe. "Yep."

"Christ." He rubs his beard. "All right. If you insist on this, then all you should do is keep your eyes and ears open around his office. Try to answer the phones. That's it."

"Why? What am I looking for?"

The toilet flushes in the bathroom and Winn snatches a *Times* crossword puzzle from the debris on the coffee table and scribbles in the blank squares. "Call me if Galanter gets phone calls from any of these characters. Or if he has lunch with them, meets with them at all. That's all I want you to do, got it? I'll take it from there." He tears out the puzzle and hands it to me. "I also wrote down the number of the pay phone at the shelter. I'm there most of the time now. If you call, say you're my cousin. Ask for Rain Man."

I look at the crossword puzzle. After a phone number, reading down is THESAURUS, and reading across is SPOOL. Underneath that is a list of names, all as Italian as mine. I feel a twinge of shame, then fear. A mobster, that close to my child?

The bathroom door opens and Artie steps out wearing a red Budweiser bath towel around his waist. "Everybody dance now!" he sings, and thrusts his pelvis expertly at us.

"Artie!" Winn shouts idiotically, lapsing instantly into character. "You're all better!"

"I *am* better!" Artie strikes a muscleman pose, his wet biceps glistening with leftover water. In the middle of his chest is a slick basketball.

"You look good!" Winn says, applauding. He leaps to his feet with joy and bunny-hops over to Artie. "Everybody, everybody, everybody dance!"

They form a conga line and dance around me on the sofa.

I sit back and laugh, marveling at how deceptive appearances can be. The man playing the fool is really a shrewd federal agent; the Ivy Leaguer is dumb enough to engrave a basketball onto his chest. And what about me? I'm somewhere in the middle, definitely involved. It's a surprise when I realize why.

I want justice.

Everybody dance now.

20

Needlepoint is usually surefire therapy. I take refuge in it at the most stressful times and have come through a divorce and even Maddie's hernia operation with a few very nice pillows. I'm hoping needlepoint will get me through high crimes and misdeameanors, but this may be too much to ask of a hobby.

I tug a pristine silver needle through a tiny white square. The yarn comes through with ease, filling in an infinitesimal block of emerald green in a rolling English landscape. I favor the smaller scrims; they demand more concentration. I stitch another itsy-bitsy square and look behind me for the local squad car, parked across the street. The skinny cop in braces sits in the front seat, engrossed in the newspaper; he looks even younger than last night, if such a thing is possible.

I check on Maddie. She swings on a swing, pumping her legs back and forth. I can see her smile broaden with pride as the swing goes higher. She's still learning to coordinate the pumping action; it's not as easy as it looks. I wave to her, but she doesn't see.

I return to England after a careful glance around the neighborhood playground. No felons anywhere, just a few children playing in the sandbox and a mother here and there. It's not busy today; it's Saturday and everybody's out running errands, which is what I would be doing if I weren't somewhere in Northamptonshire.

I look up at Maddie, still on the swings on the far side of the fenced kiddie area of the playground. She was deliriously happy the day she hit six and graduated to the big kids area, but I don't like it much. The swings are too damn high for my comfort level, and my park bench is too far away. If you think I was protective before, you should see me now.

"You're dead!" screams a little boy, and I jump. The child runs by, chasing another boy with a toy Uzi. "You have to lay down, I killed you!"

This is why I'm glad I don't have boys.

England waits while my blood pressure returns to normal. I watch the boys chase each other in the dappled sunshine around a white hobbyhorse on a steel coil, then double back around the sandbox and out toward the swings. Of course they run right in front of the swings, directly in harm's way. Don't these monsters have mothers? They survive the gauntlet of swings and run past the bench out by the tennis courts. A man in a black sweater sits on the bench; his head barely follows the boys as they run by him.

Odd.

I didn't see him when we came. There's a newspaper on his lap, but he's not reading it. I take another stitch and yank the yarn through quickly. I look up at the man on the opposite bench.

He's still there, but too far away for me to make out his features. His hair is dark, and he seems broad-shouldered underneath the bulky V-neck sweater. Something about him looks familiar. Then I remember. He looks a lot like the man I saw at the police station and the memorial service, but I can't be positive.

Still.

I turn around to the police car. It's there, but it's empty. No adolescent cop, no newspaper. I swallow hard. The cop was here a minute ago. I look down the street. He's standing in front of the borough library, talking to an old woman carrying a stack of books. He's too far away to see or hear me.

Jesus. Stay calm.

I look back at the man on the bench, watching him as he scans the playground, apparently harmlessly. His sweater is much too heavy for such a balmy day, and it's bulgy enough to accommodate a gun in a shoulder holster. He could be with the

Mob; he looks the part. Is he the same man as at the police station?

That man had a black car with Virginia plates.

I take a quick stitch and casually look over the cars along the street. There's my wagon, then another wagon and a minivan. His car isn't there; so far, so good. I glance at the library lot next to the playground. The chrome grill of a dark car peeks at me from around the library, glinting in the sunlight. I bite my lip. It looks like the black car, but it also looks like a zillion other American cars. It's parked with the front end facing me, and there are no license plates in the front. Maybe it's from Virginia, maybe not.

I can't stand this. I feel more nervous by the second.

I take another stitch and peek over at the cop. He's nodding as the old woman unloads her pile of plastic-covered books into his arms. Terrific. My yarn snags; a notch of kelly green explodes through a yellow thatched roof. I hate needle-point.

I stare at the man. He's still sitting there, but now he's checking out the swings. Maddie's not the only child on them, but he appears to be watching her. I look back at him, then at her. She's between us, but he's closer to her than I am.

Relax, I tell myself. You handled back labor, you can handle this. I weave the needle into the scrim border for safekeeping.

Maddie sails back and forth, her cotton skirt billowing each time she swings forward. The man in the sweater watches her, unsmiling.

What the hell? Is he the man from the school playground? Is he the man from the police station? Why is he watching my daughter?

Suddenly, the man takes the newspaper off his lap and stands up.

I set my needlepoint aside and stand up.

He looks up at the swings and so do I. With a start, I see that Maddie's swing isn't going nearly as high as it was; she's beginning to slow down. She slows to a low arc, dragging an untied Keds on the ground, kicking up loose, dry dirt. She's getting ready to jump off.

My heart starts to pound.

The man takes a step toward the swings.

The cop rearranges the books. The old woman takes his arm.

I feel breathless. I open my mouth to scream but nothing comes out.

The man walks right toward Maddie. Unmistakably.

My scream breaks free. "Maddie! Maddie!" I shout. I'm off in a second, running toward the swings. "Help, police!"

Maddie looks confused, then terrified. The man glances back at me, then sprints in the opposite direction.

I pick up my pace, running as hard as I can. "Help! Police!" I scream, full bore.

My panic sets off the other mothers. One of them gathers her children together, hugging them to her legs. The other, a young mother, takes off like a shot after the stranger, who's fleeing across the grassy common. She's a short-haired woman in bicycle pants, and she passes me in no time. "I got that bastard," she says, hardly puffing as she whizzes by, cowlick flying.

I keep running until I get to Maddie, who's frozen with fear in front of the swings. I scoop her up and hug her tight. Over her shoulder I watch the young mother almost on the heels of the man. I pray to God he doesn't have a gun as she grabs him by the sweater and they both fall hard to the ground.

The cop comes running from the entrance to the playground, but the young woman doesn't need his help. She clambers onto the man's back and wrenches his arm behind him. A group of teenagers playing basketball at the far side of the playground stop their game and come running over. It's a done deal by the time the cop and the teenagers reach the middle of the huge field, which is when I guess the young woman must be an undercover cop, sent by Winn just in case.

"What's happening, Mommy?" Maddie says in a small voice. "What's going on?" She wraps her arms tighter around my neck.

"That man who was running, was he the one you saw on the playground at school?"

"Yes."

I watch as the basketball players ring the prone man. "It's okay now, baby. It's all over."

"What are they gonna do?"

"They're gonna put him in jail."

"Why?"

Because he's a killer, I think to myself, and hug

her even closer. I pick her up and walk over to the crowd around the man. The cop has handcuffed him and flipped him over on his back. The woman has her running shoe at his Adam's apple. She gives me a brusque wave as I approach.

"We got him," the cop says.

Please. "You had an assist, I think, from the FBI."

The cop and the woman exchange looks over the unconscious man. "Are you with the feds?" the cop says.

"Me? Are you kidding?" The young woman laughs. "I'm a librarian."

"What?" I say. "But the way you tackled—"

"*Arrgh,*" the man moans, regaining consciousness. He's older up close but still a scumbag, like Winn said.

"He's wakin' up!" one of the ballplayers says.

The librarian presses her ribbed toe into the man's throat. "Stay right there, asshole."

"Grace?" the man says, disoriented, looking up from the grass.

"How do you know my name?"

"I gave it to you, for chrissake."

"What?"

He spits grass out of his mouth. "I'm your fuckin' father."

Bernice glares through the gate of her Fisher-Price prison, eyeing with canine distrust the stranger who is my father.

"Lucky for me that dog wasn't with you today," he says. Underneath his sweater is a ropy gold chain;

no shoulder holster, as far as I can tell. "That's a big mother dog."

"Watch your language."

"Sorry."

"You want coffee or not?"

"Yeah." He holds up his mug.

"How do you take it?" I pause over him with the pot of coffee. Maybe he needs a hot shower.

"Black is fine." He looks up at me with blue eyes that eerily mirror my own, which stops me short. I can see the years on him; the deep crow's feet at the corners of his eyes and a softening around the jowls. He must be over sixty, but he looks fifty. His hair is jet black, like Robert Goulet's; I wonder if he dyes it. I pour him some coffee, then myself, avoiding his eyes.

"You're mad, aren't ya?" he says.

"You know me so well, Dad."

He winces when he sips his coffee. "Christ, this is hot!"

I stop short of saying, Good, you burn yourself? "So what are you doing here? In the neighborhood, thought you'd drop by?"

He frowns at my sarcasm but evidently decides not to send me to my room. "Look, I wanted to see my granddaughter."

"Why?"

"I just wanted to see her, okay?"

"Why now? She's been around for six years. It's not like she's been booked up."

"I just retired." He clears his throat, but his voice still sounds like gravel. "I moved back to Philly."

"So you *were* in the neighborhood."

"I figured it was time to settle up, you know?"

"No, I don't."

"When you're my age, you'll know." He slurps his coffee, wincing again.

"We have a telephone. You could have called."

"I know, I looked you up in the phone book. That's how I knew where she went to school." He glances into the living room, where Maddie's teaching herself to make a cat's cradle with a pink string he brought her. "She's a little lady. Just like you were," he says wistfully, but I have no patience for his wistfulness.

"You scared her, you know. And me."

"I'm sorry."

I pull out a chair at the side of the table, two seats away from where he sits. Even from here I can smell his aftershave, something drugstore like Aqua Velva. He doesn't say anything for a minute, staring down into his mug. I'll be damned if I'll fill this silence. I sip my coffee.

"Okay, so it wasn't the best way to go about it," he says finally.

"On the contrary. It was the worst possible way to go about it."

"Now I got your Irish up." He laughs softly, but I'm not laughing.

"You want a drink? Little sweetener for that coffee?"

He looks at me, stung. "I haven't had a drink in a long, long time."

"Right."

"It's the truth."

"Good for you. Where do you live?"

"Philly, now. South Philly."

The Italian neighborhood. "What do you do?"

"I used to teach."

"You were a *teacher*?" I can't hide my surprise. I would have figured him for a bartender, maybe a trucker. But a teacher? "What did you teach?"

"English."

"What?" He can barely speak it. I almost spit out my coffee.

"You're surprised at your old man, eh?"

"Please. Let's not leap ahead with the 'old man' stuff. Where did you teach?"

"In high school. In Virginia."

It was his car, the black one. It's parked out in front of my house like an official Mafia squad car. "Have you been following me?"

He shifts heavily in his seat. "Not exactly. Just watching, a little."

"Why?"

"Tryin' to decide, you know. When to make my move. In the beginning, I just wanted to see what you looked like." He appraises me for a minute. "You grew up nice, pretty. Very pretty."

Let's change the subject. "So they let Italians in Virginia. You like it there?"

"No. No *calamar'*, no nothin'. I had nothin' keepin' me there, so I came back. That's my life story."

"Never remarried?"

"No."

"No other kids?"

"Not that I know of." He laughs, then spots my glare. "No."

I shake my head, and another silence falls between

us. We have nothing to say to each other; we have everything to say to each other.

"You're a lawyer?" he says.

"Yes."

"Here's a good one. You're in a room with Adolf Hitler, Genghis Khan, a lawyer, and a revolver loaded with two bullets. What do you do?"

"What are you talking about?"

He waves his hand. "It's a joke."

"Okay, what?"

"Shoot the lawyer twice." He laughs, but I don't. "Okay, strike one. Here's another. What's black and brown and looks good on a lawyer?"

"Listen—"

"A Doberman." He laughs again, his eyes crinkling at the corners. An attractive man for his age, with a kind face. Except that he's a wife beater. Did I mention that appearances are deceiving?

"You beat my mother, didn't you?"

"Did she tell you that?"

"In a way."

He exhales heavily. "*Madonn'*."

"Well?"

"I never laid a hand on your mother. Never." He points a thick index finger at me.

"Bullshit. I remember."

"You remember wrong, lawyer."

"The hell I do. Don't you dare come here and tell me what I remember," I say, my voice rising. "I know what I remember."

"Mom?" Maddie calls uncertainly from the living room. The child has been traumatized enough; now her mother is going off the deep end.

"You want to go play outside, honey?"

"No."

"You want to watch a tape?"

"Even though I watched cartoons this morning?"

"Yes."

"Yeah!" She leaps off the couch.

"You know how to put it in?"

"I do it all the time, Mom. Jeez." She rummages under the TV for her tapes.

My father watches Maddie slip a tape in the VCR. "Smart little girl."

I feel a knot in my chest. "She sure is. So was I."

He pushes his mug away and folds his hands. "You want to know why I left?"

"For starters."

He looks down at his wrinkled hands, the only giveaway as to his age. "I met your mother at the Nixon, at Fifty-second and Market."

"We're beginning at the beginning, I see."

He gives me a dirty look. "As I was saying before I was so rudely interrupted, the Nixon was one of the biggest ballrooms around. Cost a couple bucks to get in. Had a mirror ball, spotlights, ten-piece band. Soup to nuts. You had to wear a tie and jacket."

"Very classy."

He nods, missing the irony. "*Very* classy. Why your mother was there that night, I still don't know. She was from Saint Tommy More. She was a great dancer, the best."

"My mother, dancing?" I blurt out. It's inconceivable, she barely smiles.

"God, yeh." He nods. "I was there with the

goombahs, the boys from the corner. Louie, Popeye, Cooch. She was there with the Irish girls. They were all in a corner, talkin' to each other. The Italians never asked the Irish to dance, the Irish never asked the Italians to dance. They weren't from the neighborhood. Lady of Angels." He smiles, lost there for a minute. "I remember her eyes, she had gorgeous eyes. Bedroom eyes."

"So?"

"So I asked her to dance, but she wouldn't dance with me. I kept after her for the slow dance. Finally she did. I remember the floor was slippery from the powder."

"Powder?"

"Yeh. Talcum powder, on the floor. Made it even more slippery, for slide dancing. Slow dancing, you know. Big band. Ah, your mother was good. So was I. You had to be good; otherwise you'd slip on your goddamn ass." He laughs thickly. "They had a contest, too, for the best jitterbug. We won some money, coupla bucks, I forget how much."

I hear the first strains of *Cinderella* coming from the living room and Maddie jumps back up on the couch, already lost in the fantasy world of Disney. Someday my prince will come. I should burn those tapes.

"Then we went outside for a drink. You couldn't drink at these things, but we found a way to drink. We always found a way to drink. Then we got married and you came along." His smile fades. "I decided to stop then, went to AA, the whole bit. But she didn't."

I don't understand. "You mean *Mom* drank?"

"I tried to get her to stop, but she couldn't." He leans back heavily in his chair.

"But Mom doesn't drink. Not even beer."

"Maybe not now, but then she did. I tried everything. Hiding the bottles, throwing them away, pouring that shit down the toilet. I dumped her whiskey and she came at me—"

"Came at you?"

He reddens slightly. "That was the last straw. I couldn't take it anymore. I knew if I stayed, I'd go down with her. So I left. Took off. The only thing I did wrong, the thing I regret, is I left you."

My chest grows tight. I can't say anything.

"I can't even tell you I tried to get custody, because I didn't. They wouldn't have given it to me, not in those days, but that's no excuse. I heard she stopped drinkin' after I left, but I still didn't go back. We were bad for each other, we would've gone down together. And you too."

I swallow hard, disoriented. This isn't my family history. My history is altogether different: a father who drank, a no-good, and a mother who suffered. A victim, a saint. I don't know whether to believe him. I can't look at him. "You should go," I say.

"I'm not so dumb that I expected everything to be all right with us. I came because I wanted to make it up to you. I have a little money. Maybe I can help out."

"You can't. You should go."

"Maybe you need to think about it. I know I sprung this on you. You can call me any time." He puts a card down on the table. EMEDIO "MIMMY" ROSSI, CERTIFIED ESL INSTRUCTOR. "I'm startin' a little business. I teach English as a second language. To Koreans, Vietnamese, like that."

"Am I supposed to clap?"

"You're tough, you know that?" He gets up to go, but I still can't look at him. I have a thousand questions for him, but only one keeps burning in my head.

"Did you hit me?" I ask, when he's past me.

"What do you mean, hit you?"

"When you drank, did you hit me?"

"No. Never." His voice sounds louder; he must have turned around to face me. "Why?"

"I'm remembering things."

He's silent for a moment. "You'll have to ask your mother about that," he says. I hear him call good-bye to Maddie and leave by the screen door.

It closes with a sharp bang.

"*Roarf!*" Bernice says.

21

I spend a long time at the dining room table, feeling awful as Maddie sits enchanted by her tape. What is he saying? That my mother drank too? That *she* was the one who hit me?

It never even occurred to me.

I'm not sure what to do; I can't process it all fast enough. I can't even deal with the fact that I have a father now. What does a grown woman want with a father? And is there room for a mother, especially one who would wallop a child? Then a more urgent concern pops into my head.

Maddie. Has my mother beaten her, ever? My God. I close my eyes. From time to time Maddie gets bruises, but she told me they were from falls. And first grade has been so difficult for her; her first year in my mother's care. It all fits, and it sickens me. Would my mother really hit Maddie? It would be beyond belief, except that she apparently hit me, too.

When I was Maddie's age.

What's been going on in my own house? Maddie knows, but I have to pick the right time to ask her. It preoccupies me as I cook and serve dinner. Afterward, I clean up the dishes and let Bernice slobber over every plate, a silent payback.

Later, at bathtime, Maddie relaxes in a full tub of Mr. Bubble. She makes a blue rubber shark swim among plastic goldfish, hidden beneath the sudsy meringue. I sit down on the lid of the toilet, watching her. Now might be the right time.

"How's that water, button?" I say.

"Want to see a tornado?"

"A tornado? Sure."

She grabs her nose and turns over once in the tub. The water swirls around her and she comes up smiling, wet hair stuck in tendrils to her cheeks and chin. "Did you see?"

"Amazing."

She looks askance. "You weren't watching."

"I *was* watching, it was cool. Like a whirlpool, right?"

She sinks into the bubbles up to her chin.

"So Mads," I begin, as casually as possible, "what do you and Grandma do in the afternoons?" The shark plunges into a swell and Maddie doesn't answer. Maybe she's avoiding it; maybe it's a child's typical inattentiveness to adults. Or hers to me. "Mads?"

"What?"

"Do you have fun with Grandma while I'm at work?" Dumb. A leading question.

She nods and the shark leaps across her tummy.

"What do you guys do?"

"Watch TV."

I'm relieved at this answer for the first time ever. "Cartoons?"

She nods at the shark, who nods back at her.

"Tapes, too?"

"Yeah. *Yes.*"

"Don't you ever just play?"

She nods again. The shark nods, too.

"What do you play?"

"Can I have Madeline in the tub?"

"Of course not, she'll get wet," I say reflexively, then think again. Maybe Maddie can say something through Madeline that she can't say to me directly. "I'll let you this time, but not in the water, okay?"

"Yeah!" The shark dances for joy as I fetch the doll from Maddie's room and bring it back. I sit cross-legged on the rag rug beside the tub.

"Hey, Maddie," I make the doll say.

"Hey, Madeline," Maddie says cheerily. She abandons the rubber shark.

"What games do you play with your grandma?" the doll says. "Gimme the dirt."

Maddie giggles. "What's 'the dirt' mean?"

"The gossip. The news. The real truth. I want

to know everything." The doll's yellow felt hat bobs up and down.

Maddie sits up in the bathtub, focusing on the doll as if she were real. "We play lid," she says.

"What's lid?"

"It's a game, with a ball and a lid."

"That sounds boring."

Two slick knees pop through the bubbles; she wraps her arms around them. "She chases me around when she loses."

"My grandma does that, too. She's a bad sport. I hate her."

"Does she pinch you? My grandma pinches me."

I feel my heart skip a beat. "Pinches you?"

She nods. "She chases me around and pinches my butt."

"Hard?"

She shakes her head. "Just for fun. When she loses. Anyway, she doesn't catch me ever because I'm too fast. I'm faster than the boys. Do you like boys?"

"No, I hate them more than grandmas. Does your grandma ever get mad at you and yell?"

She looks blank.

"Tell me!" the doll screeches. "Tell me, you little brat! Tell me everything!"

She giggles and unsticks a wet strand of hair from her cheek. "It's a secret," she whispers, growing serious.

"A secret?"

"A *real* secret. Something Mommy doesn't even know." Her blue eyes glitter.

"A secret from Mommy?"

"Grandma said she would never find out."

I feel sick inside. "I know. Mommy's so stupid. Tell me."

"I can't. Grandma said Mommy would be mad if she found out and yell at me."

"I bet she wouldn't." The doll flops up and down in frustration, cloth mitts falling at her side.

"Uh-huh," she says emphatically. "My mom yells a lot. She says it's because she has to do everything and I don't help."

Guilt washes over me like a tsunami. "My mom yells all the time, too. She's a jerk. A big, fat, stupid jerk."

Maddie covers her face, laughing. "My mom yells *all* the time. She yells when I don't put my clothes in the hamper and she has to pick them up. She bends over twenty times a day. If she had a nickel for every time she bends over she'd be rich."

"She sounds like a big fat jerk, too."

"But know what I do?"

"What?"

"I go in the closet and take off my clothes."

"What? Why do you do that?"

"That's where the hamper basket is. I stand in the basket and my clothes fall right in." She smiles and so do I; I picture her standing in the closet in a Rubbermaid bin.

"You're pretty smart, you know that?"

"I am. Really." She rubs her nose with the palm of her hand.

"Do you love me?" the doll asks.

Maddie reaches over and arranges a strand of the doll's too-red yarn hair. "Yeah."

"Then tell me your secret!" the doll explodes, jumping around frantically. "RIGHT NOW!"

"All right, all right! Calm down!" she says, a tenuous cross between laughter and true concern. "The secret is that Grandma smokes."

"What?"

"On the porch. During *Tom and Jerry*. My mom thinks she doesn't smoke when she baby-sits me but she really does."

"That's the secret?" I try not to sound disappointed, although I didn't know my mother did this. She'd told me, with an absolute straight face, that she holds off for three hours. A good liar, from years of practice.

"Isn't it a good secret?"

"Yep. You got any other secrets for me?"

Maddie looks up, thinking. "Nope."

"I'll tell you one."

"Okay." She straightens out her knees in the tub.

"My mom gets so mad sometimes that she hits me. Like this." I squeeze the doll and bounce her head off the ledge of the tub. "Like this and this. Owww!"

"Really?" Maddie's eyes grow wide and she looks at the doll for confirmation. I make the doll nod.

"Really. It hurts."

"That's mean."

"I know. She does it when she's mad or when she drinks."

"Drinks?"

"Like a beer. Like wine or whiskey. Does your mommy do that?"

"No." Maddie shakes her head, mystified. "She just yells."

"Does your grandma?"

"No."

"Never?"

"No."

"Do you ever see her drink anything?"

"Water."

"No whiskey? It's yellow."

"No. She just smokes. It comes out her nose like a dragon."

"Yuck."

She nods gravely. "Yuck."

I feel my pulse return to normal. So the unimaginable didn't happen, and my daughter is safe in her grandmother's care. It's just the past I have to deal with. My past.

I'll get to it right after I'm finished with the present.

22

It's Sunday, and Bernice, Ricki, and I sit on the bottom row of the hard steel bleachers, watching Ricki's favorite son play soccer. Ricki's eyes remain glued to Jared while I tell her how Shake and Bake turned out to be Winn and about my father. She looks at me only when I tell her about the hit on the head in front of the courthouse, but I think that was because Jared took a water break.

"Way to go, Jared!" she shouts, cupping her hands to her mouth. "Did you see that? He almost scored!"

"He's the messiah. I'm convinced."

"Hey, watch it."

I look around the lush suburban field almost reflexively; my paranoia hasn't diminished, even though the Italian stalking my daughter turned out to be her grandfather. Apparently, there's nothing to be worried about here. Bryn Mawr, where Ricki lives, is one of the wealthiest communities on the Main Line. No killers here, only color-coordinated parents watching their kids kick the shit out of each other. I'm safe as long as I stay off the field.

"Are you gonna see your father again?" Ricki asks.

"Not if I can help it."

"You should, you know. I think it's very healthy."

"Give me a break, Rick. It's a horror show."

The wind blows a strand of hair into her lipstick and she picks it out. "I like that he came forward and found you. He's dealing with it, or trying to. Credit where credit is due."

"Please. The guy looks like Elvis. On the stamp they didn't pick."

"You should talk to your mother about what happened when you were little."

"Another winner. Masquerading as Rose Kennedy. What a joke."

She watches Jared kick the ball to his teammate. "Nice pass, honey!" She covers her mouth. "Damn. He told me not to say that anymore. Anyway, talk to her."

"I have bigger problems." I think of Armen. His killer is still out there, and this is my only Sunday without Maddie, who's at Sam's.

"You mean the judge?"

"I told you it wasn't suicide, Rick. Even the FBI thinks so."

"Don't be unbearable, please."

"You mean because I was right and you were wrong?"

"Yes, already."

"Do you say *uncle*?"

She claps loudly. "Way to go, Jared! Way to go!"

"Sometimes a train really is a train, Ricki. Trains and bagels, bagels and trains."

"Go, Jared, you can do it!" She claps. "All that matters is you getting out of that mess. You're right to let the FBI take over, it's their job. You should never have been involved in the first place."

So I lied. It was a white lie, a little white lie. Why worry her?

"I don't know what made you think you could investigate a murder all by yourself. With the Mafia yet."

Silly me. "Uncle," I say.

"Maybe I'm finally getting through to you. All that free therapy, paying off." She smiles at me, then gets distracted by the action on the soccer field. "Hey, ref, what about it? Wake up, you jerk!" The woman next to her glances over. "I heard on the radio about that death penalty case."

"Yeah, the Supremes still have it. They haven't decided yet."

"Go, Jared, charge him!"

I think of Hightower, sitting alone. I read they moved him from death row to a special cell near the death chamber. The death warrant runs out tomorrow morning at 9:03. I wonder what Mrs.

Stevens is doing today. How many mothers know the exact time and place of their child's death? Besides the Gilpins?

"The radio said they were locking down the prison tonight," Ricki says. "What's that mean?"

"It means all the prisoners have to stay in their cells."

"Isn't that what prison is?"

"They do it before executions, so the population doesn't riot."

Ricki leaps to her feet. "He scored! Way to go, honey! Way to go!" Applauding wildly, she looks down at me. "Clap, you! He scored!"

So I clap for Jared, who truly is a fine young man, all wiry legs in his baggy soccer trunks. He throws his arms into the air and beams at his mother and me, his mouth a tangle of expensive orthodonture. But somehow when I look at his face, flushed with adrenaline and promise, I think about Hightower, who had no suburban soccer field, no fancy jersey or hundred-dollar cleats. One will go to Harvard; the other will be put to death.

No justice, no peace.

Empty rhetoric, until I think of Armen and his killer.

That very night I'm on the warpath, rattling toward West Philadelphia in the dark. I'm heading for Armen's secret apartment. Someone killed him; maybe the answer is there. And I'm the only one who knows about it, so it's relatively safe. I decide to go, especially since Maddie is with Sam. I make the most of baby-sitter time; if you have children, you'll understand. I've known couples to drive around the block just to enjoy that last fifteen minutes.

I've disguised myself as the high-priced lawyer I used to be, just in case anybody's watching me: a monogrammed briefcase, overpriced raincoat, and pretentious felt hat. I check out the rearview mirror on the way to West Philly, but everything looks clear.

I open the car window into the cool night air. It still smells like hoagies at the corner of 40th and Spruce, like it did twenty years ago. I swing the car into a space and step out into a curbful of trash. Some things never change.

I lock the car and walk down Pine Street, which used to be lined with Victorian houses full of expensive apartments with hardwood floors and high ceilings. The richer students lived here when I was in school; it looks like they still do, judging from the cars parked along the street, bumper to exported bumper.

I reach the address on the checkbook and stand outside the brownstone in the dark. It's a three-story Victorian, with high arched windows and a mansard roof. A light is on on the bottom floor, showing through closed shutters in what would be the living room. I straighten my hat, climb the porch steps, and ring the bell to the front door.

A porch light comes on. An older woman appears at the window, behind bars. Her gray hair is plaited into a long braid and she wears thick aviator glasses. "What is it?" she shouts at me, through the bars.

"I'm a lawyer," I say, brandishing my briefcase. She does an about-face. The light goes off.

Good move. I take another tack. "Please, I'm a friend of Greg Armen's."

The light goes on again and she reappears, friendlier in a colorful Guatemalan shirt. "What do you want?"

"I need to come in. I'm meeting him here. My name is Grace Rossi."

She squints and I smile in a toothy way. She unlocks the several locks on the door and opens it, welcoming me into the foul odor of Indian curry. "Smells good," I say.

"Do you work with Greg?"

"Yes. I was supposed to meet him, but he's late. Do you know a way I could get into his apartment? To wait for him?"

I hear a cat meow from inside her apartment. "He didn't come today. He always comes on Sundays."

"I know, he got tied up. He asked me to stop by tonight. We just starting seeing each other."

"You want to surprise him?"

"Right."

"Interesting. Hold on," she says, winking at me in a stagey way. "He gave me a key in case he forgets it." She scuffs into her apartment in Birkenstocks and returns with a key on a ring. "He does forget it sometimes. He's kind of strange, in that cap and sunglasses all the time. I like her, though."

"Her?"

"Whoops! You didn't hear it from me! Give him hell!" she says, slapping the key in my palm; then she turns on her heel and scuffs inside. I hear the cat meow again as she closes the door.

I trudge up the stairs with a sense of dread. *I like her, though.* Who is she? The shabby carpeted stair winds around to the left, and at the top are two doors, 2A and 2B. The checkbook said 2B, so I slip the key into its lock. It opens easily, eager to reveal its secret, even if I'm not so eager to know it.

The room is dark, except for a streetlight streaming through the bay windows at the other end of the room. It looks like an efficiency, with a single bed against the wall. A chain hangs down from an overhead light, and I yank it on.

What I see shocks me.

All over the apartment, everywhere I look, are toys. Against the wall are white IKEA shelves full of stuffed animals. A plush tiger. Pinocchio. A Steiff lion. Mickey Mouse. They're crammed onto the shelves in all directions, sticking out by their cartoon feet and white-gloved hands. The lower shelves are stacked with an array of games. Candyland. Don't Break the Ice. Clue. Monopoly.

Stunned, I close the door behind me.

A child's room. Does Armen have a child? The woman downstairs said he comes on Sundays, like lots of divorced fathers. Like Sam. Is Armen divorced? Was he married before?

What is this all about?

I walk stiffly to the middle of the room and pick up a stuffed Dalmatian puppy from the couch. It looks back at me, round-eyed, blank.

Who is this child? Who is this woman?

I rummage through the stuffed animals on the shelves, then the games. Toy cats and teddy bears fly off the shelves in my wake. I feel myself getting angry, losing control. Who is this woman? Who is this child?

I tear the plastic lid off a white toy box full of blocks and root to the bottom. Nothing, except for plastic beads and a pirate's scabbard.

I move to a bookshelf next to the toy box, also white. It's full of children's books, more than most libraries, and many in hardback. I snatch them out, one by one, enraged. Why didn't he tell me, that night on the couch? I hear the sound of my own panting and watch with satisfaction as *Goodnight Moon* and *Where the Wild Things Are* fall to the soft carpet, littering it.

I take the next book from the shelf. *Eloise*. There's a pang deep within my chest; I know this book, but I have yet to buy it for Maddie.

How do I know *Eloise*?

I open it, going through it page by oversized page, trying to remember. I come to a page that at first looks ripped but unfolds at the top. I trace the trail of Eloise from a distant memory, my nail running along the dotted red line that goes up and down on the elevator. I remember a thick fingernail tracing these same travels. *See, here she goes.* The finger is yellow-stained at the edge with nicotine, and the hand is warm as my own hand rides around on top of his. My father's hand. *See, Princess?*

And then he left.

I love you.

Liars, liars all. I let the book fall to the floor.

Suddenly, I hear a noise at the windows behind me. I turn around, but nothing's there. I hear the noise again, like a rustling outside. I reach overhead and turn off the light. The room goes black just as a figure climbs onto the porch roof outside the bay window.

I back up against the wall.

The figure creeps toward the window, silhouetted in the streetlight. I feel my hackles rise. Someone is about to break in. Who knows about this apartment? Armen's killer?

The figure removes the portable screen from the window and places it on the roof without a sound. A professional. The streetlight glistens on his black leather jacket, stretched tight over a powerful back. I watch, dry-mouthed, as he jiggles the center window and it comes open in his hands.

I reach for the apartment key in my raincoat pocket, ready to drive it into his eyes. I feel the scream rising in my throat but suppress it.

The figure opens the window halfway and climbs into the room, landing silently at the foot of the single bed.

I back toward the apartment door in the dark, every nerve strained with tension. I can't see who the intruder is and I don't care. I must have been out of my mind to come here. I take a step back. Suddenly, I slip on a book and let out an involuntary yelp.

In a split second, the dark figure is barreling

across the room toward me. He slams into my chest with the impact of a freight train, knocking the wind out of me. I cry out in pain and fall back on the hardwood floor. My head cracks hard where it was bumped before.

I try to scream but a hand clamps down across my mouth so cruelly it bring tears to my eyes. The hand forces my head back down against the floor. His body climbs up on mine, pinning me to the floor. I try frantically to knee him but he's too strong. A flashlight blazes into my eyes, blinding me.

"Grace!" says the voice behind the light. "What the fuck?" The hand releases my mouth.

"Who?"

"It's me. Winn." He shines the flashlight on his bearded face. "What are you doing here?"

My head begins to ache. "Why did you attack me?" I ask him, wincing. "You hurt my head."

"What did you break in for?" He backs off of me.

"What did *you* break in for?" I pull my tweed skirt down, trying to recover my dignity. "Jesus H. Christ, I've never been so banged up in all my life. Ever since I met you."

He stands up and helps me to my feet. "Why didn't you say who you were?"

"I didn't know it was you. Why didn't you say who *you* were?"

"I didn't know it was *you.*"

"Where's your raincoat?"

He looks down at the leather coat. "Underneath." He pulls out an edge to show me, but it's too dark to see. "I found this in a dumpster a block down, can you believe it? It must've cost a couple hundred dollars."

"You've been undercover too long. Where's your rain hat?"

"I don't wear it on B and E's. You should sit down. Come on." He eases me onto the couch and tilts my head back on a crinkly bandanna he pulls from his pocket. "Rest a minute. I'll find some ice."

I grab his lapel before he gets up. "No. No ice. I hate ice."

"You need ice."

"No. What I need is to yell at you, then I need to sue you. Then I need to yell at you and sue you again."

He laughs and sits heavily on the couch next to me. The streetlight illuminates the oil slick coating his nose; I could never go undercover, my pores couldn't take it. "I'm sorry I jumped you like that," he says, "but you surprised me."

"I surprised you? I'm lawfully on the premises."

"How was I supposed to know that? I've been watching this place for over a month. The light is never on at night. I came in to catch a killer."

"Didn't you see me go to the door?"

"I didn't recognize you. You don't wear hats, and I never saw you with a briefcase. I thought you were here to see the old woman downstairs. You're off the reservation, Grace. Way off. Who's staying with your daughter?"

"She's at her father's. Sunday is father's day, apparently."

He reaches around the back of my neck. "Lift up. I want to fix this thing." I oblige and he folds the bandanna in two.

"I hate men."

"I know, we're bums. Look at me."

"Exactly."

He laughs. "Which do you hate more, men or ice?"

I feel myself smile, the adrenaline ebbing away. "Men. Armen in particular. So he was a father? Who's the mother?"

"Don't you know?"

"Of course not."

"Then how do you know about the apartment? I thought he told you."

Hurt and humiliated, the combination platter. "So whose child is it? Tell me."

He pauses. "Were you in love with him?"

I'm glad he can't see my face. "No. I was in lust with him. I didn't know him at all, obviously. If my daughter ever does what I did, I'll kill her."

"You were lonely."

"How do you know?"

"Artie told me."

I wince. "Terrific. On to more important topics. Is it his child?"

"Yes."

"And the mother?"

"You want to know? Straight up?" I feel his eyes on me.

"I can take it, doc."

"The mother is Eletha."

I gasp as if the wind were knocked out of me again. I can't say anything for a minute.

"Grace?" He touches my arm, but I move it away.

"The mother is *Eletha?* The child—"

"Is Malcolm."

Oh, God. "How do you know that?"

"She dropped him off here."

My mind reels. I think of Malcolm's picture on Eletha's desk. His lightish skin. Why didn't I think of it? Armen paid for her tuition, even. "They were married?"

"No. I checked. Never married."

Malcolm, born out of wedlock? "Does Susan know?"

"I don't know, I've never seen her here. Armen met Malcolm every Sunday."

"Since when?"

"I don't know that either. They played inside, sometimes he took him to Clark Park. Places he wouldn't be recognized. He was a good father."

My stomach turns over. "Oh, please. He was a liar."

"That's unfair."

"How do you know? What was he, Clarence Thomas? God, was I blind."

"Don't judge him until you have all the facts. I knew Armen, too. He was a good man. He went out of his way for me. He got them to let me into the Y, even got me a locker. He didn't care that I was homeless."

"You're not. And he was a piece of shit."

"You don't believe that or you wouldn't have protected him."

"I protected him? How?"

"You didn't tell me about the money. The $650,000. That's how you knew about the apartment, isn't it?"

I sink back into the couch. My head hurts even more. "How do *you* know about the money?"

"The IRS found out about the account. It was a fraction of that last year, when he declared it. Gained a lot of weight in twelve months."

"It couldn't be a bribe for *Canavan*, you know. Armen wanted the case to come out the other way."

"I know that and you know that, but the money convinced my boss it was Armen who took the bribe. They figure it's the reason he killed himself, he couldn't live with it. He killed himself in April— tax time, they figure. They're gonna pull the plug on this investigation any day now. The bad guy is already dead."

"But you saw Armen at the argument. It was him against Galanter."

"They think that was just for show. He hadn't voted yet, he was killed before he could. If I don't turn up something very soon, the investigation is over. Armen's gonna be smeared in every newspaper in the country."

"But his killer would go free."

"I know, and the world will think Armen was dirty. Including his son."

I feel stunned. It was awful before, and now it's worse. Now it's Armen and Eletha, my lover and my friend. Were they still seeing each other, sleeping together? What did she mean to him? What did *I* mean to him? "I don't know if I'm still in."

"I want you out, I told you. You're in danger."

"It's not that." I tell him about what happened with Maddie, even about my father. He's a good listener and stays quiet for a minute after I finish; the last man who listened to me that intently was Armen.

"So you're hurt," he says.

True. "I always thought he was so honest, so honorable. But here, this place. A child, Malcolm."

"He would've told you sooner or later."

"I don't know."

"Let me take it from here, you're in way too deep. All I wanted you to do was answer Galanter's phone. Now you're breaking into apartments."

"I didn't break in, I talked my way in."

He smiles. "You lied your way in. Not illegal, just immoral."

It reminds me of Armen, and our talk that night, over *Hightower*. Law and morality. *You can't separate them, why would you want to?* Then I think of his broad back slumped over his desk. Armen was murdered, and murder is wrong. Illegal and immoral. Nothing I've learned tonight changes that, and I'm still the only one who has a chance of getting to Galanter. I rise, unsteadily. "Maybe I'm not out, Rain Man."

Winn takes my elbow. "Aw, come on, Grace. I worry about you."

"Good. Somebody should."

"I mean it."

His voice has a softness I'd rather ignore, at least for the time being. "You want to walk me out or you gonna play Batman again?"

I get no answer, not that I expected one. We end up leaving by the conventional method. He waits for me on the sidewalk while I stop downstairs to return the key. The old woman opens the door carrying the cat, a chubby orange tabby. "I heard you moving the furniture!" she says slyly.

"Moving the furniture?"

She plucks the key from my hand. "You're a nineties woman, I'll tell you that!" The woman shuts the door, and the cat meows in belated agreement.

23

Monday morning I push open the glass door into the courthouse lobby. It's mercifully clear of reporters and crowds, but it looks like martial law has been declared. There are double the number of marshals, and even the lawyers and court employees have to go through the detectors. I join one of the lines, predictably the slowest moving.

"What gives?" I say to a skinny marshal, when I reach the middle of the line. Jeff stands at his side.

"New rules, on account of that circus last week."

"A little late, isn't it?"

"Tell the AO that."

In front of me in line is an older woman, thin and tall, with marvelously erect posture. Her gray hair is swept into an elegant French twist and the air around her smells like lilac bushes in June.

"Line up, now!" roars McLean, at the head of the line. His booming voice sets the woman in front of me trembling. "All bags on the conveyor belt! All bags on the belt! Sir, *sir!*" he shouts at a heavyset man in a red Phillies windbreaker.

"Shit," the man says. He surrenders the wrinkled paper bag to the conveyor belt of the X-ray machine.

"Say what, sir?"

Ray looks over from behind the machine. "Don't be roughin' up the Phils fans, McLean. We need 'em all, after last season."

The marshals laugh, including the fan. But not McLean. "I'm not roughin' nobody up. I'm doin' my job." The fan lumbers through the metal detector, and McLean motions distractedly to the woman in front of me. "You don't know who's carryin' a piece," he says. "You can't tell by lookin'."

The older woman quivers like Katharine Hepburn.

"They still haven't caught the guy who did those shootings," McLean continues, watching her place a wristwatch with a black cord band into the bin. "You can pack anywhere, even your boot." He shouts over her head to the marshal at the monitor, "Billy, you remember that joker, the one with the boot?"

Billy peers over the top of the monitor. "The cowboy."

"Yeah. Some cowboy," McLean says. "Put your purse on the belt, ma'am."

The woman watches with apprehension as her purse disappears into the maw of the machine. As the light turns green, McLean propels her through the metal detector and looks at me. "How's your head, Ms. Rossi?"

"Fine, thanks," I say warily.

"Put your purse on the belt. Go when the light turns green."

"You be nice to her, McLean," Ray says. "She's my girl. Grace, you takin' care of that matter we discussed?"

Damn. I forgot to talk to Eletha about him. How can I broach it now, when I can barely look her in the eye? "I'm workin' on it, Ray." I walk through the metal detector, but it explodes in a ringing alarm.

"Come back on through," McLean says. I walk back through the metal detector and the clamor subsides.

"What's the deal?"

"Turned up the sensitivity. Have to do our jobs right." He winks, but it's not friendly. "Take off your watch and try it again."

I snap off my Seiko, and it clatters into the bin on the counter. I start through the metal detector, but no sooner do I hit the black rubber carpet than the detector erupts in another cacophonous warning. The people in line break ranks to see what's going on.

"I think she's okay," Ray says, "even if she *is* a lawyer." The other marshals laugh.

"No, can't take any chances. Ms. Rossi's been a busy lady, checkin' up, makin' sure we're doin' our jobs."

I glance at Ray, but he looks as surprised as I do. "I was checking security."

"I know what you were doing. You wanted to know who was on duty the night Judge Gregorian bought it. Well, you're lookin' at him, and I didn't see nothin' unusual. Earrings in the box."

I drop my hoops into the bin. "Do you check the hallways?"

"Sure, I patrol."

"Did you check our hallway, on eighteen?"

"Sure did. Nothin' there."

"At what time?"

"About eleven o'clock, then again around four or so."

My mouth goes dry. By four o'clock Armen and I were on the couch. "Did you come into chambers either time?"

A smile plays around his lips. "Don't remember."

"You don't remember?"

"Is there an echo in here?"

I grit my teeth. I've deposed bigger bastards than this. "Do you usually go into chambers?"

"I check the doorknobs. If the door's unlocked, I go in. I forget if that one was open that night. Now you better get through the detector. We got a line here."

I walk through the detector, trying to remember if the door was unlocked that night. I have no idea. The alarm sounds again.

"Come on back, Ms. Rossi."

I walk back through and the noise stops. My handbag sails past me in the opposite direction. McLean looks over his shoulder at Jeff. I can't see his face but I can see Jeff's, and he's smiling.

"Now your belt, please, Ms. Rossi."

"Cut her a break, man," Ray says.

"You ain't my boss and I ain't your man," McLean snaps, then looks at me. "Only one thing left. Stand up and put your hands out straight from your sides."

"Get real. You know I'm not a security risk."

"You want to get to work today?" he says. From behind the counter he produces a hand-held metal detector, which looks like a cartoon magnifying glass. He switches it on in front of my chest.

Biiinng! It screams to life, even louder than the other metal detector. All eyes are on me, or more accurately, on my breasts. Shame and fury restrict my breathing.

Biiinnng! Biiinnng!

McLean holds the magnifying glass in front of my left breast, then moves it slowly in front of my right. It's all I can do not to hit him.

Biiinnng! Biinng!

"I thought so," he shouts, and turns off the noisy alarm. "Underwire bra." One of the marshals laughs out loud, then quiets.

I look McLean in the eye. "If this is some kind of game, pal, you won't win."

"I don't know what you're talking about," he says, unfazed.

I grab my earrings and bag and stalk ahead to the elevator, where the older woman is holding the door for me. "Here, dear," she says, in a comforting way.

I slip inside and punch the button for eighteen. "Thank you."

"What an unhappy man," she says, looking up at the lighted numbers. The elevator doors open on the second floor and she extends a bony hand. "It was very nice meeting you. My name's Miss Pershing, by the way. Amanda Pershing."

"Grace Rossi."

Her hooded eyes light up. "Are you Italian?"

I think of my father. "No."

She looks disappointed as the elevator doors close behind her. Her perfume lingers, and I travel heavenward in an elevator filled with lavender and rage. Did McLean see Armen and me together? Where was he when I was hit on the head?

I head for chambers but hear noise down the hall, coming from Galanter's chambers; it sounds like a party.

I pass the judges' elevator and linger for a moment in the hall. The sound is coming from the office of Galanter's law clerks. Maybe they're celebrating Galanter's ascension; maybe I can learn something about *Canavan*. I walk down the hall and stand in the open doorway.

There are no judges, but the clerks' office is packed with twenty-five-year-olds, crowding among the federal case reporters, laughing and talking. One of Galanter's clerks has two party hats crossed on his head in a coarse caricature of a woman's breasts.

"It's time!" somebody shouts, and then everybody starts blowing horns and noisemakers, like New Year's Eve.

"Ready for the countdown?" shouts a pretty blonde in a dark suit. She checks her watch, as do several of the others.

"Ten! Nine! Eight! Seven!"

The kids all shout, growing giddier with each second. I have no idea what is going on.

"Come on in, the water's fine!" says one of the partyers, who's older than the others. He takes me by the hand and pulls me inside. "Count with us!"

"What for?" I yell, over the din.

"Six! Five!" shouts the crowd in unison. "Four! Three! Two!"

"What are we celebrating?"

"Justice!" He raises a plastic glass. "The Court denied the stay in *Hightower.* This is the big day! 9:03!"

"One! *Zero!*"

"Good-bye, Tommy!" shouts the blonde, next to a familiar head of wiry hair.

Ben. He sees me in the doorway, and his shocked expression freezes for a moment. Then he turns his back on me.

24

"You had a phone call, Grace," Eletha calls out from Armen's office, as soon as I get into chambers. "From that reporter."

"Reporter?" I pause in the doorway to Armen's office, taken aback by the sight. Everything has been packed up. There's not a trace of Armen still visible; none of the books he loved or the objects he collected. Even the cudgel he kept on the wall has been wrapped. I feel a sharp twinge inside.

"That stringer, the one who was givin' Susan such a hard time after the memorial service." She pushes a stiff strand of hair out of her eyes, looking beautiful without even trying. No wonder

Armen loved her. "The curly guy, who needed the shave. Faber."

Are you gonna let somebody get away with murder? "I know the one. Did he leave his number?"

"You're not gonna call him back, are you?"

"Why not?"

"He's an ass. He called here, buggin' Ben, even Sarah. Artie hung up on him." She strips some wide packing tape from a roll and presses it onto a box. "I can't be bothered. I got another asshole to deal with. Did you see?" She steps aside, presenting the chair behind her like Vanna White. A long Indian headdress is draped over the chair. Its feathers are a brilliant cardinal red, with orange in the center, and the pointy tips of each plume are black. It's easily eight feet long and makes a gaudy caterpillar onto the carpet.

"What's that doing here?"

"It's Galanter's, he's the chief now, get it? Think he'll wear it behind the goddamn desk?" She shakes her head. "Meanwhile, check out what's going on down the hall. You won't believe that either."

"I saw."

"They should be ashamed of themselves. I called the clerk's office upstairs. They'll stop 'em."

"Was Galanter in?"

"He's been gone all morning."

"Where?"

"Damned if I know. He left some typing for me, like I'm his goddamn secretary."

I turn to go. "I gotta check the mail."

"How was your weekend?" she calls after me.

I think of my newfound father, then the secret apartment full of toys. "Same old same old."

"You're talkative this morning." She's puzzled by my coldness, and I decide to level with her in a way she didn't with me. Or maybe I want to pick a fight.

"Actually, I had an interesting weekend, El. Went up to West Philly."

"You? In my neighborhood? What's up there?"

"Armen's apartment."

Her mouth forms a glossy chestnut-stained *O.* "Say what?"

I close the door behind me. "I thought I knew you, El, but it turns out I don't."

She eases down onto one of the boxes. "Now don't say that."

"What am I supposed to say?"

"How'd you find out about the apartment?"

I hadn't thought about that. "I came across some papers in here the other night. A lease."

"I thought I packed all that stuff."

"You didn't tell me about Malcolm."

"You expected me to?"

"Of course, we're friends. I thought he was yours and your ex's."

She points an electric nail at me. "I never told you that. You assumed it."

"You *let* me assume it."

"You'd've blamed me."

"Blamed you? It's him I blame."

She frowns. "Armen? Why?"

"Hitting on women who work for him. First you, then me."

"Armen wasn't like that."

I look away at the bookshelves, empty and hollow. "Come on, El. I wasn't born yesterday and neither were you. It's the same old shit, just in a black robe."

"It wasn't like that."

"Wasn't or isn't?"

"Wasn't," she says firmly. "It's ancient history."

"Good. So he wasn't cheating on me, just his wife."

"We ended before he met Susan, Grace."

It sets my teeth on edge. "Then why didn't he marry you?"

"Because I said no."

"What?" It's a surprise.

"The bottom line is"—she pauses, then laughs and throws up her hands—"we fell in love, then we got pregnant. He wanted to make it legal, but I couldn't see marryin' him, takin' him away from everybody he loved. His mother. His community."

"What community?"

"The Armenians. The dinners, the church, the whole thing. It was the center of his life." She looks down. "You think his mama liked it when she met me, my belly big as a watermelon? I'm half the reason she killed herself."

"Is that true?"

"I don't know. Armen always blamed himself. So when he asked, I said no." She sighs. "Don't think I haven't regretted it, plenty of times. I even felt a little jealous of you."

"Me?"

She waves it away. "Water under the bridge. It was the right thing. I didn't fit in his life."

"Did Susan?"

She wrinkles her stubby nose. "Not really, but he fit into hers. Now *you* were different, you woulda been the one. You fit into his life and he fit into yours."

I feel a lump in my throat. I know that, inside.

"With him and me, we were betwixt and between, both of us. My family wasn't in love with the situation either. It never would've worked."

"So you took Malcolm yourself and raised him?"

"Not on my own. Armen was in on every decision, we talked about Mal all the time. He was a great father, Grace. The best."

"How'd you swing it financially?"

"Armen paid Malcolm's expenses. Now I don't know what'll happen." She flicks some imaginary dirt out from under a nail. "It's part of the reason I'm thinking about quitting school. To get another job at night."

I think of the checkbook. "Did Armen leave a will or anything?"

She laughs. "For what? He had no extra money, it went to us. You saw the apartment, he bought that boy everything. I told you he saved. Well, it was Malcolm he was saving for, for his college."

"How much had he saved?"

"About fifty–sixty grand, like I told you. Not bad, huh?" She smiles proudly, and the irony hits me full force. I can't shake the image of the

$650,000, socked away in a money fund. Did Armen hold out on her and Malcolm?

"Let's say he did have money, Eletha. Do you think he had a will? Did Susan say anything?"

"Not that I heard."

"Does she know about you and him?"

Eletha's eyes widen comically. "You crazy, girl?"

I smile, feeling my hostility subsiding. Maybe I wouldn't have told me either. "Why not?"

"Uh-uh." She shakes her head. "I didn't want to tell her, and he promised me he wouldn't. She has no idea."

"But how did he get away every Sunday?"

"How do most men get away? Work. Clubs. It became his Sunday off. We were careful during the campaign, laid low, and she found plenty to do, believe me. She was into him early on, but when she caught Potomac fever she left him behind."

"Is that when he asked for a divorce?"

She looks at me like I'm crazy again. "Armen? Never. He loved her in his bones. She's the one who called it quits."

I don't understand. "*Susan* was the one who ended the marriage, not Armen? But he told me she'd asked him to stay with her."

"Through the campaign, because she needed a hubby to smile pretty for the pictures. Otherwise, that woman didn't need him at all."

I sit down in one of the chairs at the conference table. "I don't know what to think, El. I don't understand Armen. I don't understand anything."

"You're takin' this bad, girlfriend," Eletha says. "What don't you understand, baby? Mommy make it better."

"I don't know if Armen was a bad guy or a good guy."

"A good guy. Next question."

"I don't know who killed him."

"He killed himself. Next."

I look at her in bewilderment. "How can you say that? You had a son with him."

"That's right."

"You said he was a good father."

"He was. The best."

"How could he be? What kind of father leaves his own child?" I think of my own father, though I hadn't started out thinking about him. Suddenly I need to know the answer to the question, burning like hot lead at the core of my chest. "Tell me that, Eletha. How can a father turn his back on his own flesh and blood?"

"Because he has no choice. Maybe the pain is too great to stay." She shakes her head. "Look, you left your husband, didn't you? Why?"

"He cheated on me," I say, the words dry as dust in my mouth. "It's not the same."

"Yes, it is. You loved him, didn't you? But you left."

"I had to."

"Right. You had no choice. Just because you left doesn't mean you didn't love."

I feel a catch in my throat. I can't say anything. I think of Sam, Armen, then my father. I need Ricki, fast.

Eletha folds her arms. "And I always thought you were so smart. Fancy degrees and all."

"You just assumed wrong," I say to her, and she laughs.

The marshals' smelly gym is empty; it's midafternoon. Against the wall is a huge mirror and racks of chrome free weights. A treadmill stands at the end behind some steppers. On the far wall hangs a poster of Christie Brinkley and beside it one of the electric chair. At the bottom it says: JUSTICE—FRIED OR EXTRA CRISPY? I kid you not.

"How can they have that there?" I ask Artie, who's flat on his back, pumping a barbell up and down over his chest.

"Have what?"

"That poster." I point, and his eyes follow my finger.

"Christie? She's a babe. An old babe, like you."

"The other one, whiz."

He hoists the barbell up and down, exhaling like a whale through a blowhole. "I never noticed it. They let me work out here, Grace, I don't give a shit about the artwork. Which rep am I on?"

"I don't know."

"You're a lousy spotter." He presses the barbell into the air.

I can't take my eyes from the poster. The newspaper said that Hightower's last meal was steak and an ice cream sundae. He ate the dessert first. After dinner he played Battleship with his guard, and the guard won. "Artie, if you were playing Battleship with a man who was condemned to death, wouldn't you let him win?"

"What?" The barbell rises and falls.

"Wouldn't you let him win? I mean, the man's going to die."

"I don't know, would you?" He grunts with effort, his bangs damp from sweat.

"Of course. I let Maddie win all the time. What's the difference? It's a game."

"Games matter, Grace."

"Excuse me, I forgot who I was talking to." I look back at the poster. The witnesses at Hightower's execution said he shook his head back and forth as the lethal chemicals flowed into his veins. His feet trembled and his fingers twitched for about three minutes, and then it was over. Final, unknowable, and beyond this world. "Artie, what do you think about the death penalty?"

"What is this, menopause? Hot flashes and questions?"

"Come on. Tell me what you think."

"I don't think about the death penalty."

"But if you had to say, how do you come out?"

He presses the barbell all the way up to a hook on a rack behind him, where it falls with a resounding *clang*. "It's no biggie." His arms flop over the sides of the bench.

"I thought you were against it."

"That was when I was fucking Sarah. Now that she's fucked me, it's just fine."

"You don't mean that."

He pushes his wet hair away from his forehead. "Yes, I do."

"But think about the act. The actual act of killing someone."

"I could do it, if he deserved it."

"My, we're in a macho mood."

"You started it. This isn't why I asked you to meet me in my branch office."

I laugh. He has been spending a lot of time here, I gather because he's out of work and avoiding Sarah. "All right. What did you want to talk about?"

"I wanted to tell you I was sorry about the other night. I drank too much. I wasn't making any sense."

"It's okay. I understand why it happened." Drowning your sorrows. I've done it exactly once.

"Thanks, Mom." He rubs his chest, and sweat soaks through his thin T-shirt. I remember the basketball underneath.

"You still got that tattoo?"

"Until I find a blowtorch." He sits up, straddling the bench, then sighs heavily. "Lifting sucks. I miss hoops."

"You're not playing anymore?"

"Nah. The team broke up." He wipes his forehead with the edge of his T-shirt. "You know, before Sarah dumped me she told me something. She said you thought Armen was murdered."

"I do."

"Really?"

"Really. Why, what do you think? You gonna laugh at me?"

"No. I even thought of it myself, for a minute. After the way Galanter's been acting."

It surprises me. "You suspect Galanter?"

"I didn't know about suspecting him, but if anybody did it, he did."

"Why?"

"Besides the fact that he's a dick?"

"Yes."

"Because he wanted to be chief judge. He would never have been chief if Armen hadn't died." Artie straightens up, rallying. "And remember how Bernice went after him?"

"Do you think becoming chief judge is enough of a motive?"

He snorts. "What are you, funny? It's the same as Battleship. It's *winning*."

"People don't kill to win."

"Sure they do. Plenty of people—mostly men, I admit—would kill to win. It's ambition. Raw, naked, blind, cold. Ambition."

I think of Galanter taking a bribe in *Canavan* and killing Armen to guarantee the result. That makes sense to me, in a perverse way. "I don't agree. I think people kill for money—or love."

"Love? Not Galanter, what does he know from love? He's not even married, he lives for the frigging job. He has an Indian headdress, Grace. The man is not fucking kidding."

"True."

"As chief judge, he'll get on all the Judicial Conference committees. Get to go to D.C., hobnob with the Supremes. It even positions him for the next appointment to the Court. Look at Breyer, he was chief."

The Supreme Court. I hadn't thought of that.

Combined with *Canavan,* that's one hell of a motive.

"It's a place in history, Grace."

I remember that Galanter has a collection of first editions in his office. "He would love that."

"He sure would. It's the top of the profession. They ain't final because they're right, they're right because they're final."

"But Galanter's a Republican appointee."

"The Dems won't be in forever, babe." He looks down, then shakes his head. "Justice Galanter. That's so beat. Can't you just hurl?"

I consider this, and he's right. I could just hurl.

25

slip my master key into the doorknob. It turns with a satisfying *click,* admitting me to the darkened chambers. No one's there, as I expected; it's too late even for geeks. I told my mother I had to work late, killing two birds with one stone: avoiding her and poking around. I enter the reception area and close the door quietly behind me.

The computer monitors are on, standing out like vivid squares of hot color in the dark, wasteful but helpful. ORDER IN THE COURT! WELCOME TO THE THIRD CIRCUIT COURT WORD PROCESSING SYSTEM! guides me through the reception area, where the blinds are down.

The chambers are laid out like ours, with the judge's office to the left. I walk into Galanter's office; even at the threshold it stinks of cigar smoke. The far wall is entirely of glass, like Armen's, overlooking the Delaware. The lights from the Camden side make bright wiggly lines on the black water.

In the light from the wall of windows I can make out Galanter's glistening desk, also of glass. I walk to it with more nervousness than I want to acknowledge and whip out the flashlight I keep in the car; it says WALT DISNEY WORLD. Official burglary tool, patent pending.

I flick on the flashlight with an amateurish thrill and flash it around the room. Next to Galanter's desk are the same shelves we have, where Armen used to keep the current cases. Galanter does it the same way. I look over the shelves. The circle of light falls on each stack of red, blue, and gray briefs, the colors regulated by the Third Circuit's local rules. Attached to the briefs with a rubber band is the appendix in each case and the record. That's what I'm looking for.

I sort through a bunch of criminal cases, all sentencing appeals, and a commercial contract case; the Uniform Commercial Code seems less interesting to me than it used to. Underneath the stack, at the very bottom, is *Canavan* and its record. I tug the *Canavan* papers off the shelf and settle down on the floor.

I pull off the briefs and appendix to get to the record. I expect to find a stack of blue-backed pleadings bound at the top, but the papers are

stuffed in a yellow envelope. SEALED COURT DOC-
UMENTS, says a forbidding red stamp on the
envelope. A court order is taped underneath.

Why would a district court seal this record? In
any event, it doesn't apply to me, at least not
tonight.

I plunge into the envelope, pulling out the first
part of the record. On top is the complaint, which
alleges that Canavan Flowers was driven out of
business by a group of local flower retailers. The
defendants listed Bob Canavan on their FTD-like
telephone network but never sent him any orders
to fill. The complaint is a poorly drafted litany of
the ways Canavan was starved out, but never
explains why. The young lawyer couldn't flesh out
the Mob connection. Neither can I.

A ring of florists? Galanter laughed.

I flip past the complaint and skim the appendix
until I come to the names of the wholesalers. I
take the crumpled crossword puzzle Winn gave
me from my pocket and compare it with the
papers, sticking the flashlight in my armpit. None
of the names are the same. The list of wholesalers' names reads like white bread, the list of
mobsters' like Amoroso's hoagie rolls. I
put the pleadings aside in favor of the depositions. If there's gold to be found, it'll be here.
Something that isn't what it seems.

I read the first deposition, then the second and
the third, fighting off a sinking feeling. None of
the names are the ones on the crossword; none
of the allegations amount to anything other than
common law fraud by a bunch of rather hard-

assed florists. Isn't that what Townsend said? *How is it different from a case of garden variety fraud?* Was he speaking from the casebook or the checkbook?

I start the next deposition, given by one of the vendors. An inadvertent reference to a deliveryman sounds familiar. Jim Cavallaro. I look down at the short list on the crossword puzzle:

James Cavallaro.

It must be the same man. I think a minute.

Of course.

The Mob couldn't care less about the carnations; it's in the delivery. In the trucks and the truck drivers. In an operation that runs by phone orders, the delivery is where the money is to be made. It doesn't matter what's being delivered, even something that smells like roses.

I leaf back to the other depositions, looking for references to the truckers. I scribble down the names, but there's only a few. My next step is to check Galanter's phone log to see if any of them made calls to chambers, or if there's any other connection to Galanter.

Suddenly I hear the jiggling of the doorknob in the reception area to Galanter's office. I freeze, listening for another sound, but by then it's almost too late.

The door opens, casting a wedge of light into the reception area. I flick off the flashlight and shove the record back onto the shelf. If this is Winn, I'll bludgeon him with my Pluto flashlight.

Where can I hide? I look around the room.

Galanter's private bathroom. Right where Armen's was, off a tiny hall leading from the office. I scoot into the bathroom and slip behind the door, willing myself into stillness.

Whoever's coming in has a flashlight of his own.

He strides into Galanter's office as if he doesn't have any time to lose. He casts the flashlight this way and that, throwing a jittery spotlight at the bookshelves, then at the couch and back again. All I can see of him is that he's big-shouldered, an ominous outline above the blaze of the flashlight. Too heavyset to be Winn. I withdraw behind the bathroom door, afraid.

The figure strides to Galanter's desk. His back is to me as he aims the flashlight on the papers piled neatly on the glass surface. He touches each pile; his hand is hammy as it falls within the flashlight's beam. He seems to be looking for something, rapidly but with confidence. He's been in this office before, it seems. He had a key, unless he picked the lock.

His hand moves over the desk like a blind man reading Braille. He finds something and picks it up. I squint in the darkness. He holds a wrinkled piece of yellow paper in the beam of the flashlight. It must be a phone message; we use the same ones. They're printed on thin paper so they'll make a carbon copy. They tear constantly.

"Fuckin' A," the man says, in a voice I almost recognize. He takes the paper and slips it into a pocket.

Who is this man?

I get my answer when he turns around. In one

terrifying instant he passes in front of the bathroom on the way out. I don't see his face clearly,
but the mustache is a giveaway, as is the glint of
an official marshal badge.

Al McLean.

My mouth goes dry. I hold my breath as I hear
the outer door to chambers open, then close
behind him. He jiggles the doorknob to make
sure it's locked.

McLean. Christ. And he was the one on duty the
night Armen was killed. I wait in the bathroom a
minute, not surprised to be perspiring. I wipe my
forehead and tiptoe into the office. I want to know
what McLean was looking at, and what he took.

I walk over to the polished desk, stand in the
same position he did, and flick on the flashlight.
Everything is upside down, all the papers and
correspondence that tie a circuit judge to the
outside world. In a stack on the middle pile is a
group of yellow message slips, written in the
careful script of Galanter's secretary, Miss Waxman.
The first two messages are from Judge Foudy
and Judge Townsend. PLEASE CALL BACK, the secretary has checked. But the three messages after
those are from Sandy Faber.

The reporter. The same one who's been phoning me and everyone in our chambers. The latest
message, recorded at 4:58, says IMPORTANT! in
letters so perfect they could be printed.

What did Faber find out? And whose message
did McLean take?

It could be Faber's, since the three preceding
it were from him. But it ain't necessarily so; the

odds are worse than a flip of the coin. I decide to check the phone log tomorrow; it will have copies of each message. It's too risky to stay tonight.

I set the messages down the way I found them. Underneath is a small squarish envelope, its address the tiny Gothic typescript characteristic of only one institution: the Supreme Court of the United States. *Hobnob with the Supreme Court,* Artie said. *Position himself for the next appointment.* I open the stiff envelope.

What's inside is a surprise.

A note from Associate Justice Antonin Scalia, thanking Galanter for his recommendation letter on behalf of Ben Safer. Incredible. Ben doesn't even clerk for Galanter. I read it again, then slip it back in the envelope. I stack everything up the way it was, three-inch messages on top, small cards under that, letters next, then briefs. Strict size order, calibrated to telegraph CONTROL.

Boy, am I going to hate working for Big Chief Galanter.

26

Galanter's office gleams in the morning light, all sparkling surfaces with sharp edges. Glass glistens in front of the many photos of him with other judges; his collection of rare books rots behind locked glass doors. Even the furniture is shiny, covered with a polished cotton in navy stripes. It's more the domain of a corporate CEO than a judge with a public-record income of $130,000. I always thought Galanter had family money; I never knew it was money from the Family.

The problem is, he isn't hiring.

"I have my own clerks," he says, looking down

at me from behind his desk chair. His cigar sits in a Waterford ashtray on the desk. "They're all full-time."

"But you get a part-time assistant as chief judge. It's in the budget already, for the administrative work."

"My law clerks can handle it until I hire one. Judge Gregorian waited several months to hire you, as I recall."

"The Judicial Conference meets soon. You'll need to be briefed."

"I can read." He thrusts my memo at me, a heavy hint to scram. I rise from the stiff-backed chair.

"I'd recommend that they get to the misconduct complaints first, then. There are eight backed up, and Washington likes us to stay on top of them."

"Washington?"

"They monitor the complaints, even keep a report on their disposition by all the chief judges. You don't want to make that list, it's a black mark. In Washington." I turn to go, hoping he'll call me back. I get as far as the door, ten feet farther than I predicted.

"You say there are eight, eh?"

"Last time I looked. We set them aside to do *Hightower,* and they just kept on coming."

"How long do they take?"

"The research, a while. Then we get the record and review it. That takes time too. At least a week per complaint."

He puts his hands in his pockets, rocking slightly on his heels. "I don't have the space for you. I'm gutting your office when I move. It needs redo-ing."

Fuck you very much. "I can work in your law clerks' office."

"No."

Good thing I have a strong ego. "I can work in the library on the first floor."

He examines his nails. "Of course, I would hire my own assistant eventually."

"I want to get back to practice anyway."

"I'd have no time to supervise you."

"I don't need supervision, just a paycheck." A sympathetic note, to make him feel like the regent he thinks he is.

"Miss Waxman?" he calls out the door. His oppressed secretary materializes at the other entrance to his office; she's probably been hovering there, waiting for him to bark. A civil service retirement is the only reason this sweet-faced soul would stay with such a tyrant. "You two have met, haven't you?" Galanter says.

"Sure. Hello, Miss Waxman."

Built like a medium swirl of soft ice cream, she nods at me but says nothing.

"Give her the drafts as you finish them, then I'll take it from there. If I need you, I'll call."

"Fine." I start to go, then do Peter Falk as Columbo. "Where should I put the drafts so I don't have to bother you? I used to put them in a box on our secretary's desk."

He looks at Miss Waxman. "Miss Waxman, make a place on your desk for a bin."

She nods.

"I could show you what I mean, Miss Waxman," I say to her.

She glances at Galanter for permission, and he dismisses us with a wave that says: Women, so concerned with the details! Then he picks up the phone. "Close the door," he says.

I close the heavy door and meet Miss Waxman at her desk in front of the door to the law clerks' office. Next to her computer keyboard is the phone log I need to see, with the standard four message slips to a page. Galanter couldn't have gotten too many calls this morning, so the copy of the message McLean took should be on the top page.

"I thought it would help if I knew where to put the papers," I say, moving closer to the open log book. "I don't know how you do things here."

She nods slightly. Her bangs are arranged in tiny spit curls around her face; an aging Betty Boop, down to the spidery eyelashes. "We do them the way the judge wants them," she says in a soft voice.

I look at the log. The top four messages are: Judge Richter at 9:00, Judge Townsend at 9:15, Chief Judge Wasserman of the Second Circuit at 9:16, and one at 9:20 from Carter at the Union League. Damn; a busy morning. It's not on the top page; it must be on the page underneath. I touch the spot next to the log. "Do you think it should go here? It just might fit."

"If you think that's okay, Miss Rossi."

"Please, call me Grace."

"I wouldn't feel comfortable."

"Please. We'll be working together."

She nods deferentially; the master-slave relationship, she understands it perfectly. This I can't abide. "Where would *you* like to put the box, Miss Waxman? It's your desk, after all."

"I don't know." Her brow knits with worry, cracking her pancake makeup into tectonic plates. Sometimes free will is not freeing. "I just don't know. Whatever you think, Miss Rossi. Grace."

I pat the surface near the log again and spot a photograph of a wicker basket full of silver toy poodle puppies, with frizzy gray pompadours. "Maybe here?"

"No!" she blurts out. "But, I mean, if you want to."

"No, that's all right. Whatever you want."

She touches her cheek. "It's just that . . . my dogs are there. Their picture. I like to see them when I work."

"I'm sorry. I don't want to hide the picture."

"But still, if you—"

"Please, I understand. I have a dog too." And now I have an idea. A wonderful, nasty, awful idea. I feel like the Grinch. "It's a big dog, though."

"I like big dogs too," she says. Interest flickers in her pale gray eyes.

"Actually, I adopted Judge Gregorian's dog, Bernice."

"You did? I heard she was given to the Girl Scouts."

"No. She was at the Morris Animal Refuge."

A horrified gasp escapes her lips. "Why, that's a *dog pound*."

"I know."

She gazes at me with an awe better directed at Madame Curie. "Well, aren't you kind!"

I look away guiltily and pick up the dog picture. Its frame is flimsy, from a card shop. The puppies look at me with abject trust, like their mistress. "They're so cute, Miss Waxman."

She beams with a mother's pride. "They do all sorts of tricks. I taught them. They're smart as whips."

"They look it." Coal-black eyes, little button noses.

"This one grew up to be a champion." She points at the one in the center, but how she can tell them apart I'll never know; each one looks as yappy as the next. "That's Rosie, my baby. My champion."

"A champ? Really?" I take an invisible deep breath and let the picture slip from my fingers. It hits the carpet and the frame self-destructs on impact. I feel like shit on toast, but it had to be done.

"Oh! Oh!" Miss Waxman exclaims, hands fluttering to her rouged cheeks. She bends over instantly to rescue the picture, and I flip the top page of the phone log over.

"I'm so sorry," I say, reading the four preceding telephone messages, recorded in carbon copies. All four are from Sandy Faber. I counted only three messages from Faber on Galanter's desk, so that means the one McLean took was from Faber too. "I hope it's not broken."

"It came apart," she wails.

"I feel terrible." I flip a page back, then another. A bunch of judges. Cavallaro and the other Mob names would be farther back, presumably before the *Canavan* argument, but I don't have time to look now. I turn back to the top page. "Here, Let me help."

"That's all right, I have it." Waxman finishes gathering up the frame, and when she straightens up, her eyes are glistening with tears.

I feel awful. "Let me fix it, Miss Waxman. If I can't, I'll replace it. I'll buy you fifty, I swear." I take the assembly from her with a gentle tug.

"It doesn't matter. I can get another," she says, ashamed of her reaction.

"Let me try." I replace the piece of plastic in the square well, then put the photo over it and close the back. One of the brass clips has gotten bent, so I bend it back with a thumb. I breathe a sigh of relief for my immortal soul. "There you go. I really am sorry."

She turns it over in her hands. "Why, it's good as new!"

"It wasn't hard."

"I could never have done that."

"Of course you could have, Miss Waxman." I touch her shoulder, soft in a nubby chenille sweater. "Maybe we can have lunch sometime."

A look of horror skitters across her face. "Oh, no, I eat at my desk."

"Every day?"

"Yes."

"Why?"

"The phones. I have to get the phones." She nods.

"Can't the law clerks get the phones? We take

turns in our chambers, so everyone can have lunch."

"Judge Galanter doesn't think law clerks should answer the telephone."

"Why?"

She looks blank. Ours is not to question why.

He wants to keep the calls confidential, I bet. "I guess he has his reasons."

She purses her lips, inexpertly lined with red pencil. "He says you don't need a legal education to answer a telephone."

I wince at the insult to her, but her expression remains the same. "We'll see about that, Miss Waxman."

She smiles uneasily.

I spot Artie making copies at the Xerox machine on my way back to chambers. "Just the hunk I want to see."

"The Artman. Making copies. Copy-rama," he says, lapsing into an old routine from *Saturday Night Live*. "At the Xerox."

"How are you doing, handsome?"

"Gracie Rossi. Single mother. Former lawyer. Very horny." He grins and makes another copy.

"I get it. Now cut it out."

"You're no fun," he says in his own voice. He flips a long page over and hits the button. "What are you doin' in the enemy camp?" He leans over confidentially. "Find any evidence?"

"Not yet. Listen, you busy tonight?"

"Me? It's atrophied, babe. It's fallen off. It's

lying in the parking lot across the street. You know that speed bump? That's it." He laughs.

"Artie, you'll be okay. You'll fall in love again."

"I'm not talkin' about love, Grace. I'm over love. I'm talking about jungle fuckin'."

I pretend not to be shocked, it dates me. Besides, I have something to accomplish. I need to talk to Winn, face-to-grimy-face. "Listen, since you're free, how about you come to my house for dinner tonight? You can even bring your sidekick."

"She broke up with me. Had a crush on my friend, what can I say? I had her body, not her heart." He shakes his head. "Can you believe I loved her for her *mind? Me?* It's gorky."

"You're growing up. Anyway, I meant Shake and Bake."

"The Shakester. The Shakemeister. Shake-o-rama," he says, singsong again. "Real smelly. Schizophrenic."

"Wash him up first, okay? So he doesn't terrify Maddie. Or Bernice."

"The Madster. Little cutie. In the first grade."

"Artie, stop."

He comes back to reality and hits the button. "You really want me to bring Shake and Bake?"

"I thought it would be nice. Do my part, sort of." White lie number 7364.

"Is your kid ready to meet the oogie-boogie man?"

"I married the oogie-boogie man, pal."

He smiles. "What are you makin' for dinner?"

"What do you care? I can beat Frosted Flakes."

"Hey, last night I had Cocoa Krispies, from the Variety Pak. You know those little boxes?"

"Maddie likes those, too. So come to dinner. You can have Lucky Charms for dessert."

"You want to make me a good-bye dinner?"

"Good-bye? I didn't say that." I feel a pang: too many good-byes lately.

"Yes, ma'am. I'm outta here. Headin' for the junk blondes in NYC. I picked out a crib this weekend." He doesn't look so happy about it. "This is the lease."

"So when do you go?"

"Next week. Cravath's taking me early."

"You're in the army now."

"Tell me about it." He looks at his lease with contempt. "You have to be a lawyer to understand this friggin' thing."

"You *are* a lawyer, Artie. Starting next week, people will pay a hundred and fifty bucks an hour for your time." I think of the basketball on his chest.

"Suckers." He laughs. "So will you look this over for me?" He holds up the lease, a standard form.

"The landlord always wins. That's all you have to know."

"That's just what Safer said." He shakes his head. "What a dick. He's in there, sittin' by the phone."

"Why?"

"Waiting for that call from Scalia."

"They call?"

"Except for Rehnquist. He got turned down once, so he makes his secretary call."

I think of the letter I saw on Galanter's desk. "Think he'll get it?"

"The Eight Ball says yes. Isn't that so lame?"

"It's a toy, Artie, remember?"

He looks at me, dead serious all of a sudden. "It's always right, Grace."

I almost laugh: $150 an hour. Don't say I didn't warn you.

Later, after work, we drive to my house together. Artie sits in the front seat and Winn sulks in the back, in an apparent psychotic funk because Artie made him take off his rain bonnet. When we reach the expressway, Artie turns to the news station for the basketball scores, but Winn wants the Greaseman, another misogynist with a microphone. He reaches between the seats and presses the black button for the Greaseman's station.

"On!" he says. "We want the Greaseman."

Artie punches the KYW button. "No Greaseman. Greaseman sucks."

"Greaseman. Greaseman!"

"Be good, Shakie," Artie says.

The news comes on as we sit stalled in the bottleneck going west. The expressway narrows to a single lane at the Art Museum, even though it's easily the most heavily traveled route west out of Philly. A row of red taillights stretches out in front of me all the way to Harrisburg. "Why would they design a road like this? It makes no sense."

Artie looks out over the Schuylkill, the wide river that runs alongside the expressway. Its east bank is home to a lineup of freshly painted boathouses; the white lights trimming them glow faintly. Single rowers scull down the river and disappear into the sun, now fading into a dull bronze. Here and there an eight picks up the pace, with a skiff running alongside it and a coach shouting through an old-fashioned tin megaphone. "I'll miss this shitburg," Artie says.

"It's not a shitburg."

"How do you know? You never lived anywhere else."

"Why would I want to?"

"KYW . . . news radio . . . ten sixty," Winn sings, in unison with the radio jingle. "All news all the time. All news all the time."

Artie turns up the volume. "Go Knicks."

"Go Sixers," I say, and catch Winn sticking his tongue out at me in the rearview mirror. His face changes as soon as we hear the first news story.

"A Caucasian male," the announcer says, "found murdered in the early morning hours, has been identified as Sandy Faber, a reporter who worked for several Delaware Valley newspapers. The Mount Laurel, New Jersey, man was beaten to death after he used an automated teller machine in Society Hill. Police have no suspects, though they believe robbery was the motive."

My God. I find myself gripping the steering wheel to keep my wits. Faber, killed. And

McLean in Galanter's office last night, taking his phone message. I look at Winn in the rearview mirror, but he's still in character.

"Bye-bye Greaseman," he says sadly. "All gone."

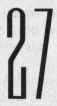

27

I tell Winn the story while I pop chicken with rosemary into the oven and check on Maddie, who's in the backyard shooting hoops with Artie. Artie's hogging the ball again, so I knock on the window. He coughs it up with reluctance while I start to scrub some new potatoes, then drop them into hot water and finish the story.

"Back up a minute, Grace. What were you doing in Galanter's office?" Winn says, pacing in front of the counter. His ratty clothes are clean so he looks merely poverty-stricken, more like a grad student. "It could've been you that was murdered last night, not Faber."

"He was after Faber, not me. He knew just

what he was looking for. I bet Faber was getting closer to Armen's killer. I wonder if McLean was working with Galanter somehow."

"You shouldn't have been there."

"Do you think he was working with Galanter or not?"

"You're not a professional. You have no training." He paces back and forth in the cramped kitchen; Bernice watches him, swinging her massive head left, then right.

"But if McLean were working with Galanter, why would he have to steal the phone message? Galanter would just give it to him, wouldn't he? Unless they thought of it later, after hours."

"Grace—"

"But Galanter could've called Faber at the paper, using a general number." I look out the window, thinking. Maddie is shooting foul shots, none of which reach halfway to the basket; Artie, retrieving the balls, is learning to take turns. "No. Faber wasn't a staffer. He was a stringer, he works on his own. So he couldn't be reached at the paper. But why didn't they call him at home, look him up in the phone book?"

"Grace, you're not listening." Winn stops pacing and folds his arms. Bernice rests her head on her front paws.

"Neither are you."

"Yes, I am. Faber wouldn't be in the Philly phone book because he lived in Jersey. They said it on the radio."

"There you go! So maybe Galanter did have something to do with Armen's death, he wanted to be chief judge so bad. Or maybe McLean was working alone."

"Grace, you have to slow down." He rakes a hand through his hair; it looks a lighter brown now that it's been washed. "I told you not to go prowling around at night. First Armen's apartment, now Galanter's office."

"I work there now. It's my office, too."

"No, it isn't."

I open the oven door and check on the chicken. Bernice sniffs the air with interest. "I thought I did pretty good. I even figured out the Mob connection."

"That was my end of the deal, not yours. You could have called me. I would have explained it to you."

"I couldn't have read the *Canavan* record in the daytime. What did you expect me to do?"

"I told you to keep your eyes and ears open at work. That's all I wanted. I didn't think you were going to turn into Wyatt Earp."

"Nancy Drew. My role model, not yours."

He frowns deeply. "Look, the phone log was okay, the breaking and entering was not. Got it?"

"What are we fighting about? We just caught the bad guy. Let's call the police."

He throws his hands up in the air. "Grace, I don't want you in any deeper. How you gonna explain what you were doing in Galanter's office? I don't want you identified."

"All right, then you report it. Call your boss."

"My boss, why? We think McLean may have murdered a reporter at a money machine. It doesn't have anything to do with the DOJ investigation. Murder's not even a federal crime."

I sit down on the stool next to Bernice, curled up in her new sixty-dollar dog bed. The aroma of rosemary chicken fills the room, but it doesn't suffuse me with the homey feeling it usually does. "I have an idea. How about you report it to the Philadelphia police and I'll be your confidential informant? I tell you what I know, you get an arrest warrant for McLean. Just keep me confidential."

"You, an informant?"

"Why not?"

"Confidential informants are slime."

"You don't know what I'm capable of. I knocked over a picture of poodles today—on purpose."

He smiles. "Life on the edge."

"It'll be enough for probable cause for Faber's death. It's a start."

He rubs his beard thoughtfully. "We could take it a step at a time. *I* could take it a step at a time."

"Do we have enough for a wiretap? It's the same standard, isn't it?"

"Down, girl. Wiretap of who? McLean, maybe, but not Galanter. All we have on him is a marshal going into his office, which is what he's supposed to do."

"But he took a message."

"That doesn't prove anything about Galanter, even assuming McLean fesses up. Trap-and-trace procedures are strict, Grace, you know that. It's not like on TV, with phone taps installed as soon as you suspect somebody. Remember the Fourth Amendment?"

I pull a pad out of the junk drawer. On the top it says DENNIS KULL—YOUR REALTOR IN MONT-GOMERY COUNTY. "Let's start already. Take a letter, Maria."

"What?"

"Take a statement from me, okay? Let's get to work before the kids come back in."

He takes the pad grudgingly and begins to write.

"Wait, I didn't dictate yet."

"Oh, you didn't, huh? Well I'm dictating, not you. Sign this." He tears off a piece of paper and slides it along the counter to me. At the top it says CONTRACT. Underneath that it says I PROMISE NOT TO GO ON ANY MORE SECRET MISSIONS OR WINN CAN TAKE ME TO THE PARTY OF THE FIRST PART.

I smile.

"Sign," he says, handing me the pencil. "I'm not interested in losing my most confidential informant."

"It's not a valid contract. There's no consideration."

"Ha! You'd take money from a homeless man?"

"It doesn't have to be money, it could be anything of value. Not that you have anything of value either."

He reaches into his pocket and offers me his battered photo of Tom Cruise. "My most prized possession. Now sign."

"You're kidding."

"Nope."

"If I sign your statement, will you sign mine?"

"Yes."

So I sign. It's not enforceable anyway.

The kitchen fills up with the homey smell of fresh-baked rosemary chicken.

Winn's phone call comes at the worst time, when I'm rushing like a madwoman to get Maddie to school. I leave her at the front door holding her Catwoman lunch box, run back to the kitchen, and struggle over the gate penning Bernice in the kitchen.

"They arrested McLean this morning," he says.

I feel a thrill of excitement. "They got the bad guy! All right!" Even Bernice wags her tail.

"Your identity remains a secret. Even from my boss, the president."

I'm juiced up, like I just won a jury trial. "So tell me what happened."

"Mom, we have to go," Maddie calls from the door. I've been pushing her all morning, and now she's going to push back.

"Tell me fast," I say to Winn.

"They picked him up at home, no muss no fuss. He denies taking the message. He's mad as hell."

"You saw him?"

"Through the two-way mirror. The man has a temper and a history of some pretty rough street fights."

"I'm not surprised. He doesn't deny being in the office, does he?"

"Mom," Maddie says, coming into the dining room, far enough from Bernice to feel safe. "We have to go."

I hold up my index finger, the universal sign for please-let-Mommy-talk-on-the-phone. Bernice sticks her head over the gate, begging for Maddie's attention.

"He admits to being in Galanter's office," Winn says, "but he claims he was just checking. He was on duty that night. Said he heard a noise."

"I take offense. I didn't make any noise."

"I know, master burglar. He has no good alibi for the time Faber was killed. Says he was off by himself, fishing."

"In Philadelphia?"

"On the Schuylkill."

I laugh. "Real believable."

"Right. The boats fuckin' dissolve, the fish don't stand a chance."

Maddie says, "Mom, I'll be late. I don't have a note."

I check my watch. She's right. "Wait a minute, Winn. When does he say he was fishing?"

"At dawn, the same time Faber was killed."

"Also the same time Armen was killed."

"That doesn't mean anything."

"What's the connection to Armen? Did they find out anything?"

"No."

My heart sinks. "But then why would McLean kill Faber? I thought it was because he was investigating Armen's death. Getting closer."

"Wrong motive, and I'm not sure Galanter had anything to do with it either. We may be back at square one."

"What?" It comes out like a moan.

"McLean had it in for Faber. Turns out they had a couple of run-ins last week, with all the press coverage of *Hightower*. Faber stepped over the line trying to get a story and it pissed McLean off. He's an ex-cop, you know. They all are."

I remember McLean taking off after Faber at the memorial service.

"Last month, McLean caught Faber bothering the U.S. Attorney and roughed him up. Faber reported him for it and they were considering discipline. McLean was about to lose his job."

"Jesus." I think of the reporter, beaten to death, and reality sinks in. Catching McLean doesn't bring Faber back or erase the violent way he died. And Armen is still a question mark.

"Mom, she's staring," Maddie says, watching Bernice anxiously. "Is she gonna bite me?"

I scratch Bernice's head. "No, honey, she loves you."

"You love me?" Winn says. "I knew it. Tell me what it was that turned you on. Was it my body odor? The tartar on my gums? My tattoo?"

I laugh. "Basketball tattoos don't do it for me, pal."

"It's not a basketball. You don't know what it is."

Maddie narrows her eyes. "Is that your boyfriend, Mom?"

I silence her with a glare. "I gotta go, Winn. I have to take Maddie to school."

"But we love each other!"

Maddie dances around, singing, "Mommy has a boyfriend, Mommy has a boyfriend." Bernice watches her, wagging her tail harder.

"Is that Maddie?" Winn asks. "What'd she say?"

"Nothing."

"She likes me, you know. She told me after dinner."

I hold the phone close to my chin and wave to Maddie to stop, but she doesn't. Who raised this child? "I have to go, Winn. We're late."

"All right, but stay out of trouble. Call if you have to, cuz."

"Fine."

"No more funny stuff, remember our contract. Things are heating up. Anything can happen. If McLean didn't kill Armen, whoever did is still out there."

Maddie skips around the dining room table. "Mommy has a boyfriend, Mommy has a boyfriend." As soon as I hang up, the child says, giggling, "I'm telling Daddy."

"The hell you are," I say, and chase her around the table.

28

Wednesday is my alleged day off, but I decide to go in until Maddie gets out of school. I drop her off, still the only mother who walks her child all the way into line, and drive into town.

I rack my brain about McLean and Armen the whole way in; somehow the two must be connected. Al McLean was a cop, Winn said. Where do a cop and a judge meet up?

In court.

Cops are in court all the time as witnesses. Maybe Armen let a defendant go free on appeal, somebody that McLean had testified against in the trial court. It's just a hunch, but it's not a bad one. I hit the courthouse with my brain churning.

The marshals look grim at their stations behind the security desk and at the X-ray machine. They have to know about McLean's arrest. Ray is nowhere in sight, only Jeff. He barely nods as I walk through the detector. I head upstairs alone and unlock the door to my office. I want to do some research on Lexis before going into chambers.

The joke is on me.

I open the door to my office and it isn't there anymore.

The bookshelves, previously full of duplicate case reports and green pebbled volumes of Pennsylvania statutes, are empty. Dismantled overnight. The rug has been torn up, exposing a cement floor covered with yellowed streaks of sticky gum. All the furniture is gone; only my desk and computer remain, not counting the view.

I'm gutting your office, Galanter said. He even paid overtime. He must really like me.

I step through the tacky goop, my pumps sticking at the soles, until I reach my desk. I sit with my feet stuck straight out until I find a legal pad to rest them on. At least my papers and computer are still there. I log on to Lexis and the modem sings to me. A glittering double helix comes on, the logo of the legal research company. Don't ask me why.

WELCOME TO LEXIS! says the screen. Machines

greet us everywhere in the modern workplace; it's the people we can't find. PLEASE TYPE IN YOUR SEVEN DIGIT IDENTIFICATION NUMBER.

I watch the polite sentence disappear. Ben, computer maven, has rigged it so we don't have to log on each time. The only downside is you have to erase the last user's research.

YOUR LAST SEARCH REQUEST WAS FREE SPEECH AND ARTNETT. DO YOU WANT TO CONTINUE WORKING ON IT? Y OR N?

Probably Sarah's. I press N, then punch in GENFED, then 3CIR, to retrieve only cases in the Third Circuit.

The screen says, READY FOR YOUR SEARCH REQUEST.

"Give me a minute, whiz," I tell it. I'm not as speedy on this program as I should be; Lexis was born about the same time Maddie was, and my refresher training's no match for a 486 chip. I squeeze my eyes shut and think. Assume Armen decided a case when McLean was a cop, and McLean was a witness of some kind. That means I need cases that will contain both names. I open my eyes and type in AL MCLEAN AND WRITTENBY (GREGORIAN).

In a nanosecond the screen says, YOUR REQUEST HAS FOUND NO CASES.

Shit. So there's two possibilities: a dry hole or a lousy drill. Guess which is likelier. I double-check the search request. Wrong. Al's name is probably Albert, or Alan. If he testified in court he would use the more formal name. I type in AL! MCLEAN AND WRITTENBY (GREGORIAN). It should retrieve all incarnations of Al imaginable. I sit back, proud of myself.

Not for long. YOUR REQUEST HAS FOUND NO CASES.

Damn it! I sigh at the computer. It's in there somewhere, I feel it. Every judge has enemies; they make at least one with each case. In desperation, I type in MCLEAN AND WRITTENBY (GREGORIAN).

The computer says, YOUR REQUEST HAS FOUND ONE CASE.

"Yes!" One case is all I need. Excited, I squint at the template above the keys and hit .fd, which is computer for gimme gimme gimme!

Clermont v. Brewster comes up. An old case, 1983. Armen was on the panel and wrote the opinion. But it's not a criminal matter. I don't understand.

I type in .fu, which stands for full case and not what it usually stands for.

The case comes up in full. I type .np to get to the next page, then the next, deflating slightly with each new screen of white-on-blue text. There's no police testimony in it at all; it's a medical malpractice case. A woman, Elaine Brewster, sued a doctor for not diagnosing her skin cancer early enough to save her life. A jury awarded her a whopping $15 million. On appeal, the Third Circuit reversed. Armen, writing for the panel, found the evidence of the doctor's negligence was insufficient to go to a jury, a sympathy vote but legally indefensible.

I hit .np and the next page pops onto the screen.

Then I see it. Highlighted in bright yellow by the computer.

Mr. McLean.

A man who testified in the trial court about the plaintiff's pain and suffering, but not in his capacity as a cop. He testified that the plaintiff had been a beautiful woman, spunky enough to keep her own name after marriage. Elaine Clermont. The disease reduced her to an invalid, her skin blackened and eaten away.

The woman was his wife.

McLean lost his wife to cancer and he lost $15 million to Armen. That's it.

I ease back into my chair, staring at the screen. I should be happy, but I'm not. Too much pain, too much death. I imagine McLean going to Armen's to kill him. Bernice would have known McLean from the courthouse. So would Armen; he would have let him in without question. But Armen wouldn't have remembered McLean from a ten-year-old case. He never saw McLean testify in the first place; the appellate court bases its decisions on a record. Armen would have assumed McLean was his protector. He would have assumed wrong.

But why would McLean wait ten years to get Armen? I don't know the answer, but I intend to find out.

My hand is shaking as I pick up the phone to call Winn. It's not hard to convince the young girl who answers the phone that I'm Winn's cousin, I sound pretty depressed. I tell Winn the story and after he gets over the initial surprise, his tone turns cautious. "How do we know it's the same McLean?" he says.

"What do you mean?"

"You said the computer searches the name exactly, right?"

"Right."

"So how do we know it's the same man?"

"How many Mr. McLeans can there be who had a case before Armen?"

"Maybe one, but that's not the point. The question is, can we charge this McLean just because a guy with the same name had a motive to kill Armen?"

"But it's *him*."

"McLean is a common name."

"Not really." It sounds feeble, even to me. I went to high school with one.

"Does it at least say he was a cop?"

I scroll through the case. "No. It identifies him as the husband, that's all. He's only mentioned in the opinion for a paragraph."

"Does it say his age?"

"No. But the wife was thirty at the time. That would be about right."

"Only if you assume she married a man about her age, but an assumption's not enough to charge a man with murder. The whole thing could be a coincidence. After all, why would McLean wait ten years to kill him? Can't we verify it somehow, get the actual record instead of just the opinion?"

Of course. I should have thought of that. "The record will have the trial transcripts, all his testimony. Address, work history, the whole thing."

"Where's the record now?"

"The case was from the Eastern District of Pennsylvania, so the record would be downstairs in the district court file room. It's in this building, unless it's archived."

"Can you get it? I mean without your standard B and E."

I smile. "We order district court records all the time. We call on the phone, they deliver them to chambers."

"When will you have it?"

"In four hours."

"Four *hours*? I thought you said the file room was downstairs."

"This is the federal government. They have to fill out forms and type up receipts. If I went downstairs and got it myself, I'd have the answer in fifteen minutes."

"Do it the normal way. I want everything by the book."

"It's not a Miranda warning, Winn."

"McLean's already in custody, what's the difference? It's more important that it be done right."

"I'd do it right. It's perfectly safe. Let me get the file."

"Grace," he says, "I want no suggestion that you tampered with the records. I want the chain of custody to be clear. Order the record, please. Keep the reason to yourself. Don't go running in and telling everybody you caught Armen's killer."

"Come on."

"You come on. Now order the record and call me when it comes in."

"Mighty pushy for a Quaker."

"You love me anyway."

"Bullshit."

"And one other thing. There's a loose end."

"What?"

"It doesn't explain Armen's bank account. Or *Canavan*."

"Do I have to do everything for you?" I say to him before I hang up.

Then I look at the phone, thinking. He's right. It doesn't explain the money, but that was *his* investigation. My investigation is just about over.

We celebrate Ben's big news at a picnic lunch on the grassy mall between the Liberty Bell and Independence Hall, just catty-corner to the courthouse. Ben got the call from Justice Scalia this morning and was so delirious he even became likeable, helping all of us box the last of the case files. For a time it was like when Armen was alive and we all worked together, despite the clerks' bickering. My spirits were high, fueled by my certainty that the record would prove me right about McLean. I felt so good I sprung for hoagies all around.

"They call this a sub in New York," Artie says, inspecting his sandwich with a frown.

"What do they know? We invented it," I say, wiggling my toes in the grass. Behind my digits is Independence Hall, the most beautiful building in the world, in its own subtle way. Its muted red bricks have a patina that only two hundred years can bring, and its mullioned panes of glass are bumpy; perfectly imperfect even from here. A long line of schoolchildren piles two by two out of Congress Hall, the right wing of the building, where Congress used to meet.

"Look around you, Artie. This is a real city, a city where people can live. It's beautiful, and there's history everywhere."

"Except for that," Sarah says flatly, her long granny skirt spread out on the grass. She points over Ben's shoulder at the new housing for the Liberty Bell, a structure of sleek concrete with corners that stab out onto the cloudless sky. "I hate that building. They call it a pavilion, but it looks like a Stealth bomber."

"Something the matter with Stealth bombers?" Ben says, smiling.

Eletha picks a paper-thin onion out of her hoagie, her nails working like pincers. "It's not that bad, Sarah. It's just new." She drops the onion onto a pile of its brethren.

"That's the problem." Sarah raises her voice to be heard over the tourist buses gunning their engines next to the pavilion. "It should be compatible with the surrounding architecture and it's not."

"I agree, they should've left the bell where it was. It belongs in Independence Hall." I remember how angry I was when they moved the Liberty Bell from Independence Hall. Now Independence Hall has to face its bell's new home; it's like sitting across the table from your ex's trophy wife. For eternity.

"You mean they didn't consult you?" Artie says. "You, Miss Philadelphia?"

"Isn't it terrible? I don't know why they think they can run this city on their own." I tear into my cheese hoagie.

"So Ben," Eletha says, "the clerkship begins in September?"

He nods and sips his coffee.

"What'll you do till then?"

"I'm working on an article."

"What about?" she asks, fishing out another onion.

"The European Convention on Human Rights."

"Human rights? You?" Sarah says, bursting into tactless laughter.

Ben smiles easily; not even Sarah can bother him today. "I've been doing some thinking on the subject."

"*You?*" she says, still laughing.

"Real nice, Sar," I say. "What are *you* going to do next? And you better say join the Peace Corps."

"How about joining Susan's staff? Is that good enough?"

"Not since she got my name wrong," Ben says, and Eletha laughs.

"Is she still in Bosnia, finding facts?" I ask.

Sarah nods, and I hope she forgets that I accused the woman of murder. Nancy Drew, my ass. She had a roadster, not a station wagon.

"So Artie," Eletha says, "are you all ready for Wall Street? You pack your toys?"

Artie looks down at his hoagie. He seems out

of sorts today, quiet. "Guess so. Off to peddle my soul."

"For how much?" Eletha asks.

"You don't want to know, girlfriend."

"Yes I do. Hit me with it."

"Just shy of one hundred large."

Eletha almost gags. "You're kiddin' me!"

"Not including the endorsements. Justice. Just do it."

"Justice?" I say. "On Wall Street?"

"*Isjdjr! Keidnbu!*" shouts a young man with flyaway blond hair, who troops with a park ranger onto the lawn behind Ben. Suddenly, a group of tourists is thronging around the man and the ranger, a bobbing mass of blond heads. "*Keird ishdsn!*"

"What the fuck is this?" Artie says. "Our neighbors to the north?"

"I would like to propose a toast," I say, ignoring the interruption. I hoist my Diet Coke in the air. "To all of us, even Ben. And to justice." I'm thinking of McLean, behind bars.

"Perfect!" Sarah says. "To all of us, even Ben. And to justice!" She hoists her Evian bottle to Eletha's paper cup.

"To all of us, even Ben," Eletha says. "And to justice, and happiness."

Artie raises his bottle of Yoo-Hoo. "There is no justice or happiness. To all of us, even Ben, and to Patrick Ewing."

"*Kirs eushjk!*" shouts the young man. He points to the Liberty Bell, visible through the pavilion's glass wall. Crudely embossed letters at its top say

ALL THE LAND AND UNTO ALL THE until the sentence disappears around the cast-iron curve. Tourists encircle the bell, but a park ranger will prevent them from touching the rough-hewn letters. I touched the letters once, when the ranger wasn't looking; they felt cool and ragged.

"Thank you, all of you," Ben says. "It's very nice. You're all very . . . kind."

Artie bursts into laughter. "Don't choke up or nothin', dude. It's not like we meant it."

"Artie, be nice," I say. "Good things happened today for a change." I think of my successful Lexis search. Wait until they find out Armen was murdered. Will it make it worse or better? Which way does it make me feel?

"God knows, we needed it," Eletha says, taking a slug of her iced tea.

"Welcome to Philadelphia, ladies and gentlemen," the park ranger booms, then launches into his spiel with official enthusiasm. The tourists frown up at him almost instantly. Either the sun is bright or they don't understand English with a Philadelphia accent. My guess is they've seen the sun before.

"I have some good news of my own," Eletha continues, shouting to be heard. She sets down her cup in the grass and inhales deeply. "I'm a free woman, as of today. I broke up with Leon."

"Really?" I say. I was wondering what she meant about happiness.

"I told him this morning, no more shit. Life is too short to take shit from any man."

"Good for you!" Sarah says, drawing a sharp

look from Artie. There's an awkward silence, and I think of my promise to Ray.

"Don't hang it up too fast, Eletha," I say. "Have I got a man for you."

"So have I," Ben says, leaning over. "Chief Judge Galanter is single."

Eletha laughs. "That'll be the day! Shoot me before I get to that point. Shoot me, child!"

I think of Armen and stop laughing slowly. The others don't seem to notice.

Sarah says, "No, Eletha, you got it backwards. Shoot *him*."

They all roar with laughter, even Ben. I force a smile. What does it feel like to be shot? What is the last thing Armen felt? Did McLean hold the gun to Armen's temple? Force him into the chair? I look away to where the park ranger is addressing the tourists and tune him in.

"There were no bell foundries in the colonies at that time period," the ranger says, "so rather than send it back, these resourceful colonists, who had previously made only pots, pans, and candlestick holders—"

"Grace?" Artie says. "You with us?"

I push it out of my mind. We got him now. That's justice, even if it doesn't bring Armen back. "Sure."

"Who's bachelor number one?" Eletha asks.

"What?"

"Who did you want to fix me up with?"

"Oh. One of the marshals."

Eletha shudders. "One of the marshals? Forget it!"

"Back in the saddle, Miss Thing," Artie says. "I love a man in uniform."

"What's the matter with a marshal?" Sarah says.

Eletha leans forward. "You know what I heard? One of the marshals was arrested this morning. For the murder of that reporter."

Sarah pales. "You mean the stringer? The one who was calling us?"

"What?" Ben says, setting his hoagie down in its shell of waxy paper. I concentrate on the grease spots soaking the paper from the inside and try to look as shocked as he does.

"That's unbelievable," Artie says, between mouthfuls of corned beef. "Which marshal?"

"Al McLean, the big one."

"How did you hear this?" I ask her.

"Millie, from the clerk's office. So no marshals, honey. Not for me. No way."

"But it's Ray Arrington. He's a teddy bear."

"Ray? A *what*?" Artie says, chomping away. "Gimme a break! You ever see him on a basketball court? The man is a maniac. He almost knocked Shake and Bake out."

"Ray?"

"The Shakester had a bruise all down his side."

"Poor schizophrenic," Ben says. He stows his empty coffee cup in his hoagie wrapper and rolls them up together. "We should get back to the office. It's been over an hour."

Eletha and Sarah look at each other and laugh. "What are they gonna do, fire us?" Eletha says.

"I want to work on my article."

But Sarah doesn't hear him. "We're free. We have

no work, no job, no office." Her face falls suddenly. And no boss, is the thing we're all thinking, but nobody says it. Artie wraps up the remains of his lunch in silence and Eletha watches him, her eyes unfocused. I feel a lump in my throat and raise my can in a silent toast.

"I agree," Sarah says softly and touches her drink to mine. Eletha raises hers, too. Only Artie doesn't say anything. I can't catch his eye.

Ben clears his throat. "We'd better go back. Grace still has a job, you know."

"Don't remind me." I've indentured myself for nothing, unless I want to help Winn's bribery investigation. "Anyway, today I'm off duty."

"So why'd you come in?" Sarah asks. She gets up, then helps me up.

"I don't know. We don't have much more time together. I thought I'd say good-bye." It comes out of its own force, and even though it's not the reason I came in, I realize how true it is. The lump comes back.

"Awww," Sarah says, and to my surprise gives me a warm hug, which Eletha joins.

"Group hug!" Artie says, rallying. He wraps his long arms around Eletha and presses us all together. I'm somewhere in the middle, trying to swallow the damn lump.

"Come on in, Mr. Human Rights," Sarah calls out.

"I'll pass," Ben says, but I hear the smile in his voice.

"*Isjdhyk mejsgr!*" shouts the young man. "*Kkkrk!*"

29

sit at my desk with the form letter in my hand, reading it to Winn:

> We have been unable to locate the record in this matter in our archives or file room. This is not out of the ordinary with older case files and we will continue our efforts to locate it. We regret any inconvenience this may have caused you.

"You know McLean took it, don't you?" I say.
"Possibly."
"Possibly?"
"The government never loses anything?"

"A court record? Not often."

"Ever?"

"Not often."

Winn is silent.

"Charge him anyway, Winn. The lawsuit existed. His wife existed. He can't hide the facts, even if he can steal the record."

"Fuck. This slows us up."

"How? Ask him about it. Say to him, Did your wife die of skin cancer? Did she sue the doctor? Was the fifteen million dollar award taken away by Judge Gregorian?"

"He's not answering questions, Grace. He's got a lawyer already."

Shit. Of course. Shoot the lawyer twice. It stumps me for a minute.

"You say we don't need the record, but if the record doesn't matter, why would McLean steal it?"

"Because he's stupid. Because he didn't count on anybody doing legal research on him."

"How would he steal it? Would he be able to?"

"Sure. The marshals have master keys, that's how he got in Galanter's office. The files are kept in number order by year. Even an idiot can find a record."

"Fuck!"

"Let me be the confidential informant again. I'll make another statement. Describe everything that happened in Armen's office, the way McLean acted to me at the metal detector, even my research and the clerk's letter. It's enough to charge him, isn't it?"

"It's a close question."

"Winn, he killed Armen because of the court case, then he killed Faber because he was close to finding out. A verdict that big would make the papers. Faber probably did his homework and found out about the wife's case. Hell, he could find it easily on Nexis. I could do it myself, right now. Faber was calling our chambers all day."

"Relax, Grace."

"Charge him. It's enough. I'm a lawyer, I know. Are you gonna let him get away with murder?"

"It's close. I don't want to go in half cocked."

Man talk. "You got another idea?"

"Yes. Is there any other place records would be?"

The thought strikes like a thunderbolt. "The appendix! The appendix is a duplicate of the record. For a trial with that much money at stake, I bet it's complete."

"Where would the appendix be?"

"Every judge on the panel would have gotten one, including Armen. It's an old case but Eletha would know if we have it." My brain clicks ahead. I didn't see the older cases in the boxes we packed this morning, but Eletha could have packed them earlier. "She said Armen saved everything. We just finished packing this morning."

"Go get 'em, tiger."

"It's about a million boxes."

"Dig we must."

Easy for him to say. He doesn't have to deal with Eletha's reaction when I tell her what I'm going to do.

*   *   *

"You want to do what?" Eletha shrieks at me, astounded. She stands protectively in front of the boxes that stack almost to the ceiling in Armen's office.

"Shhh!" I look toward the clerks' office, even though the door is closed. "You can go home. I'll do it. I already called my mother to pick up Maddie at school."

"Are you out of your goddamn mind?" Long fingers clasp at her chest and she breathes deeply, in and out.

"Eletha, don't do the Lamaze thing, not for me. You can go."

"You want to rip open all my boxes? We just finished!"

"I'll put everything back."

She shakes her head. "No. I won't let you do it. No way. No file is important enough to ruin all that work."

I wish I could tell her why, but Winn made me swear. "I'll redo it."

"Galanter wants this stuff out of here! I told him we'd be done tomorrow, you know that. That's why I worked my ass off all morning! All *week!*"

"I know, but I need it."

"What for?"

"A misconduct case."

"What misconduct case is ten years old? Don't bullshit me, Grace. We're friends."

I take her by the shoulders. "Listen, trust me. I can't tell you anything more."

"Why not?"

"Eletha, it's the most important file in the world."

"No file—"

"This one is."

"Are you outta your mind?" Her dark eyes watch me with hope.

"No."

"But I got class tonight, and Leon sure ain't gonna sit anymore."

"That's all right. I have to do it myself."

"Galanter wants in—tomorrow. It'll take you all *night*."

I remember the last time I was here in this office until dawn. "That's okay."

I look around at the boxes and so does she. It's daunting, like moving an entire house in only one night. Twice. I wonder if I'll be able to get it done in time. If I can't, screw Galanter. He may not be a killer, but he's still a jerk.

"I know what you're thinkin'," Eletha says to me, wagging a finger. "It's gotta be done by morning. GSA is comin' in to take up the rug."

"All right, all right."

"You want me to come back after class? It's over at ten."

"Nope. You got Malcolm."

"I'll bring him. He can sleep on the couch."

"No, thanks."

"Suit yourself." She shakes her head, mystified. "Start with those boxes against the wall." She gestures to about forty-five boxes, taped closed and stacked up like children's blocks. "Those are the case files. Everything over there"—she points against the back wall behind Armen's desk—"is old stuff, papers, and some older files. There could be some older case files in there, too."

"Okay." I eyeball the boxes in the back. Thirty, easy. Christ. I remember when I left Sam: all my stuff and Maddie's in a storage bin, and it still wasn't that high. "No problem."

She points at the conference table and the chair against the window, both of which are heaped with brown paper packages. "That's all the Armenian stuff. I put bubble paper underneath that brown paper, you know. You won't be needin' any of it, so don't unwrap it."

"I won't." Each package is labeled in black Magic Marker, some cryptically. STATUE. ANOTHER STATUE. PRAYER RUG. FRAMED THING. BIG THING. I laugh at BIG THING, lying horizontally across the chair near the window. "What's that one?"

She wrinkles her nose. "You know, that big thing?"

"No, I don't, El. I have no idea."

"You do too. That wood thingie he had hangin' up, like a baseball bat."

Now I remember. The cudgel. "Oh, yeah. That big thing."

"Right. It weighs a ton. Leave it alone, all of it."

"I will. I promise. Hey, where's the Indian headdress?"

"Oh, that?" She grins. "I lost it."

"You what?"

"I can't remember where I put it, for the life of

me. I guess it just got lost in the shuffle." She scratches her sleek head, then bursts into laughter.

"Eletha, what did you do?"

"It serves his ass right, doesn't it?"

I have to agree.

"Okay. I gotta go, but I'm gonna do one thing for you. Make you a pot of coffee."

"Deal," I say and get to work.

I open box after box, digging into each with cheap government scissors. I go through the case files; each is a manila folder containing Armen's notes, a set of briefs, and an appendix. Unfortunately, they don't seem to be in chronological order, or in any order at all; I don't stop to read Armen's notes, even those not written in Armenian. I can't afford the time; I'm trying to nail his killer.

The afternoon wears into the evening and I go through cup after cup of coffee and box after box of files. Eletha pops her head in to say good-bye when she goes; then Artie, Sarah, and Ben, who's still carrying a briefcase. I tell them I lost some papers, and they all offer to help, even Ben.

I check my watch. Maddie's bedtime. I decide to call home, then Winn after that. I punch in the numbers to my house.

Maddie answers the phone, then proceeds to work me over. "But *why* do you have to stay, Mom?" she asks, her thin voice rising on the other end of the line.

"I told you, honey. Because it's an important case. I have to work on it."

"Why can't somebody else work on it? Why does it have to be *you*?"

"Because I'm the only one who can."

"Are you with your boyfriend?"

I laugh. "Of course not. I don't have a boyfriend, I'm working. Now tell me what you're gonna read with Grandma before you go to bed."

"I'm too sick to go to school tomorrow, Mom. Madeline feels sick too, her forehead's hot. She's *burning*."

I ease into the chair next to the conference table. "You'll be fine in the morning. You just need to sleep."

"But my head hurts. My neck is swollen."

"Honey, listen. We'll see in the morning, okay?" I tug a box over to the chair and cross my legs on top of it. "I'll check if you have a fever."

"You have to use the thing. The glass thing. Grandma says you can't tell with your hand, not really."

Thanks, Mom. "Maddie, I've never used a thermometer with you and I've never been wrong. I can tell with my hand."

"No, you can't. It's not science."

I look out the window into the night. The orange lights are twinkling again, running in thin strips to the river, the way they were that night. I was sitting right here, but tonight is different from before. It's raining hard, a spring downpour, and Armen is gone. The streets below glisten darkly.

"Mom?"

"Tell you what. Remember last week, how you wanted to wear your party dress to school and I said no?"

"The purple one?"

"Yes. Well, I'll let you wear it tomorrow, just this one time, since it's a special occasion."

"What special occasion?"

I think of the case file; it's in here somewhere. "We'll make one up. Happy Thursday."

"You're silly."

"I am. I get it from you."

She giggles. "Mom, I have to go now. The commercial's over."

"What, are you watching TV? It's after nine o'clock!"

"It's Disney."

"Disney is still TV. What happened to reading?"

"Just Donald Duck, then we have to turn it off."

"All right, but after that it goes off. Now go get ready, you don't want to be too late to bed."

"Yes, I do," she says, hanging up.

I press down the hook and am about to try Winn when I see a dark form reflected in the window. Someone must be in the doorway behind me. I hang up and twist around in my seat.

The gun is the first thing I see.

I scramble to pick up the phone.

30

"Hang up, Grace," Ben says. He closes the door behind him and locks it from the inside. "Hang *up*."

The phone clatters uselessly onto the hook. "Ben?"

"Surprise! Did you find the file yet?"

"What? How—"

"Lexis. The computer saves the last search request, remember? I saw it after lunch when I logged back on. Nice search request, by the way. You're improving." He moves to the head of the conference table and points the gun at me.

I'm terrified. My mouth turns to cotton. No one is around. Eletha is at class. God knows where Winn is, or security. "How did you get that gun past the metal detector?"

"I took the judges' elevator." He smiles down at the gun, handling its heft with satisfaction. He looks strange, unhinged. "I bought this the other day. Isn't it nice?"

"What are you doing, Ben?"

"It's not what I'm doing. It's what you're doing." He slips a finger inside his jacket, pulls out a small piece of white paper, and holds it up. "Your suicide note. Sign it." He places the paper in front of a brown package that reads PHOTO OF A MOUNTAIN. "Oops, I almost forgot." He puts a rollerball pen on top of the paper.

I don't touch the letter or the pen. I can't believe this is happening.

"Please sign, Grace. Make it easy on yourself."

My own suicide note. A fake suicide. Oh, no. "Did you kill Armen, Ben?"

"Yes."

I can barely catch my breath. I assumed wrong.

"I didn't plan to, if that's any consolation."

"But why?" It comes out like a whisper.

"Why did I kill him? What's the difference?

"I want to know, to understand."

"I wanted that clerkship."

I stare at the paper. It's almost inconceivable. "You wanted a clerkship that bad? A *job*?"

"It's the Supreme Court of the United States, Grace. I've been preparing for it my entire adult life. I'll teach after that, then on to the appeals court. I intend to end up on the high court myself. I wasn't about to let *Hightower* stand in my way."

"It was Armen who stood in the way."

He flinches slightly. "Sacrifices had to be made."

Armen: a sacrifice for a young lawyer's ambition. "But you could've gotten the clerkship anyway."

"Why take a chance?"

I don't understand. I feel sick with fear and dread. "You got the clerkship, so why this? Why me?"

"It's your own fault. You were the one digging around. You dug up McLean, now there's a glitch. It's only a matter of time before he points the finger at me."

"Did McLean kill Faber?"

"The reporter? Yes, at my suggestion. Faber was too close to finding out."

Two men dead. I feel stunned. "Was McLean the one who hit me on the head?"

"No, that was me. Now open the letter and sign it. I want no question later that you wrote it."

I feel myself break out into a sweat. The lethal black eye of the gun barrel is almost at my head; I think of the gunpowder star the detective found on Armen. "What does it say?"

"That you hired McLean to kill the reporter. You see, Faber had found out that you had killed the chief."

I look up at him behind the large gun barrel. "Why would *I* kill Armen?"

"Sexual harassment is a terrible thing. He raped you that night in the office."

"He did no such thing!"

A smug smile inches across his lips. "I heard. You were very willing, McLean said."

"You—"

"Of course, McLean was all too happy to help you cover up the murder. He's been nursing his hate for a decade. He thinks the chief ruined his life, so it didn't take much convincing to get him on board. I bought him a few drinks and pointed him in the right direction." He levels the gun at me. "Sign, please."

I pick up the paper and unfold it. It's neatly typed, and the last line makes me sick inside:

I love my daughter very much.

I stare at the paper. *I love my daughter very much.* Maddie. She'll think I abandoned her. I know how that feels. I fight back the tears; I'd beg if it would do any good. "She needs me, Ben," I said hoarsely.

"You were the one who wouldn't let it lie."

I look at the note. The typed letters seem to swim before my eyes against a vast backdrop of brown packages. PRAYER RUG. STATUE. ANOTHER STATUE. Then I remember the label on one of the other packages. BIG THING.

The cudgel. It's on the chair by the window. Eletha called it a baseball bat. How will I reach it? I need time to think. Stall him.

"You have a problem, Ben. I don't have a gun like Armen did."

He laughs abruptly. "He wasn't very good

with it, Grace. I had the letter opener, but he couldn't bring himself to shoot me. I grabbed his hand and pointed it at his own head. It was over in a minute."

Poor Armen. I imagine the scene with horror. I can't speak.

"Don't think too badly of me. I did give him a last chance to come out the right way in *Hightower*, even brought him a draft opinion. We discussed the case law for some time, even the policy issues. It was sort of a final appeal. For him, and for me."

He makes me sick, outraged. "How are you going to pull this off, Ben? You going to make me shoot myself, too? Your fingerprints are all over your gun."

"Oh, you won't use my new toy, Grace. You'll jump."

I feel my mouth fall open. My mind reels. "From where?"

"The window." He gestures with the gun barrel.

I wheel around toward the window, petrified at the thought. Then I glimpse the cudgel right near the window, on the chair. Armen said it was used to kill. Can I kill? "Ben, you don't mean this."

"Yes, I do."

My blood runs cold. "But the windows."

"I'll break them. They're just a single layer of glass, not even thermapane. This building was built in the sixties."

"But the marshals will hear it."

"Not from inside. We're eighteen floors up. Even if someone sees it, they'll think it's the wind from the storm and phone GSA. They should be here by tomorrow morning." He cocks the trigger on the gun and it clicks smoothly into operation. "Sign the paper. Now."

He's thought of everything. I feel a stab of stone cold fear, then will myself to stay calm. Remember Maddie. Use the cudgel. It destroyed families, now it will protect one. "I'll sign it," I tell him, "but ease off the trigger. You want them to find me shot?"

"Now you're thinking." He relaxes on the trigger and I pick up the pen. My hand is trembling as I read the letter one last time. What if I can't get to the cudgel. What if I blow it? "Hurry, Grace."

I scribble my name, then lift the pen from the paper. Just in case, underneath I write, *I love you, Mads. You are the best*. I blink back the tears that seem to come.

"Get up," Ben says. "Stand near the window."

Good, you bastard. That's just where I want to be. My whole body shivers. Get a grip. I'm not within arm's length from the cudgel, not yet. It's too close to the window.

Still aiming the gun at me, Ben crosses the room. He picks up a chair and swings it into the wall of windows. The huge panel shatters instantly into brittle shards; cracks race all over the pane like nerve endings, electrified. Breathing like a madman, Ben hurls the chair into the cracked window again, at full speed. It bounces off with a crashing sound. The glass explodes into a million pieces. Slivers fly in all directions. The window collapses and falls away, hurtling down the side of the courthouse, leaving a jagged opening like the mouth of a dark cave.

Wind and cold rain blast into the office, gusting hard off the Delaware. Glass particles and loose papers flutter wildly around the room in crazy currents. My hair whips around. The rain soaks my face and clothes. Glass stings my cheek, my forehead. The room seems to hang in the middle of the thunderstorm. Wind buffets my ears.

"Walk to the window!" Ben shouts against the wind.

I brace myself and step closer to the cudgel near the window. The wind howls. The rain drenches me.

"Now, Grace! Jump or I push you out! Your choice!"

I take another step to the window. The city glitters at my feet. The cudgel is at my right, and behind it is Independence Hall, lit up at night. I face the wind and take one deep breath, then another. One, two . . . three!

I grab the wrapped cudgel by its end and whip it full force into Ben's face. It makes contact with a dense, awful thud. I drop the weapon, horrified.

Ben staggers backward, shrieking in pain and shock, blood pouring from his mouth and teeth. His jaw hangs grotesquely and his hands rush to it. His gun slips onto a pile of broken glass. I dive for it a second before Ben does and scramble to my feet, my own hands cut and slippery with blood.

I point the gun at him as he lies on the floor,

in the whirling holocaust of splintered glass and paper. "Stay down!"

But he won't. He staggers to his feet, moaning in agony. It's a wild animal sound, as loud as the wind. Blood runs in rivulets between his fingers.

"Stay back! Stay away!" I can barely look, but he keeps coming toward me, backing me up against the conference table. I hold the gun up. I don't want to shoot him, please don't make me. "Ben, stop!"

Suddenly, he stops and shakes his head, still cupping his chin. His suit is heavy with rain and blood. His dark eyes brim with tears as they meet mine, and for an instant he looks like the Ben Safer I remember.

"Ben, I'm so sorry." I start to sob. "You'll go to a hospital, they'll fix it."

He shakes his head again, then turns toward the window. I feel a cold chill as soon as I understand what he's going to do.

"Ben! No! Don't!" I scream into the rain, but he won't hear me.

He runs headlong toward the darkness, and when he reaches the edge of the carpet, he leaps mightily into nothingness and the thunderstorm.

The next sound I hear is a heartless clap of thunder, then the shrillness of Ben's scream.

And my own.

31

I wake up in silence and semidarkness. There's a bed table at my side and a boxy TV floating in the corner. Moonlight streams through the knit curtains, casting a slotted pattern on a narrow single bed. A hospital room. I lie there a minute, flat on my back, taking inventory.

I am alive. I am safe. I wiggle everything, and everything works.

I hold up my hands in the dark. There are bandages on some of my fingers. My face aches, the skin pinching like it doesn't quite fit. I can only imagine what I look like. My fingers go instinctively to my cheeks. The surface is rough under-neath, cottony. More bandages.

I hear myself moan, remembering slowly how I got to be here.

It comes back to me like a gruesome slide show, with hot white light blinding me between each freeze frame. Ben, entering with the gun. *Click*. The suicide note. *Click*. The cudgel at the window. *Click*. Independence Hall at my feet.

Oh, God.

Poor Ben. I hurt him, and he died a horrific, painful death. And Armen, dead too. Even Faber, beaten to death. It's too awful to dwell on. I feel wretched and totally, miserably alone, until I turn over. There, asleep in a shadowy corner near the door, her silvery head dropped onto a heavy chest, is my mother.

Who else. She has been here for God knows how long. She probably arranged for Maddie to go to Sam's.

I lie still and look at her sleeping in a hard plas-tic chair. Even in the dim light I can see she's fully dressed. A matching sweater and slack set, cheap leather slip-ons, and stocking knee-highs, which she buys in gift packs. Her chest goes up and down; her shoulders rise and fall. In her hand is a paper cup, sitting upright on her knee, even though she's sound asleep. On the cup I can make out a large blue circle.

I know that circle. Pennsylvania Hospital, at Eighth and Spruce.

My mother was born in this hospital in 1925, and it was here that she gave birth to me, and I, in turn, to Maddie. One after another, each picking up the thread and advancing it, like an unbroken line of stitching in a fabric's seam. Three generations of us, each making her own way. Raising her daughter in her own way, without men. A tribe of three women only.

How curious.

Our blood, our very cells, must be constitutionally different from other families. Families of four, for example. Or families that go on camping vacations in minivans and watch their kids play Little League. Families that leave the city they were born in, to divide and scatter.

Normal American families.

We're not like them, like on TV, with a mom and a dad. Nor are we ethnic Americans: happy-go-lucky Italians or the truly Irish, raucous on St. Patty's Day. We are not of those tribes, of those races. We are something else entirely. We are our own invention. We are what we do.

And what we do, what one of us in particular is doing, is sleeping. In an inhospitable chair, clutching a full cup of water. The full cup of water is significant, an act unto itself, and my heart tells me who the water is for.

For me, when I wake up.

It will be the first thing she offers, because she cannot say *I love you* as easily as she can hold out something to drink. Because she cannot say *I worry,* she issues orders and commands. And when she felt pain and loss, she could not say that either, so she drank whiskey. And lashed out in rage.

I understand that now, watching her sleep in the chair. I understand, too, how blessed I am to have her wait while I sleep, with a cup of water on her knee. I don't feel a need to confront her any longer. There's no reason to shake my fist in her face, to call her to account. That much is past, not present.

That much is over.

Let it go.

The door opens and a nurse comes in, luminous in a white uniform that seems to catch and hold the moonlight. She walks directly over to the bed and looks at me with concern. She bends over and whispers, "Are you in pain?"

I am not in pain. I was in pain when my face looked fine. I shake my head.

"Are you hungry?" A single lustrous pearl dots each earlobe in the darkness. She smells like Dove soap and White Linen.

I shake my head, no.

"Do you need anything?" Her teeth are white and even. Her breath is fresh, like peppermint Life Savers.

"No. Thanks."

She pats my shoulder and leaves.

I feel myself smile at her receding silhouette. This is her job and she does it well, but her shift will end soon. My real nurse, the one snoozing at the switch, stinks of cigarettes, but ten to one she's been sitting there for a long, long time. Her shift never ends, as mine will not.

I should let her sleep, but I owe her a rather large apology.

"Ma," I say, and she stirs.

"Honey?" she says hoarsely.

Her eyes aren't even open before she offers me a cup of water.

32

"Will you look at that!" Artie says in amazement at the kitchen window. We all gather around and look out at my backyard. I'm so happy my face hurts.

"I can't believe it," Sarah says. "She never did that before, even for Armen."

"She's gonna do it again," Eletha says, casual today in a sweater and jeans.

We all watch as Bernice rolls over like a champ and comes up smiling. Miss Waxman stands over the dog like the Ubersecretary and gives Bernice a treat, delivered professionally to the mouth.

Bernice snarfs it up and sniffs the grass for left-overs.

I open the window and yell through the screen, "Way to go, Miss Waxman!" It stings my cheeks, but the woman is working miracles out there. "Isn't she great, Maddie?"

Maddie rolls her eyes. *Duh,* Mom.

"Wish I had a dog like that!" Eletha says. "Boy are you lucky, Maddie!"

"Roarf!" Bernice sits and barks at Miss Waxman, who frowns at her charge.

"No!" Miss Waxman says, her voice resonant with authority. Her transformation is as radical as Bernice's, and probably as ephemeral. "No talkie!"

Artie shakes his head. "Did she really say that?"

I elbow him in the basketball. "Give her a break, it's working. What have you done for me lately?"

"I brought you a get-well present."

"You did? Where?"

"It's in the living room. Wait." He runs heavily out of the kitchen and Sarah laughs.

"Wait'll you see this."

"What is it?"

"You'll see." She smiles as Artie lumbers in with a package wrapped in Reynolds Wrap.

"Nice paper, Weiss," Eletha says.

Artie thrusts the present at me. "It was either this or the Hanukkah paper."

"Thanks, Artie," I say, peeling back the foil like a microwave dinner. Underneath is a shiny black plastic I've seen before. "A Magic Eight

Ball all my own!" I'm actually touched, which shows how soft I'm getting in my dotage. I give him a hug.

"It's mine, you know," he says, smiling.

"Really? Yours?"

"Putting away childish things, Artie?" Sarah asks.

"You know me better than that, Sar. I got Etch-a-Sketch now."

Sarah laughs, and so do I.

"What? It's more fun than Legos, and it doesn't hurt when you step on it."

Sarah and I exchange looks. Her expression is unreadable as usual, but mine is full of deep and powerful significance. My eyes telegraph: You are crazy to let this wonderful man leave your life, because there are not that many wonderful men around. I'll tell her later if she doesn't read eyes.

"Of course, the Etch-a-Sketch is okay," Artie says, "but it's still not my favorite toy." He grins at Eletha. "Doctor, lawyer, Indian chief."

"Don't you tell on me now," she says, laughing evilly.

Sarah looks from one to the other. "What are you two talking about?"

It takes me a full minute to figure it out, but that's because I'm such a stinky detective.

"Look, Grace!" Miss Waxman calls from the backyard.

We all look out the window. Bernice is heeling perfectly as Miss Waxman walks her back and forth. This is not what it looks like when Bernice walks me.

I wave to Miss Waxman. "Unbelievable. The dog is Rin Tin Tin."

"Who's that?" Sarah says.

"Forget it."

"Tell her about the Edsel, Grace," Eletha says.

"One more wisecrack and the dog is yours, El. And I know what you did," I say, pointing my newly bejeweled fingernail at her. Eletha painted my nails while I was in the hospital, and each one is a masterpiece of turquoise polish with a sapphire in the center.

"Hey, girl, you owe me, from that fix-up with Ray."

"You went out with him?"

"Lunch. Then he pounced." She shudders.

"Oh, no."

"Told you," Artie says. "Man's an animal."

"I'm sorry, El. I thought he was nice."

"He slobbered worse than Bernice." She snaps her fingers. "Wait a minute. I just got an idea."

"What?"

"Maddie hates Bernice?"

"Right."

"Ask Miss Waxman to take her."

I look at Eletha, astounded.

The perfect solution.

Tears pour from her eyes. Her face is flushed. She hiccups uncontrollably. I'm afraid she's going to lose dessert, right there at the dining room table.

"Mads, I don't understand. You hate Bernice."

"I don't hate Bernice!"

The dog looks over the plastic fence, forlorn as a child in a custody fight.

Miss Waxman, shaken, sets down her teacup. "I'd give her a good home, dear. She could play with my poodles."

"She'd be happier, Mads," I say. "She wouldn't be so lonely during the day." And I wouldn't have to hurdle a fence every time the phone rings, or share my bed with the Alps.

"She'd have friends, Maddie," Artie says.

"She doesn't need friends!" Maddie cries.

"Everybody needs friends," Sarah says.

Maddie only cries harder. They have no way of knowing it, but we're not talking about the dog anymore. I hug Maddie close.

"Maybe we should keep Bernice," I say.

Miss Waxman nods. "Of course, whatever you want. She's a very fine animal."

"A *fine* animal," Eletha says. "If Bernice were my dog, I'd never give her up."

Maddie's sobbing slows down and she buries a tear-stained face in my neck. "I can be her friend," she says.

"Now there's an idea. You sure can."

"Can I go upstairs now?" she whispers.

"Sure." I pat her on the bottom and she runs out of the room. I plop into my chair and take a slug of frigid coffee.

Artie snorts. "Way to go, girls. Called that one right."

"Sorry, Grace," Eletha says sheepishly.

"It's not your fault," I say. "I should have known."

"I'm so sorry," Miss Waxman says. "It's all my fault. It's my inexperience with children."

"No, it's my fault." I touch her hand. "My child, my fault."

"Only women have conversations like this," Artie says. He digs into the apple pie Eletha brought.

"Well, it's all right now," I say. I push my hair back and drink the icy coffee. "We have the dog. Someday she'll get out of the kitchen." I look over at Bernice, and her tongue rolls out. "Maybe."

Miss Waxman looks at Bernice indulgently. "Maybe if you take it a step at a time."

"How?"

"Move the animal into the dining room, let the child play near her when she's in the living room so they get used to being around each other."

I think of what Maddie said. *Maybe I could be her friend.* "Then what?"

"You might want to buy her some toys."

"She has plenty of toys."

"I think she means the dog," Sarah says, smiling faintly. "Don't you, Miss Waxman?"

Miss Waxman nods and sips her tea with delicacy.

Oh. I knew that. Add it to the bill.

"Of course," Miss Waxman continues, "not everyone takes to animals, but it seems like Maddie will."

"I'm sure," I say. Just not in my lifetime.

"Like Judge Galanter," Artie says ruefully. "Bernice almost ate him, did you know that, Miss Waxman?"

Miss Waxman shudders. "Judge Galanter was *quite* unhappy about that."

"I bet he was. He almost lost his nuts."

Miss Waxman clears her throat, and a frown crosses Sarah's face. "Why was she after him, I wonder. Remember that, Grace?"

"Yeah. Odd."

"Dogs don't like Judge Galanter," Miss Waxman says.

"Neither do people," Artie says. "Does he have any friends, Miss Waxman?"

"Artie," Sarah says, "don't put Miss Waxman on the spot."

"She can tell me to pound sand if she wants to." He turns to Miss Waxman. "You can tell me to pound sand if you want to."

"Tell him to pound sand," Eletha says.

Miss Waxman's mascara'd eyelashes flutter briefly. Ten to one, she's never heard the term.

"Does he have a friend in the world?" Artie asks.

"Well, he doesn't have . . . many friends."

"I heard he eats alone. He doesn't even meet anybody for lunch."

"Like Ben," Sarah says. Eletha winces and so do I, at the fresh memory of that horrible night. Artie blunders on, retriever puppy that he is.

"Name one for me, Miss Waxman. One friend."

She thinks a minute. "He has an older brother, a banker."

"Beep!" Artie says, like the buzzer in *Jeopardy*. "Doesn't count, that's family. Anyone else?"

She pauses. "There's a Mr. Cavallaro. He met him for lunch, once or twice."

I look up. I am hearing things. "What did you say, Miss Waxman?"

"A Mr. Cavallaro? Mr. James Cavallaro?"

But I'm already running for the kitchen drawer, where I keep the crossword puzzle.

I have a feeling it's on its way to being solved.

33

I sit in the darkened back row of the courtroom, where Winn sat that first day. Susan will be speaking here in not too long, at yet another press conference, this one about the bribery scandal. Galanter has been indicted and will be impeached if he doesn't resign. The entire Third Circuit feels the sting of disgrace collectively. Even the court crier is somber as he stands aside, watching TV technicians adjust the lights that will illuminate the dais; interlopers, spotlighting our shame.

Senator Susan Waterman leans on the back of

the pew in front of me. She looks sophisticated in a checked Chanel suit, with her hair smoothed back into a classy French twist. Power hair. "How do you know about the money?" she asks.

"I found the checkbook. How do *you* know about the money?"

"You're wondering where he got it." She doesn't answer my question, but I'm not the one in control of this meeting even though I asked for it.

"Yes, I'm wondering where he got it."

"He got it from me."

"Why?"

"For the child." She glances at her preppy aide, the laconic Michael Robb of Bath, Maine, who's discreetly guarding the courtroom door. "His child with Eletha. Did you know he fathered a child?"

"You know about Malcolm?"

"Of course."

"Eletha thinks you don't know."

"I know that. Armen agreed not to tell me, and he never did. My campaign manager found out before I ran for office, during my vetting. He's the one who told me. I kept it from Eletha—even from Sarah."

"But not Armen."

"Of course not."

"Were you hurt?" She seems so cool, I can't help but ask.

"No. It was before we met, how could I be? He always wanted children and I didn't, so I couldn't begrudge him."

Eminently reasonable. "Why did you give him the money?"

"For the child's education."

"How much did you give him?"

She checks her new Rolex. "Six hundred thousand. The rest he saved."

"Six hundred thousand dollars? That much?"

"He needed it for the child. I'll make sure Malcolm gets it when the estate is settled." She claps her hands together to end the meeting; I notice that her funky silver bangles have been replaced by a thick gold bracelet. Power jewelry.

"You gave him six hundred thousand dollars for the education of a child he had with another woman?"

"Yes."

"I find that hard to believe."

"That's your problem."

"Come on, Susan, let's talk. It's just us girls. What did Armen have that you wanted, that you paid him for?"

She checks her watch again. "I don't have time for this."

Which is when I finally figure it out. Remind me not to quit my day job. "That's it, isn't it? Time."

"What?"

"Armen gave you a year. You wanted him to stay with you through the campaign, and you knew he needed money for Malcolm. So you paid him. You bought him for a year."

"I needed him," she says, and I see a glimmer of the lethal ambition that drove Ben.

It scares me. I say exactly what I'm thinking, unfiltered. "What did Armen see in you?"

"I'm an idealist and so was he."

"An idealist? What are your ideals?"

"I am a liberal, freely admitted. I'm working for child care—"

She doesn't want children.

"For the poor—"

That jacket is double my rent.

"I'm working for the American family."

"You can't *buy* a family."

The courtroom door opens and the preppy aide lets Sarah slip through, but Susan doesn't seem to notice. "You resent me," Susan says.

I get up to go. "No. Mostly, I don't understand you."

"Do you know how important it is for women to get into government? Do you realize the effect we have, the role models we provide?"

"I think I do."

Sarah comes over, looking vaguely senatorial herself. "Grace, how are you?"

I give her a warm hug. "Get out while you still can, Sar."

She looks at me, puzzled, as I head for the swinging doors.

"Good-bye, Michael," I say brightly, on the way out.

"Good-bye, Grace," he says. "And have a nice day."

I do a double-take.

*   *   *

His gaze is direct; eyes clear and intelligent, with a hint of crow's feet at each corner. His mouth, now that I can see it without the underbrush, looks full, even sweet. His brown hair is trimmed, with longish sideburns. He's not hard to look at as he sits at the conference table, next to the FBI bureau chief, the U.S. Attorney, Senator Susan Waterman, my favorite mayor, and the acting chief judge of the Third Circuit, Judge Morris Townsend, awake for the occasion.

"*That's* Shake and Bake?" Sarah says, crossing her legs.

"Isn't he awesome?" Artie says, with an admiring grin. "You oughta see him play. As fine as Earl the Pearl."

"He does look . . . different," Miss Waxman says.

Eletha cracks up. "Real different."

Susan gets up and makes a speech, blah blah blah; the U.S. Attorney and the others all make speeches, blah blah blah. God knows what they say, and who cares. It all sounds the same, each one taking full credit for an investigation in which I heard it was Winn who ended up strapped to a body mike, pretending to be Nick the Fish. On a tip by a secretary who trains toy poodles.

Please.

The FBI bureau chief takes the podium again and a thousand flash units go off, motor drives whining like locusts. He sips his water and says, "I would like to introduce Special Agent Thaddeus Colwin, who has been investigating this matter in an undercover capacity. You'll understand that we can't give you the details, because every secret we divulge is one less weapon in our arsenal against crime. Suffice it to say that we are extremely pleased with the results of the investigation. Special Agent Colwin?"

Winn gets up, and the courtroom bursts into applause. He smooths down a pair of wool pants uncomfortably, and by the time he reaches the podium he's blushing. "There's something I have to say before you start shootin'."

The crowd laughs.

Sarah recrosses her legs.

"I'm happy that this investigation turned out so well, but I can't take the credit for it. The real credit should go to two other people."

I feel nervous; they promised to keep me out of it. The FBI chief looks as worried as I am; Winn is supposed to hand the credit up, not down.

"One of these persons chooses to remain anonymous, and I keep promises to my confidential sources. However, I have made no such agreement with the other person, and she is one of the kindest and bravest ladies I ever met. She testified yesterday at the government's probable cause hearing, so now her identity can be divulged. Her name, friends, is Miss Gilda Waxman."

I look over at Miss Waxman. Her hands fly to her cheeks; her eyes brim with astonished tears.

"Please stand up, Miss Waxman," Winn says. He claps for her, and so does everybody else.

"Oh, my. Oh. Oh," she says, from her seat. The woman has never had a moment in the spotlight in her entire life. She looks as if she's about to have a heart attack.

"Stand up, Miss Waxman!" I say, half rising to grab her soft arm and pull her to her feet.

"No, I couldn't. Really." She tries to sit back down, but Artie covers the seat cushion with his large hand, palm up.

"Come on, good-lookin', sit down," he says, wiggling his fingers. "I dare you."

She swallows hard, then faces the courtroom and her fans. She looks uncertain for a minute, then breaks into a shy smile.

34

I turn the Magic Eight Ball over in my hands and read the bottom.

Yes, definitely, it says. Its white letters float eerily to the black surface. I'll try again. There are only twenty possible answers; it shouldn't take that long to get the answer I want, and I am a patient woman. I shake the ball and look at the bottom.

It is certain.

Where are all the negative answers? Must be defective. I listen to the stone silence coming from Maddie's room. She's boycotting me because I won't let her invite her grandfather to her class play. Should I invite him? I shake the ball and turn it over.

Most likely.

Hmmm. I'll rephrase the question; I didn't go to law school for nothing. Should we never see Maddie's grandfather again? I shake the ball harder, then rotate it.

My reply is no.

"Damn!" I say aloud, and Bernice raises her head. "Why don't we take him, Bernice? He and Grandma could duke it out in the auditorium. You bring the camcorder. We'll be on *Funniest Home Videos.*"

I set down the Eight Ball next to the card my father sent Maddie today, which started this whole thing. A short hello, then a list of Italian words, with their meaning. Girl: *ragazza.* Dog: *cane.* Cat: *gatto.* Seems that Emedio "Mimmy" Rossi and his grandaughter got to talking about languages at recess that day. Now Maddie is convinced she wants to learn Italian.

Love: *amore.* I have to admit, it's a pretty language.

"Mom?" Maddie calls faintly from upstairs. Bernice looks toward the stairway at the sound.

"What?"

"Can you come up?"

"Sure." I put down the card, and since Bernice is still *cane non grata* outside the kitchen, I climb over the gate. It catches me neatly in the crotch. Either Bernice goes free or I get taller.

I head up the stairs to Maddie's door, which is plastered with stickers of butterflies, frogs, porcupines, and metallic spiders. Here and there is a much-valued "oily," the goopy stickers that are all the rage with the younger set. Me, I had crayons, eight in all. "Did you want me, Mads?"

"You can come in," she says grudgingly.

"Good." I turn the knob, but the door doesn't move much.

"Maddie, is something blocking the door?"

"Wait a minute." I hear her dragging things around inside. She must have barricaded the door again with her Little Tikes chairs; they never show that particular use in the catalog. "Okay," she says. "You can come in now."

I open the door and it shoves aside the clutter behind it, including a chair, a white stuffed gorilla, and about three hundred multicolored wooden blocks. "So, how are we doing up here?"

She holds out her palm. "Look."

In the center of her hand is an ivory nugget. I pick it up in wonder. The front edge is the bevel I recognize and the other end is a fragile circle tinged with blood. "Wow! Your first tooth, Maddie."

"It didn't even hurt."

"How'd it come out?"

"I pulled it out."

I recoil. "Really?"

She nods.

"Let me see your mouth. Smile."

She snarls in compliance, and sure enough, there's an arched window where her front tooth used to be. Then she snaps her mouth shut like a baby alligator. "I'm still mad, you know. This isn't a make-up."

"I understand. Let's get the tooth ready for the Tooth Fairy."

"I'll take care of it. It's mine. Give it back." She holds out her hand.

"Don't be fresh." I put the tooth in her palm.

"Thank you," she says, and walks over to her play table. It's covered with play lipsticks, plastic jewelry, art supplies, and old scarves I've given her for dress-up. She plucks a blue paisley scarf from the pile and wraps the tooth up in it. Then she writes with a crayon on a scrap of pink construction paper.

"What are you doing, honey?"

"I have to write a note."

"No, you don't. You put the tooth under your pillow, and the Tooth Fairy leaves you some money."

"I wasn't talking to you."

So cute. My daughter's first tooth and we're not on speaking terms. "That's quite enough, miss. Would you like a time-out?"

"Well, I *wasn't* talking to you. I was talking to myself."

"Fine, but you may not be rude."

She turns around in her bare feet and thrusts the paper at me. It says, in wobbly red letters: I DON WAN $. T R T G RD. THAN YU. "I don't do lower case."

"It's very nice. What's this part say?"

"It says, I don't want money." She points to the end. "Thank you."

"Why don't you want money?"

"I want her to bring my grandfather to the play."

I sigh in the martyred way my mother taught me. "Why, Maddie? Why does it matter so much?"

"Because everybody else will have a daddy there and I won't. Everybody else will have a grandpop there and I won't. Everybody else has sisters and brothers and I don't." Her lower lip trembles. "All I have is stupid old red hair and freckles that everybody makes fun of."

I look down at her blue eyes, on the verge of welling up. There's nothing in the book about this.

Suddenly, I hear a rustling down in the kitchen, then the *click-clack* of nails on the stairs. I turn around just in time to catch Bernice before she plows into Maddie. She must have jumped the gate.

"She's out!" Maddie screams, backing up against her play table.

"I got her. So you busted out, huh, Bernice?"

"Put her back in the kitchen!"

I hold Bernice by her new ten-dollar collar with its gold electroplate heart: G. ROSSI, it says. The dog wriggles with joy at her liberation from the kitchen. Her tail wags so hard that her hindquarters go with it, a living example of the tail wagging the dog.

"Aw, Maddie, let's leave her out a little. She's sick of the kitchen. She wants to be with us."

The dog swings her head from me to Maddie. It may be my imagination, but Bernice's expression is as close to hopeful as a draft horse can get.

"She's staring at me again," Maddie says. "Why does she have to stare?"

"She wants you to be her friend."

"I can see her teeth."

"So she has teeth, Maddie. You have teeth, she has teeth. Dogs lose baby teeth too. Did you know that? Just like you."

"So what?"

A tough nut. "Why don't you ask her to sit, like Miss Waxman taught her?"

"She won't do it for me."

"How do you know? You never tried. Give her a chance."

Maddie looks at me, then at Bernice. "Now you *sit!*" she shouts.

Miraculously, Bernice sits. Right on the spot. Her tail goes *thump thump thump* on the hardwood floor.

"She did it!" Maddie says.

"She's a good girl. Ask her to do something else. What else did Miss Waxman teach her, do you remember?"

Maddie locks eyes with an excited Bernice. *"Roll over!"*

Bernice drops heavily to the floor and rolls over an array of wooden blocks; she finishes lying flat on her belly and begging for more.

"Look at that!" I say. "Now tell her she's good."

"Good dog!" Maddie says sternly.

"Now see if she'll give you her paw."

"What do I say?"

"Say, 'Give me your paw, Bernice.'"

"What a stupid name," she says, but even her pseudo-cool can't hide her excitement at Bernice's response. *"Bernice, give me your paw."*

Bernice looks blank but scrambles to a sitting position, panting. Her eyes remain on Maddie, rapt.

I rack my brain. What did Miss Waxman say? "Try 'Shake.'"

Maddie straightens up like a toy soldier. *"Shake! Now!"*

I begin to wonder about the dark side of my little angel, but Bernice doesn't seem to mind. On cue, the dog lifts a furry foreleg and paws at the air between her and Maddie.

Maddie's eyes grow panicky. "What's she doing?"

"She wants you to take her paw."

Bernice puts down her paw, then raises it again.

Maddie looks at me, then back at Bernice. "Will she bite me?"

"Of course not. Come on, Maddie, just touch it. She won't bite you. I promise."

Bernice puts down her paw and raises it again in the air.

Maddie reaches out tentatively with her fingers, her child's hand just inches from Bernice's soft white paw. I flash on Michelangelo's depiction of God creating Adam, which doesn't seem half as significant for western civilization.

"Just touch her, Maddie. She wants to be your friend."

Maddie bites her lip and reaches closer to Bernice's paw.

Bernice whimpers and rakes at the air.

"Go ahead. *Touch* her, Maddie."

"Can I?" she says worriedly.

"Yes, go ahead."

And finally, she does.

35

We sit uncomfortably in the darkness, on the carpeted steps that serve as seats in the elementary school auditorium. To the left is my mother, her face carved from a solid stratum of granite, like the dead presidents hewn into Mount Rushmore. Her hair has been sculpted into curls and is as rigid as her gaze, which does not waver from the stage, much less look at me. I figure that we will speak again in the year 3000 or when she quits smoking, whichever comes first.

Making a cameo appearance to her left is Tyrannosaurus Ex, Sam, in a Burberry suit with a stiff white collar. I told him I would picket his law firm if he didn't come today. He gives me a billable smile when I look over.

Next to him is Ricki, looking entirely entertained, and not only by the class play. She has brought along her three sons so the requisite brothers will be present, and has even offered me half price on the therapy I will need to recover from today. That's what friends are for, she said with a smile. And she forgives me for lying to her, and even for returning the blue Laura Ashley dress.

To my right, of course, is a man who looks like Robert Goulet and smells like the perfume counter at Thrift Drug: my father. He's the only one having fun at this thing. He guffaws at all the punch lines and claps heartily after all the songs. He nudges me in the ribs four times, whenever Maddie enters in her costume, knocking the camcorder into the back of the man in front of me. When I finally ask him to stop, he says out loud: "Wadja say, doll?"

So I don't ask again. I put the rubber rectangle of the camcorder to my eye and watch my daughter take center stage. Dressed as a carrot, naturally, she joins hands with her new friend, Gretchen the tomato, and they take the hands of a bunch of broccoli and several tulips to sing about the things that sprout up in the spring, tall and proud in the warm sun.

Like children.

In no time at all I'm in tears, looking through the rubber eye of the camcorder, hating that it will record my sniffles with Japanese high fidelity. In the background will be a group of first graders warbling faintly about springtime.

I find myself thinking of Armen, then Sam and my father. And how sometimes it doesn't turn out like it's supposed to.

Love dies, people die. Mothers and fathers break apart, the ties that bind unraveling as freely as a ball of yarn, with one tie remaining: the microscopic skein of DNA that resurfaces in our children, in permutations never imagined. Maddie's the only tie between Sam and me; I'm the only tie between my parents. We all relate to our children, but none of us to each other.

The tears wet the eyepiece of the costly camcorder, and I have to set it down in my lap. My father puts his aromatic arm around me, and then my mother does the same, which only makes me cry harder.

For all we lost.

For all we never had.

Sam passes me a monogrammed handkerchief and I try to recover, grateful for the darkness. Meanwhile Ricki looks like she wants me on Prozac, and the carrot is hugging the tomato. The house lights come up, threatening to expose my hysteria, but in the light I can see that everyone else is crying too. I'm just another hysterical mother in an audience of hysterical mothers applauding their baby vegetables.

Maddie finds me in the crowd and grins, gap-toothed.

I clap loudly for her, hands over my head. I

look over and my father is doing the same thing. Scary.

My mother puts a note on my lap. On the front it says GRACE ROSSI. "What's this?" I ask her.

"Sam passed it down to you."

"Sam?" I look over at Sam, but he's whistling for Maddie, doing his best impression of a real father. I pick up the note and something falls into my lap.

It's a new photo of Tom Cruise. The note says:

> Roses are red,
> Violets are blue,
> Maddie's adorable,
> Wanna see my tattoo?

I look past Sam and over the parents, teachers, and kids. Underneath the EXIT sign, in the back row of the auditorium, is a handsome man in a black raincoat.

And no rain bonnet at all.

ACKNOWLEDGMENTS

—————◆—————

Kay Thompson's wonderful character, Eloise, likes to make things up. So do I, which is important to keep in mind as you read this book. Even though I have worked for the Third Circuit Court of Appeals, doing the very same job as my character Grace Rossi—indeed, in the very same courthouse—*Final Appeal* is fiction. None of the characters are real, although they are realistic, and the plot, though plausible, is entirely imagined.

The first thanks go, as always, to my agent, Linda Hayes, and to my editor extraordinaire at HarperPaperbacks, Carolyn Marino. I am blessed in knowing these terrific women and in becoming their friend, even if I never write another book. But since I intend to write other books, I'll be the grateful recipient of their judgment in knowing what makes a book work, their insight into how to improve a manuscript, and their commitment to me and my writing. Not to mention their sensitivity to my care and feeding. The Old Testament would call what they have lovingkindness, which is proof that there is still some writing that cannot be improved upon.

Heartfelt thanks also go to my boss, Chief Judge Dolores K. Sloviter, who is the absolute best the federal judiciary has to offer. Her dedication to public service is an example for me every day, and we are all lucky to have her. I mention her here especially because she has been more supportive of my part-time writing and full-time mothering than I could ever have hoped.

Thanks, too, for their support, to Martha Verna, Anne Szymkowski, Mary Lou Kanz, and the law clerks, Seth, Theresa, and the strikingly handsome Jim (and before them Alison, Larry, and Jessica). I am grateful as well to the other employees of Third Circuit—Bill Bradley being the ringleader of a conspiracy that includes Marisa Walsh and the staff attorneys; Toby Slawsky, Lynne Kosobucki, Pat Moore, and the Circuit Executive's Office; Doug Sisk, Brad Baldus, and the clerk's office; and the librarians, who have been so supportive.

Thank you very much to Alison Brown at HarperPaperbacks, a whiz of an editorial assistant who made some dead-on suggestions about an early draft, and who has helped in many other ways. Many thanks to Laura Baker at HarperPaperbacks and my local publicist, Laura Henrich, who are both wonderful. Janet Baker, my copy editor on all two occasions, is awesome; even from afar, she never forgets Philadelphia. A quick story: in *Everywhere That Mary Went,* Janet corrected me on exactly where along Route One you begin to smell the cow manure. This is a copy editor you can only dream about, and she is mine.

When Grace Rossi wandered out of my range of expertise, I sought help from United States Attorneys Joan Markman and Amy Kurland (who was kind enough to let me collar her on Fifth Street), Special Agent Linda Vizi of the FBI, Detective McGlinchey and others of the Philadelphia police, the federal marshals and court security officers (Mssrs. King and Devlin, as well as Tony "Hole-in-One" Fortunato and his cohorts), and the staff at the medical examiners office of Philadelphia. Not to mention Brian J. Buckelew, man of many talents, and my friend David Grunfeld. All errors and omissions, of course, are mine. By the way, needlepoint really does relieve stress, and you're guaranteed one pillow for every life crisis. Ask Barbara Russell of Barbara Russell Designs in Chestnut Hill.

Special thanks, too, to Reverend Paree Metjian and his family, who taught me about Armenian pride and culture. I feel honored to have been even a fictional member of that community.

Finally, I am indebted to my friends, especially Rachel Kull and Franca Palumbo, who found the time to read an early draft of this book and to offer suggestions and encouragement. I owe them both a tankerful of milk, and much more.

As for my family, they are where it all started and where it all ends.

FINAL APPEAL

READERS GROUP GUIDE QUESTIONS

1. *Final Appeal* is a winner of the Edgar® Award, the highest honor for a mystery novel. What did you like the best about the book in terms of its plot, character, and structure? For example, did you think the characters were complex and the chapter endings suspenseful? Why or why not?

2. What do you think about Grace's decision to have an affair with her married boss? If she had waited even one more day, until after divorce papers were filed, would that make you feel any different? How risky is a workplace romance, and where do you draw the line?

3. Did you like Armen's character, and why or why not? Was he really a good guy? Did you agree with all of the decisions he made? How much of a factor was his Armenian background and upbringing on his decisions? Did you like the idea of Grace and Armen as a couple? Do you think he really could have fallen in love with Grace after only three months?

4. All of the parents in *Final Appeal* are flawed, although some more than others. Grace has to face an ugly truth about her own parents and reevaluate her childhood. Did you agree with Grace when she questioned her daughter, or did you think she was being disloyal? How do you think her own childhood impacted her role as a mother? Should Grace forgive her father? Is it ever too late to rekindle a relationship with a parent?

5. Why do you think Eletha is such a strong character? Did you like her, respect her, or agree with all her decisions? How did her decisions affect her child? Do you consider her a good mother and a good friend, and why?

6. Sarah says "The death penalty is revenge masquerading as justice." What do you think about this statement? Do you think the defendant in the book deserved a second trial because the judge misread the directions to the jury, or is it just a loophole that will cost the taxpayers more money? The Hightower case plays an important role in the plot. If you were writing the end of the book, how would you have resolved the Hightower proceedings? Is it possible to separate law from justice, or law from morality?

7. Why do you think *Final Appeal* has such an interesting cast of characters? Who was your favorite character, who did you dislike, and why? Do you think Grace and her new love have a future together, or it will be difficult for her to date while she has a young child? How soon should you introduce your child to someone you are dating? How hard is it for a single parent to find time for themselves, especially if they are working?

8. Do you think judicial misconduct is widespread, or is it just a few bad apples? What do you think would help cut down on judicial bribery? For example, would it help if we gave judges a higher salary? Do we need to have a better system for tracking judiciary conduct, and if so, what would that system be like?